"I'm not Michelle.
My name is Josephine!"

William smiled. "I know." He draped an arm around her shoulders. It was awkward comforting her. Now that she was conscious, his heart struggled to protect itself.

Josie eased out of his arms. "So you believe me?"

"Of course I do."

"Thank you," she said softly. "I'm surprised that you helped after . . ."

Their eyes met again.

He couldn't ignore the pain and uncertainty reflected in them. "You needed my help."

Her gaze fluttered down to her hands. "No one would listen to me. They just kept drugging me to the point where I couldn't think."

He watched as she fidgeted with her hands.

"They were stealing my life."

By Adrianne Byrd

DEADLY DOUBLE
IF YOU DARE

ADRIANNE BYRD

DEADLY
DOUBLE

HarperTorch
An Imprint of HarperCollins Publishers

This is a work of fiction. Names, characters, places, and incidents are products of the author's imagination or are used fictitiously and are not to be construed as real. Any resemblance to actual events, locales, organizations, or persons, living or dead, is entirely coincidental.

HARPERTORCH
An Imprint of HarperCollins*Publishers*
10 East 53rd Street
New York, New York 10022-5299

Copyright © 2005 by Adrianne Byrd
ISBN: 0-06-056539-X

First HarperTorch paperback printing: June 2005

HarperCollins®, HarperTorch™, and ❦™ are trademarks of Harper-Collins Publishers Inc.

Printed in the United States of America

Visit HarperTorch on the World Wide Web at www.harpercollins.com

10 9 8 7 6 5 4 3 2 1

To Raymond Johnson,
I'll always love you.

"Kidnapping is a federal offense," Dr. William Hayes muttered into the dark October night. From the stolen laundry van, he took a deep breath and wished like hell he had a cigarette. Maybe a jolt of nicotine would stop his hands from shaking.

A pair of headlights beamed in his rearview mirror. Frightened, William tensed as his breath hitched in anticipation of the Atlanta police. A moment later, he slumped against the headrest when a car traveled past him.

Keystone Mental Institute loomed in his side view mirror. "I've lost it," he mumbled, then reached for the glove compartment. In the back of his mind, he held the crazy thought that a pack of

Benson & Hedges would magically appear. Even that didn't make sense—he'd stopped smoking years ago.

William removed his white cap and ran a shaky hand through his dark hair, then met his blue gaze in the rearview mirror. "You're going to jail," he told himself. The traffic light turned green, and he took a left out of the hospital's parking lot.

The white uniform was a little too snug for his liking, and the glue from his fake beard itched like crazy, but right now he had to force both to the back of his mind.

His anxieties mounted as he caught every red light in a two-mile stretch. Fulton County also seemed to be crawling with police cars. The pressure to obey the speed limit was intense.

A soft moan floated from the back of the van. *Was she waking up?* "Dear God, not now." He instinctively glanced back, fearful of what he might see, but relaxed when nothing met his gaze.

A horn blared.

He jumped and eased off his brakes when he saw that the light had turned green. The car behind him moved into the left lane and flew past him.

"Another cop car." He shook his head and had a devil of a time convincing himself that it wasn't an omen.

Thirty minutes later, he pulled into the Oil Drop

repair shop and drove to where the cars, vans, and trucks were either waiting for repair or pickup.

William parked next to another Machemehl Cleaners' van, shut off the engine, and collapsed against the headrest. For a few minutes, all he could do was listen to his heart pound against his rib cage.

Another moan accompanied a rustle of movement, and William was instantly alert. The night was a long way from being over and, if he wanted it to end without the click of handcuffs, he needed to get on the ball.

He unhooked his seat belt and rushed to the back of the van. In a large roll-away tub of clean sheets, William stared down at the drugged woman he'd just snatched from Keystone.

Silvery moonlight streamed through the back square windows and gave the caramel beauty's sickly pallor an angelic glow. Then again, maybe he still viewed her through the eyes of a lovesick twenty-one-year-old.

He brushed away a thick lock of black hair in order to study her heart-shaped face and smooth cheekbones. Sixteen years had done little to change her features . . . and her effect on him.

A barrage of tender emotions attacked his conscience, but he pushed them all aside and focused on the task at hand. He leaned over and checked her vitals.

Her faint but steady pulse comforted him and gave him the courage to continue as planned. Inches from the tub, William retrieved his leather duffel bag and quickly changed out of his white uniform and into loose jeans and a flannel shirt.

He glanced out the back windows and assured himself that the lot was empty before he opened the doors. When he did, a gush of cool air whipped inside. Another soft moan fell from his patient's lips, and William prayed the night's elements wouldn't further damage her condition.

Jumping down from the van, he rushed over to his parked Lincoln Navigator, tossed his duffel bag into the front passenger seat, and opened the back door. He quickly returned to the van and extracted his patient from the tub.

Her deadweight was a challenge, but he summoned the strength to carry her to his vehicle. The backseat was already prepared with clean sheets and pillows, and he made quick work of getting her situated.

Another trip to the van, and he erased all evidence of his thievery, especially his masterful job of hot wiring. Who knew this rebellious teenage skill would come in handy again?

A few minutes later, he was on his way. The moaning increased in both duration and frequency and, again, William found himself worrying.

"We're on our way," he said. "Don't worry. It won't be long now."

More moaning.

Small droplets of rain splattered the windshield and quickly turned into a heavy downpour.

"This is not an omen," he recited with little conviction. He turned onto I-85 south and estimated that he would reach Pine Mountain in the next half hour; but ten minutes into the drive, he rolled to a stop behind a long, curving line of traffic.

The moans transformed into restless whimpers, then finally "Josephine" was whispered from her cracked voice.

William's heart squeezed at the name. He turned in his seat to glance at the woman lying behind him.

She fidgeted while her head tossed restlessly among the pillows.

"Shh, now. Try and get some rest."

She quieted down.

He eased back around in his seat and expelled a long, tired breath. There was no point in continuing to beat himself up about the night's events. What was done was done. It was too late to turn back. He would have to stay the course.

Minutes later, his vehicle approached flashing blue-and-white lights. Dread seeped into his body as gloom and doom monopolized his thoughts at what looked like some kind of police checkpoint. His head slumped into the palm of his hand. "Lord, help me."

After eighteen hours, Dr. Meredith Bancroft decided to call it a night. Life as a workaholic had its drawbacks; then again, so did being married to one. It was nearing 2:00 A.M., and Meredith wouldn't be surprised if she beat her husband home—again.

A zombie, she headed toward one of the exits, carrying her briefcase, with her arms loaded down with patient charts. Hopefully, she would get a chance to review most of them while she worked at the institute's sister location in Duluth.

Meredith had been at Keystone since the day they'd opened the doors thirty years earlier. Back then, it was a big deal for an African-American

woman to make partner in such a large organization. It was the first of many milestones for her.

"Calling it a night, Dr. Bancroft?" a male voice
boomed down the hall.

Meredith turned and spotted Theo Watts, a
charismatic man who looked more like a football
player than a male nurse, waving from the opposite end of the empty hall. "Yeah. You guys try not
to work too hard." She waved back.

"Nah. You know how we are on third shift.
We're about to give Alana her farewell cake. You're
not going to join us?"

"No. I've already said my good-byes and gave
my gift. Right now I just want to get home and
crawl into bed before my pager starts buzzing."

He laughed and gave another departing wave.
"Then go and catch some Zs. I'm sure you'll be
back here before my shift is over."

She rolled her eyes. "You're probably right.
Night." Turning, Meredith pushed through the
doors of the institute and stepped out into the wet,
velvet night. Cursing her luck for not having an
umbrella, she bolted down the dark sidewalk like
a fireman five minutes late for a fire.

"If I get home by two-thirty, I can squeeze in
about five hours of sleep," she muttered under her
breath. Then she remembered that she needed to
feed the cat, pay a few bills online, take a shower,

and God help her if her husband wanted to have sex. "Maybe four hours."

Meredith reached the employee parking deck as her mind raced with more stuff she either had to take care of before going to bed or before she made it back to work at eight in the morning.

The light rain picked up velocity, and she was completely drenched by the time she reached her black BMW. After fumbling for her keys, she pressed the unlock button from a key chain remote. Sliding behind the wheel, she dumped her briefcase and charts into the passenger seat.

"I thought that you would never get off."

When cold steel pressed against Meredith's temple, she gasped as her gaze flew to the rearview mirror. The stranger's face was obscured, but his presence was immeasurably terrifying. "What are you doing in here?" Her hand trembled as she placed it over her heart. "What do you want?"

The intruder laughed, and Meredith's skin became a blanket of goose bumps at its high cackle.

"I tell you what," the intruder's silky voice said with an eerie calm. "Why don't you just hand me your security badge?"

Meredith swallowed. "I can't do that."

"Of course you can," the stranger said, leaning forward. "Or I can just shoot you and simply take it."

Meredith shivered, and her heart swelled with fear. "What is this all about?"

"You don't need to concern yourself with that right now. Just hand over the badge."

Think, Meredith. Think.

"How do I know you won't kill me once I hand it over?"

"You don't."

Meredith swallowed again and tried to make out her captor's features in the rearview mirror. However, the night cloaked the figure as though they were one entity.

"I'm going to count to three," the voice informed her. "One—"

"Okay, okay." Meredith's hand fluttered to her breast pocket and snatched off her ID, which also doubled as a security badge, and held it up. Immediately, it was snatched from her fingers.

"Now, that wasn't so bad."

Meredith swallowed and pretended she didn't hear the added coldness to the stranger's voice.

"Hand me your keys."

"What?"

"Come on, come on. I don't have all night."

Trembling, Meredith quickly found her keys, but hesitated before handing them back.

"Don't try me. I *will* shoot."

Meredith handed over the keys.

The dark figure emitted another cold laugh.

"Good girl. Now, we're going to get out of the car together. ¿*Comprende?*"

Drawing a deep breath, Meredith nodded. Since she was still breathing, she held more hope of actually surviving the night.

"Okay. On the count of three, we're going to open our doors slowly. You do anything foolish, and you're dead. Got it?"

"Got it."

"All right. One . . . two . . . three."

Meredith opened her door. A few minutes later, she was standing in the rain at the trunk of her car.

"Get in."

She didn't move. Instead, her eyes darted around in search of something or someone to save her.

"My patience is wearing thin," her mysterious captor droned in what seemed like a bored voice.

"I'm extremely claustrophobic."

A sliver of moonlight gleamed against the gun. "Well, how do you feel about being shot?"

Meredith gave the small trunk a quick survey before drawing a deep breath and climbing in. Carefully, she curled her five-foot-seven frame in order to fit before glancing up again. This time, the moonlight streamed across her captor's face.

"Good-bye, Doctor."

Two quick, muffled shots ended Meredith's life.

* * *

The closer William drew to the swarm of blue-and-white lights, the sweatier his palms became and the harder his heart tried to wedge itself in the middle of his throat. As he approached the first police car, he caught sight of red-and-white lights, then orange and white.

"An accident," he mumbled under his breath, then relaxed. Soon after, he felt guilty for having felt relieved when someone was probably hurt.

"Help me," the woman's soft voice said. "Please."

"Shh, now," he comforted, and gave a quick glance behind him. As he drove through the thicket of blinding lights, he swore his entire life passed before his eyes. Might as well. His actions that night were surely another form of suicide.

As his vehicle inched along the highway, William was finally able to make out an overturned car near the concrete median. A few feet from that, a white truck had its driver side smashed in, and the road was covered with shards of glass.

He made a quick prayer that no one was hurt; but seconds later, he saw a covered body being lifted into an ambulance. William's gaze remained glued on the image until the paramedics closed the rear doors.

A loud bang directed his attention to the hood

of his SUV, and his gaze jumped to a police officer in a rain slicker.

"Keep it moving. Keep it moving," the cop yelled, as he waved him through.

William rolled his eyes and eased off the brakes. He had just kidnapped a patient and he was rubbernecking an accident in front of the police. Great.

When he passed by a slew of officers attending the accident and directing traffic, he couldn't escape the feeling that everyone was really watching him—wanting to see how far he was going to go with this. He glanced up through the rain at the ink black sky and sighed with relief when a helicopter and a bright spotlight didn't appear.

After he passed the accident, traffic dissipated like magic, and twenty minutes later a large, painted sign welcomed them to Pine Mountain.

Pine Mountain was an affluent place even among the wealthy. The small town surrounded Callaway Gardens, a place where addicted golfers—like William's brother, Larry—descended during the summer months. But since it was mid-October, William was fairly certain the town's population was reduced to just the locals.

"We're almost there," he said over his shoulder. He didn't expect a response, but realized his patient hadn't made a sound since they were back at the accident. While wrestling with whether he should pull over to check on her, the faintest whisper reached his ears.

"Josephine."

Another killer strode through the halls of Keystone Mental Institute. Hidden safely behind a doctor's coat and a stolen ID badge, the imposter made it easily into the secured area of the hospital.

The killer's steps slowed as laughter tumbled down the hallway. Instinctively, the intruder ducked into a nearby room.

"We're sure going to miss you around here, Alana," a man said as he passed by.

"I'm going to miss you guys, too," Alana responded.

A few seconds later, their voices grew faint, and the killer waited a little longer before stepping out of the room. With a renewed sense of urgency, he rushed down the hall in search of Michelle Andrews in room 1526.

More voices drifted down the hall.

Fifteen twenty.

"That had to be the best red-velvet cake I've ever tasted," a woman praised off in the distance.

1522. 1524.

His objective was to kill the girl and meet his partner downstairs in ten minutes. His hand

closed around the knob of room 1526 just as someone was emerging from around the corner.

The killer ducked inside the dark room with a
large measure of relief and waited for the hall to
fall quiet again.

Something was wrong: the silence.

Turning away from the door, the killer removed
the gun from inside the lab coat.

The silence grew deafening.

Reaching out blindly, not daring to switch on a
light, the killer sucked in a gasp of disbelief when
his gloved hands discovered an empty bed. For
the first time that night, fear seized him.

"Goddammit, Josephine."

Turning onto a dark graveled road, William slowly maneuvered his Navigator up a rocky incline. Unable to see through the surrounding fog, he clicked off his high beams and caught sight of a deer as it dashed into a thicket of trees.

The road was littered with deep potholes, and the patient's mutterings became clear sentences with each jostle of the backseat.

"Josephine. Stop calling me . . . Michelle. Somebody help."

Her distress tugged at his heartstrings. "I'm doing all I can," he promised.

Finally, they approached the end of the unpaved road where a two-story, blue-gray, wooden house materialized as if by magic. In the dark, it looked like something right out of a horror movie, but in actuality, William knew it to be filled with love and many happy memories.

He rolled to a stop in front of the closed garage door and grabbed the remote from the visor. After jabbing the open button several times, he was mystified why the door refused to budge.

"Great," he mumbled. Cutting off the engine, he climbed out of the vehicle.

At least the rain had diminished to a light drizzle, and he didn't have to worry about his clothes sticking to his body. When he reached the garage, he struggled to open it manually, but remembered his brother, Larry, telling him that the partition had jammed sometime before his leaving for vacation, and he wasn't going to call a repair service until his family returned shortly before Christmas.

"Damn."

William jumped at the clap of thunder but relaxed when lightning flashed and illuminated the house. When he turned back toward the SUV, the raindrops suddenly quickened, and the wind picked up speed.

"Just get her in the house," he said, feeling a new wave of frustration seize him.

After rushing to the vehicle's back door, he wrenched it open. If he hurried, he could get them both inside before they were soaked completely.

He climbed in and positioned himself to lift her when what he saw stopped him in his tracks.

Beautiful pearl-shaped tears leaked from the woman's thick lashes as she once again wrestled against an invisible force. He wondered about the demons that chased her in her sleep, then put the thought aside.

"Everything is going to be okay," he assured her, then slid his arms beneath her body.

Instantly, her eyes flew open, and the unmistakable look of fear filled them. His arms fell away as their gazes met.

Her horrific scream filled William's ears a fraction before a good right hook clocked him across the chin. His head snapped to the side and crashed against the window.

The screaming morphed into a mad wail and grew distant within seconds.

William blinked but had trouble shaking the stars from his eyes and the pain from his temples. When his vision cleared, she was gone.

"Christ!" He scrambled out of the SUV and was instantly drenched by the night's sudden heavy downpour. "Wait! Come back!"

Racing after the wailing escapee, William felt his heart hammering inside his chest when he realized that she wasn't heading back down the gravel road, but into the thicket of trees where God only knew what lay in wait.

"Josie," he yelled, chasing after her and quickly receiving a solid whack across the cheek from a limp tree branch. He flinched at the raw sting but kept moving.

It was a marvel how fast she moved barefoot across slippery leaves and sharp, jagged rocks poking up sporadically from the earth. Surely, she couldn't see where she was going, because the rain and darkness made it impossible for William to make out anything.

Then the wailing stopped.

She's hurt.

His fear helped accelerate his pace and allowed him to dodge through the wet, heavy maze with surprising agility. "Please, God, don't let it end like this," he prayed.

From his peripheral vision, he saw a flash of white lying on the dark ground. His heartbeat nearly stopped. "No," he moaned weakly, and raced toward the disheartening sight.

Dropping to his knees beside her, William reached out to turn her still body over for inspection, prepared for the worst.

Gently, he rolled her over. The slow rise and fall of her chest sent a wave of relief through his tense body.

Lifting his head, he squinted up against the rain to see a thick tree branch and assumed that it was the cause of her being out cold.

Gathering her close, he lifted her into his arms and struggled through pure hell to find his way back to his brother's mountain hideaway home.

Detective Ming Delaney woke to a light tap on her shoulder. While stifling a yawn, her eyes took in her husband Conan's bodybuilder frame and amused expression.

"One of these mornings, I would actually like to wake up with you next to me." He leaned down and kissed her forehead.

Confused, she straightened in her chair and her stiff joints popped like a skyful of firecrackers on the Fourth of July.

"What time is it?"

"Seven."

"A.M?"

"As usual," he responded with a wry smile as he passed her to head for the kitchen. "Coffee?"

"Yeah, sure." She raked her fingers through her curtain of ink black hair and pressed her hand against her chin so her neck muscles would ease into place. Seconds later, the wonderful aroma of coffee wafted out to the dining room and caused a smile to curve the corners of her lips.

"Maybe if I put the coffeemaker in the bedroom, it would solve all of our problems."

"We don't have any problems." Ming rolled her

eyes as she stood up from the chair and removed her gun and badge from the table. "I'm taking a shower."

"Glad to hear it." He poked his head around the breakfast bar. "You want pancakes or waffles?"

"Surprise me," she said, flashing him a wink and a smile before disappearing into the back bedroom. Once there, she peeled off layers of clothes and turned on the shower to full blast.

For Ming, heaven was a showerhead with ten different control settings. She couldn't count the number of times a puzzling case came together during an Herbal Essence moment.

However, she paid a price for being obsessed with her work. Her husband could testify to that. Though she would also argue that he had known what he was getting into when he married her, it didn't stop her from feeling guilty.

Their marriage was hard enough when considering that both of their families opposed the union. Throughout Ming's life, her father praised all the opportunities America offered, but he in no way condoned a daughter of his marrying outside her race.

And as for Conan's family, they pretended to be the so-called opened-minded ones who always used terms like "you people" and "well, over here in America." Her poor husband spent more time apologizing for his family's arrogance than anything else. Holidays with the Delaney and Lee families could be described with one word: hell.

Reaching for the shampoo, Ming allowed her thoughts to travel back to work and the Thornton case. Usually, the death of a wanted felon wouldn't raise too many eyebrows down at the department, but the how and where Daniel Thornton died had Ming suspecting that this wasn't simply a drug deal gone bad.

Yet, those close to Thornton had a severe case of hear-no-evil, see-no-evil. No one knew anything. And the man's girlfriend was committed to Keystone Mental Institute shortly after his death.

Ming couldn't help but believe that the incidents were too coincidental to be ignored.

Shutting off the shower, Ming acknowledged a tinge of disappointment for not discovering any new clues in the case, but her Herbal Essence routine didn't perform its magic every morning.

Donning her favorite pink robe, Ming, wet hair and all, went to join her husband in the kitchen. But before she could settle down to her stack of buttermilk pancakes, the phone rang.

"Placing any bets?" Conan asked, peeking over his morning paper.

"It could be for you," she said, with little conviction. She grabbed her coffee and headed over to the wall unit near the refrigerator. "Maybe it's your mom complaining about my lackluster domestic skills again."

He chuckled. "What domestic skills?"

"My point." Ming smiled as she lifted the receiver. "Hello."

"Lee, I hope I didn't wake you."

Ming rolled her eyes at the sound of partner Tyrese's voice. "What's up?" There was no point insisting that he stop calling her by her maiden name. He would just pretend to forget.

"You've finally got your wish," Tyrese chirped.

"What are you talking about?"

"Keystone. We have a homicide . . . and a possible kidnapping. Thornton's girlfriend seems to have managed a disappearing act."

Ming stiffened. "I'm on my way."

"What are we going to tell the sister?" Dr. Rae Coleman asked Marcus Hines, Keystone Mental Institute's practice administrator. "I say we wait until we talk to our lawyers."

"Already on it," Marcus said, pacing the worn patch of carpet in front of his desk. If he weren't already balding, he would've been pulling his hair out for the past few hours. Instead, the few hairs horseshoed around his pale head were graying by the second.

Usually a quiet and reserved man, Marcus knew his quiet charm was what won him points with doctors and patients' families. Staring at an Ecosphere and listening to a Frank Sinatra CD usually relieved work-related stresses.

Not that day.

"What are the police saying?"

"At the moment, I don't know any more than you do."

"Which is nothing."

"Bingo."

Rae clasped her hands behind her back while her forehead wrinkled. "Poor Meredith. I just can't believe no one saw anything."

"We're pretty sure everything happened during a going-away thingy for one of the employees. Everyone claimed they visited the cafeteria for no more than a few minutes at a time for cake and ice cream."

"Just long enough for some crazy person to murder one of our prominent doctors and snatch a patient."

"Assuming the two incidents are related."

"How can they not be?"

Marcus shrugged and felt his lower abdomen bubble with anxiety. There was no sense in trying to take anything for it. No pharmaceutical company had developed a powerful enough drug to placate his rattled nerves.

When a light rap sounded at the door, his heart plummeted to his knees in fear of more bad news.

At the rate he was going, he would have to check himself in as a patient before the day was out.

"Come in," Rae instructed, when Marcus failed to do so.

Dr. Ambrose Turner gently pushed the door open. His brilliant head of flaming red hair was always a focal point for attention, second to the intriguing blue of his eyes. "The press is here," he said in his usual thick English accent.

Marcus didn't know how he managed it, but he gave Ambrose a quick nod and watched as he disappeared back behind the door.

"Boy, that was quick," Rae mumbled, and adjusted the black-rimmed glasses that made her look like an intense owl.

"Too quick," Marcus added, returning to his desk—maybe guzzling a bottle of Mylanta *would* bandage his intestinal problem.

"Should we talk to Ms. Ferrell before she actually hears about her missing sister on the news?"

He glanced over at Dr. Coleman, halfway wishing he could stuff a sock down her throat in order to stop her from stating the obvious. "Yes, I suppose we should."

"But before we talk with our attorneys?"

Marcus took a deep breath and trained his full attention on her. "It seems that we have little choice in the matter, Dr. Coleman. Now, I hate to delay you from your patients any further—"

"No, no. This is definitely more important—"

"There is nothing more important than the care of our patients, Dr. Coleman," he said, forcing steel and patience, of which he was bankrupt, into his voice. "I'm rather surprised to hear you say such a thing."

A rush of burgundy bloomed against Dr. Coleman's creamy cocoa complexion as she raised her five-foot-two frame from her chair.

On any other day, the morning would have been a routine dance of harmless flirtation between the two, but this implausible crisis changed all of that.

Rae's reluctance to leave was nothing more than a sad attempt to gather enough juicy details to crown her queen of watercooler gossip for a day.

"I guess on that note, I'll leave you to deal with Ms. Ferrell on your own."

Marcus's temples throbbed at the woman's name. The woman was more than a handful, especially since she opposed her sister's transfer to the facility in the first place. He could practically smell the pending lawsuit.

"I'm more than capable of dealing with Ms. Ferrell," he said, and winced at the hollowness of his words.

Dr. Coleman laughed. "Sure you are." She headed for the door, but before her hands landed on the knob, there was another knock.

"Come in," Marcus shouted. His irritation was at an all-time high.

When Dr. Turner's burning bush reappeared, Marcus suspected the good doctor was actually eavesdropping.

"Yes, what is it?"

At Dr. Turner's grave expression, Marcus braced himself to hear that the police had discovered that another doctor had been murdered and stashed in the trunk of their car, but instead Ambrose delivered worse news.

"Ms. Josephine Ferrell is here to see you."

William didn't dare go to sleep.

Instead, he'd spent the first few hours in his brother's home tending to the needs of his patient. So far, the hardest part was changing her out of the wet hospital gown and into a full-length flannel number he found in his sister-in-law's dresser drawer.

His professionalism was challenged while he glanced at a body he once knew intimately. Even now, as she lay sleeping, he was drawn to her fragility and innocence.

William stared at her full lips and could feel his body give in to a magnetic force, but shame was an equally powerful weapon in his arsenal, and he backed away.

He sighed and rechecked the dilation of her eyes, satisfied with his assessment of a mild concussion.

Once he'd finished tending to the cut along her right brow, he went to change out of his disguise and clean up.

All the while, his mind never strayed far from the woman in the other room. He exhaled a heavy breath and hung his head low beneath the steady stream of hot water.

"Josie," he murmured, as water trickled down around his face. The sound of her name had a way of ripping open a wound he'd long thought healed. More than a decade had passed since he experienced pain with such intensity.

"A man should never wear his heart where his ribs can't protect it." His father's voice rang clearly in his head.

William didn't listen the first time around, but conceded that at this point in his life it was sound advice.

Scrubbed clean, he finally shut off the shower and slid into one of his brother's robes. Minutes later, he was back beside her bed, staring at a face seemingly untouched by time. His eyes lifted to the full-length mirror on the other side of the bed to stare at his own reflection.

Time had done a number on him.

Through good genetics, at thirty-seven, William

possessed a full head of dark, wavy hair—though there were growing shocks of gray along the temples. He had the long hours at Grady Hospital to thank for the permanent thin grooves etched around his eyes. Character lines, someone told him. For years, he had dealt with people commenting about his strong resemblance to George Clooney—except for the color of his eyes. Where the popular actor's were a dark brown, William's were a bright baby blue.

What would she see when the drugs finally wore off? How would she feel?

Expelling a weary breath, he stood and crossed the plush carpet for his leather duffel bag and withdrew something else he'd snatched from Keystone: a medical chart.

Another look at the name on the chart and an avalanche of questions, possibilities, and doubts buried his good intensions. Suddenly, he had a vivid image of prison bars clanking with a note of finality.

"Stop it," he commanded. "You're doing the right thing."

He returned to the chair next to the bed, made another quick assessment of Josie's vitals, and settled back for a good read.

"Michelle Andrews," he read, and was unable to stop his glance from briefly sliding over to the bed. *Patient transferred from Northside Hospital after stabilization of an apparent suicide attempt.* His eyes lingered on the word "suicide." In no way did it describe the woman he knew. It was much like trying to force a large square box into a small triangle. It just didn't fit.

Toxicology reports lethal levels of lithium, Prozac, and Tegretol. William shook his head and struggled through the rest of the report. *Hair strands from subject are inconclusive to history of abuse. Patient shows a lack of awareness to time and place and often shows high levels of agitation when called by her name. Behavior may be due to mental illness.*

William lowered the chart and thought back on his first day at Keystone Institute six weeks before and remembered his reaction when he'd walked into Ms. Andrews's room. It was perhaps the first time in his life that he was rendered speechless. When Dr. Turner inquired if he was okay, he forced his professional mask on and resumed his work. But in the days that followed, he couldn't get Michelle out of his mind and her striking resemblance to Josephine Ferrell.

Closing his eyes, the sights and sounds of Paris some sixteen years ago welcomed him back like an old friend. . . .

Rushing to get out of the rain, William and five of his closest friends ducked into Le Petite Opportun. They were looking for a jazz club and were pleasantly surprised that they had stumbled onto a nice one.

"Hey, looks like getting lost was a blessing in disguise," Bernard Watson announced with a beaming smile.

Bernard's girlfriend, Brenda, rolled her eyes. "Nice try. Seeing that you're the one that got us lost in the first place."

"There's a method behind my madness," Bernard assured.

The rest of the group, William, Ryan, and Eddie, laughed and rolled their eyes before turning and seeking a table large enough to seat them all.

A bass started up with a smooth melodic beat that had William immediately tapping his feet, and when the gentle tickle of the ivories came into play his mind searched for the name of the haunting tune.

Unexpectedly, the soft, silky voice of an angel flowed over a microphone. William's eyes flew to the stage, where a gorgeous caramel beauty held him spellbound.

Willow weep for me. Willow weep for me. Bend your branches down along the ground and cover me.

Despite being dressed in all black, the sultry singer's hourglass figure was obvious in a tight turtleneck and form-fitting stretch pants. Her eyes remained closed as she continued to belt out the tune. It was as if she'd experienced every word of that sad fable of lost love and, as a result, he was sure that everyone in the room felt it.

At the tug on his arm, he lowered himself into a chair without taking his eyes from the stage.

Her lush lips were something to behold, but it was the gentle flutter of her lashes that caught his attention. Given the depth of which she sang, he wanted them to open and reveal the mirrors of her soul or tears to slide from them.

A hand waved in front of his face, forcing him to blink.

His friends snickered among themselves.

"Looks like someone is on the prowl again." Brenda chuckled and wiggled her eyebrows playfully at William. "I guess this means he's gotten Sammy out of his system."

"Thank God," Ryan muttered.

Before William could respond, the rest of the group chimed in their agreement. His brief fling with Samantha Godfrey during his last semester at school started out well but quickly cooled into friendship.

"However," Bernard said. "I say the honey onstage might just be what the doctor ordered."

Miffed, Brenda popped him on the back of the head and scowled when he looked at her incredulously.

"What?" he asked, rubbing his head.

William just smiled and returned his attention to center stage.

Weeping willow tree, weep in sympathy. Bend your branches . . .

"She's something else," he marveled. "Something else."

Eddie leaned forward in his chair and spoke in his heavy Caribbean accent. "I didn't know you had an eye for the sistas."

"I have an eye for beauty."

A petite blonde approached the table with a wide smile and tray. "*Bonsoir. Vous êtes américains?*"

"Yes, we are," Brenda answered brightly. "Do you speak English?"

"Yes, I do. Would you like to place your order now?"

"Excuse me," William interrupted. "But may I ask who's performing?"

The waitress turned, glanced up at the stage, then turned back to him with a shrug. "I don't know her name, but I've seen her several times."

"What's the name of the band?"

"Actually, it's open mike night. Everyone's welcome to sing."

"You mean she's not a professional?" Bernard jumped into the conversation, only to receive another pop on the head.

"Why are you so interested?" Brenda sassed.

Whatever else was said, William didn't hear it. He was on his feet and moving toward the stage. He didn't plan what he was going to do next, he just allowed instinct to take over.

The song ended to a hearty round of applause, and William tapped the piano player on the shoulder and politely asked if he could take over.

Concluding she had a love for Billie Holiday, he knew just the song to play next. "I'm a fool to want you," he sang slyly.

The singer turned to him and met his stare as he repeated the opening line.

She brought the microphone to her lips and picked up where he left off. "To want a love that can't be true."

And just like that, the world melted away.

While he realized that his voice was no match for hers, their notes still complemented each other as they continued the song of longing.

He had never seen anyone like her.

She removed the microphone from the stand and sauntered toward William like a seductress on the prowl. And despite the melancholy tone of their song, a small smile lifted the corners of his lips as he watched her.

When she reached the piano, the faintest scent of her perfume tickled his nose, and he knew that he would remember the sweet fragrance for the rest of his life.

His fingers drifted over the final notes of the song just as she sat on the piano bench next to him and smiled. Not only did she look good, she smelled like flowers and sunshine. Was that even possible?

Their performance played out as if it was a well-rehearsed act, and the resulting round of applause finally dissolved their private world and jarred them back to reality.

"You're pretty good," she whispered to him before nodding at the audience.

"Thank you." Pleasantly surprised by the husky lilt of her voice, he continued to smile. "But you're *very* good."

Together they stood from the bench and worked their way off the stage before he extended his hand in an awkward introduction. "William Hayes."

When she slid her small hand into his, he was more than aware of its softness.

"Nice to meet you. I'm Josephine Ferrell, but please call me Josie."

Ming's leather jacket did little to warm her against the early-morning chill. She uttered no complaint as she supervised the forensic team and the questioning process outside Keystone.

Detective Tyrese Simmons made his way over to her, shaking his head and flipping through his small notepad. Partners for five years, Ming and Tyrese had found their own rhythm when working a crime scene, but for the most part he was the brawn and she was the brain.

"Any ideas?" he asked.

She frowned and glanced at her own notes. "Nothing inspiring, one dead doctor and a missing patient."

"Not just any patient but Thornton's girlfriend. How do you feel about coincidences?"

"Never been a believer." Flipping the notepad closed, she drew in the morning's cold air while contemplating a connection between this case and the Thornton case. "Maybe Thornton's murderer believes the girlfriend knows something—or has something."

Tyrese shrugged. "Well, they sure went through an awful lot of trouble."

"And had a lot of luck on their side: an empty parking lot, a farewell party, and no witnesses inside the hospital."

"Luck or calculation. Could be someone on the inside," Tyrese added.

Ming looked over at him as he gave her a sheepish smile.

"What can I say? Even I get an idea every once in a while."

Ming shrugged. "I guess stranger things have been known to happen." From over her partner's shoulder she spotted a six-foot-six brickhouse of a man approach with tears in his eyes.

Whatever Tyrese was saying he stopped in midsentence and turned to see what had caught her attention.

"Hi, I'm Detective Delaney," she said, moving toward the man. "Did you know the victim?"

The giant nodded as his kind brown eyes continued to swim through shallow films of tears. "I'm Theodore Watts, lead nurse on third shift. I believe I might have been one of the last people to see Dr. Bancroft before she was killed."

Ming's brows stretched upward while simultaneously flipping her notepad open again. "When was the last time you saw her?"

"Early this morning. I-I think it was sometime around 2:00 A.M." He wiped at a stray tear.

Surprised at the large man's waterworks, Ming cast a quick glance back at her partner, only to be rewarded with another shrug.

"And your relationship with Dr. Bancroft was strictly . . . professional?"

Sniffing, he nodded. "She was a wonderful doctor. Definitely a favorite among the staff."

Ming nodded but continued to scrutinize the man while he relayed the events of his last encounter with Dr. Bancroft.

"Did you notice anything odd about her behavior? Was she nervous or jumpy even?"

Theo thought the question over before he responded. "No. She seemed normal."

He seemed genuine, but in murder cases, Ming had discovered that there was a world of great actors outside of Hollywood. "If we have any further questions is there an address and phone number where we can contact you?"

Theo, as he liked to be called, gave them his

contact information and before he left the two agents he stole a glance over to the yellow crime tape around Bancroft's BMW. "It's a real shame. I hope you catch whoever did this."

Ming studied him again. "We'll do what we can."

Theo nodded as his eyes glazed over, but he spared the two agents more tears as he turned and walked away.

"That was interesting," Tyrese said. "Do you think that he was lying?"

"About what part?"

"The strictly professional colleagues part. He seems awfully torn up about this."

Ming's gaze remained locked on the departing giant as she mulled over her answer. "I'm not quite sure what I think. Right now I'm focused on finding Michelle Andrews—preferably alive."

Josephine Ferrell held her temper in check as she was escorted into Marcus Hines's office, but as her eyes met the practice administrator's, she actually felt her skin crawl with irritation.

"Ms. Ferrell," he began with an unsure smile. "What a surprise. I was just about to call—"

"Spare me," she said, sliding open her midlength, coffee-and-cream chinchilla to settle her gloved hands against her hips. "The first thing I want to know is how your *reputable*—that was the word you used last week, wasn't it?"

Mr. Hines cleared his throat and gave her a slow nod.

"Good. I didn't want to get it wrong. How is it that your *reputable* institution failed, not only to provide the best possible care for my sister, but also managed to lose her in the process?"

Once again, Hines cleared his throat, but squirmed all the same beneath her hard gaze. "Ms. Ferrell, I know that you're upset."

"Pissed."

"Very well. I know you're pissed. But I want to assure you that we're doing everything we can to get to the bottom of what happened here last night."

Josephine's lips curled as utter loathing for the short balding man hit her like a whip. "And what about *finding* my sister?"

Hines paled to the point of looking ghostly. "Of course, we're working closely with the authorities in locating Michelle."

Josephine's sneer turned into a wicked smile. "Are you now?" She glided over to a vacant chair in front of his desk and took her time settling into its soft cushions. "May I ask when exactly were you going to tell me about all of this?"

He hesitated a second too long.

"After discussing your position with your attorneys?" she guessed, and waited to scrutinize his reaction. "Maybe you're worried that I'll sue the hell out of this two-bit organization?"

"Now, Josephine—"

"Ms. Ferrell."

Hines plopped into his own chair, seemingly unprepared to handle this sort of dilemma. "Ms. Ferrell, the practice was first trying to ascertain the full scope of the situation. We wanted to first make sure that Michelle wasn't somewhere else on the fifteenth floor before we informed you that she was indeed missing."

"So you thought that you simply misplaced her?"

A flash of annoyance flickered across his features. "We didn't misplace her."

"As far as you know," she countered, without missing a beat.

He paused as if needing to do a mental count to ten before continuing. "Ms. Ferrell, I understand that you're angry . . ." He caught her daggered stare. "Pissed," he corrected. "But there is a certain protocol that we must adhere to—"

"Meaning that this has happened before?"

He hesitated again, and Josephine waited patiently for his answer.

"Years ago, we had a patient who wandered from the facility."

One delicate eyebrow arched as she measured the nervous man before her. "Wandered off?" She suffered through another bout of his clearing his throat before he got around to clarifying his statement.

"It was a good ten years ago. Since then we've implemented security measures to prevent something like that from ever happening again."

"And yet my sister is missing."

"But she didn't wander off," he countered.

"And how did you come to that conclusion?"

"You need an ID badge to scan in and out of the fifteenth floor. Period. So, whoever took your sister knew exactly what they were doing."

"Took her?" Josephine blinked, then leaned forward in her chair. "Why would anyone want to *take* my sister?"

Hines patiently braided his fingers on his desk. "I don't have an answer to that."

Fire lit her eyes. "It doesn't seem you know much of anything, if you ask me."

"The likely answer might have something to do with Michelle's personal life," he boldly added. "The unfortunate thing is that it may have cost the life of one of our doctors as well."

"That's crazy," she retorted indignantly. "Maybe Michelle stole a badge and left on her own. Did you ever think of that?"

"Given her condition, I doubt that."

"But you don't know for sure. Do you?" she asked, evenly.

"No." Hines held her heated gaze as he continued. "But I suspect otherwise. The police have been here several times, wanting to question Michelle about an ex-boyfriend. A drug dealer, if I remember correctly. Given her current medical condition, we were able to decline the request until a court order of some kind was obtained."

"When in the hell did all of this happen?"

The room sweltered from the woman's intensity, and Hines adjusted his tie in a vain attempt to get comfortable. "The early part of last week."

She straightened her shoulders. "And why wasn't I informed?"

"With all due respect, Ms. Ferrell, but until you present a power of attorney naming you executor of medical decisions for Michelle, this facility has no legal obligation to inform you of anything. Given her propensity to violence whenever you visit, it's clear to me that there is some bad blood between the two of you."

"How dare you," Josephine snapped, smashing her hand on his desk.

Hines jumped in his seat. "Ms. Ferrell, I'm going to have to ask you to contain yourself."

She stood. "Go screw yourself."

Her venom struck him hard, but he maintained

his professionalism. "Please sit down, Ms. Ferrell. While I understand your position—"

"I highly doubt that." Josephine headed toward the door. "I'll be back with my lawyers and your damn power of attorney." She jerked open the office door and promptly collided with a tall Asian woman.

"Excuse you," Josephine snapped.

"Ms. Andrews?" Ming asked astounded, and then cut a questioning looking across the room at Marcus Hines.

"What?" Josephine stepped back and rubbed her hand along her temple.

"Detective Delaney." Hines cleared his throat as he came around his desk. "This is Ms. Josephine Ferrell. She's Michelle Andrews's sister."

Ming's gaze returned to the woman before her. Remembering the photograph taken from Thornton's wallet, she asked, "Are you and Michelle twins?"

Josephine smiled tightly. "As a matter of fact, we are."

"Josephine is a beautiful name," the twenty-one-year-old William said, accepting Josie's hand and lifting it to his lips to place a kiss against her knuckles.

Her cheeks darkened prettily as she smiled. "Something tells me you're a dangerous man, Mr. Hayes."

"William or Will, if you prefer."

She slid her hand from his. "Not Billy or Bill?" She turned and maneuvered through the tight space between the club's tables and patrons.

"My father is Bill," he answered, and followed close behind her.

"So you're a junior?"

"Actually, I'm the fourth. William Charles Hayes IV."

She stopped and turned back toward him with a glowing smile. "My father's name is Charles."

"Really?" Pleased that he'd said something to capture her attention, he relaxed and smiled. "I hope that's a good thing."

"It's not bad." She gave him a quick wink. "Would you like to join me and my friends?"

He followed the wave of her hand to a crowded table of women.

"Well, actually, no," he said, mustering a straight face.

Disappointment crept into her features. "Oh? Are you here with someone?"

Until that moment, William had forgotten about his table of friends and turned to see them watching him from across the room. "Yes and no," he answered, returning his gaze to hers. "What I would like to do is either grab our own table or go somewhere we can be alone."

Josie lifted a quizzical brow. "I hardly know you."

"That's the whole point," he said. "It is a chance for us to get to know each other."

She held his serious gaze while the band struck up a smooth instrumental number. "I'm curious, William. Is this charm or cockiness?"

"It's definitely not cockiness. I'm terrified you're going to say no."

"You should be." Her smile was slow to return as she made a casual glance around. "Where would you like to sit?"

Relief and excitement swelled in his chest. "How about we grab something toward the back? I want to make sure we're not disturbed." When her eyes sparkled up at him, his heart muscles tightened.

"All right," she said.

A few minutes later, William and Josie sat opposite one another at a small round table and grinned like a couple of teenagers.

"Okay, you've got my attention." She crossed her legs and settled her hands in her lap.

"Now I don't know where to begin," he admitted. "I'm not usually tongue-tied around women."

Again her right brow lifted quizzically, and he concluded the act was a habit. "Picking up women in smoky jazz clubs is something you do often?"

He blinked. "Oh, no. I've never done *this* before."

"So where do you usually meet women?"

Cornered, a rush of heat crept up William's face and enflamed his ears. "Is there any possible way I can rewind the clock so I can take my foot out of my mouth?"

"Afraid not."

Her melodious laugh had the same effect on his

heart as her smile. Not to mention that something in his stomach was performing acrobatic somersaults each time his gaze leveled with hers. "Okay. Fair enough. I tend to meet women at school or at the hospital."

Another smile. "You scope out hospitals?"

It was his turn to laugh. "I work at one."

"Oh? What do you do?"

"I'm a first-year medical student."

Josie's features colored with surprise. "Ooh, a doctor. I'm impressed."

"Well, not yet. But that's the plan."

"*Bonsoir. Vous désirez?*"

William glanced up to see the same petite blond waitress from earlier.

"*J'aurai un verre de votre meilleur Chardonnay,*" Josie answered.

William was impressed with how she shifted from English to perfect French. "I'll have the same," William informed the waitress before returning his attention to the woman across from him. "It's your turn. How do you usually pick up men?"

"I don't." She lifted her right hand to flash a diamond ring.

"You're engaged?"

"I'm afraid so." Her smile widened.

The waitress returned, set down their drinks, and scurried back to the bar.

"Then why are you here with me?" William asked, picking up his glass.

"That's a good question." She took a sip from her glass. "I don't know. Maybe I find you charming?"

"That's not it," he said. He was determined not to crash and burn.

She took another sip of her drink, but kept her gaze glued to his over the rim of her glass. "I like you," she said finally. "You have an honest face. You even remind me of someone."

He nodded. "Yeah, yeah. George Clooney on the *Roseanne* show."

She frowned. "The what show?"

"Roseanne—Roseanne Barr."

"We don't get a lot of American television over here," she said. "Sorry."

He frowned. "You live in Paris?"

"Yes. I'm studying music at the Sorbonne."

"Ah. I assumed that you were vacationing like me."

"Well, you know what happens when you assume."

He shrugged with a smile. "All right, you got me. But you are American. Where are you from?"

"Actually, I've lived all over, but I was born in Georgia."

William's eyes rounded. "That's where I'm from. Atlanta?"

"You're looking at a Grady baby."

"Well, I'll be damned. I had to travel halfway around the world to find the girl next door."

"God has a sense of humor sometimes."

"And a master plan," he added.

Josie chuckled. "You sound like a hopeless romantic."

"Guilty." He leaned back in his chair. "So where is this fiancé of yours? I can't imagine anyone being crazy enough to let you out of his sight."

"He's doing some work in Johannesburg for the summer."

"South Africa?"

"Yes."

"Good." His confidence grew. "Now all I have to do is get you to fall deeply, madly, and completely in love with me before he gets back." He held out his glass.

"I highly doubt that."

"I'm going to take that as a challenge." He winked, then clinked their glasses together . . .

Ming crossed her arms and blocked the exit from Hines's office. "Twins. Growing up I wished I had a twin."

"It has its benefits." Josephine mimicked her stance. "Are you the one investigating my sister's disappearance?"

Ming was taken aback by the obvious hostility in the woman's narrowed gaze. "Yes, ma'am. I am." She glanced at Hines again, then addressed Josephine. "I would've come up sooner had I known you were here. Do you mind answering a few questions?"

"Do I have a choice?"

The response further confused Ming. Here was a woman whose sister had either wandered off or been taken from the institution, and she was acting like answering questions was going to interfere with a manicure appointment.

"It shouldn't take too long," Ming said.

Josephine's gaze meticulously swept over Ming. "Okay. Shoot," she said, holding her ground.

"Mr. Hines," Ming said, but didn't pull her gaze away from Josephine, "may we borrow your office for a few minutes?"

"By all means." He joined them at the door. "Please take all the time you need."

Ming read relief in the administrator's expression and stepped aside before the man actually bowled her over, trying to get out. She smiled and moved farther into the room. "Would you like to have a seat?"

Josephine waited until Ming closed the door before she turned and walked to a vacant chair in front of the large mahogany desk.

Intrigue and confusion twisted inside of Ming as she took her time to move over to the desk.

When she settled behind it, she reached inside her leather jacket and pulled out her notepad.

"Had I known Michelle had a sister, I would've contacted you sooner," she said, wondering why she *didn't* have this piece of information.

"Not many people know."

Ming frowned. "Why is that?"

Josephine paused as if to weigh her words. "Until a year ago, Michelle and I didn't know the other existed."

The response generated only a mild surprise from Ming. "So you don't know your sister that well?"

"Not as well as I would like to."

"In this past year, how much time did you spend with her? Do you know her friends, boyfriends, or anyone who might want to cause her harm?"

"Can't say that I do." Josephine opened her handbag and withdrew a pack of cigarettes. "Do you mind if I smoke?"

"Not at all." Ming spotted an ashtray and pushed it toward her. "Does the name Daniel Thornton mean anything to you?"

Josephine lit her cigarette. She took her time as she drew a deep drag and blew out a long stream of smoke. "Never heard of him."

"He was Michelle's boyfriend." Ming studied her.

"Really?"

Ming nodded. "At least according to Thornton's friends."

Josephine shrugged while boredom glazed her eyes.

"Daniel Thornton was a slippery felon—at least that's how we viewed him down at department." She waited, but when she received no response from Josephine, she continued. "He was murdered about six weeks ago. He was found dead under a tree in Grant Park."

"Sounds like he was in a dangerous profession."

Ming gave her a sardonic smile. "True. But despite the bullet in his chest, the autopsy report states that he drowned. Strange, wouldn't you say?"

Josephine blew out another stream of smoke. "I suppose, but I fail to see what any of this has to do with me or my sister."

"Your sister is missing, and a dead doctor was found in the parking lot. Michelle might know something about Thornton's death. My notes say that Michelle attempted suicide the day after Thornton's body was found. It's possible whoever killed your sister's boyfriend is responsible for killing a doctor here and kidnapping Michelle."

Josephine laughed. It wasn't a light, amused sort of thing, but a head-back hearty cackle that further shocked Ming.

"You know what I think?" Josephine leaned forward and snubbed out her cigarette. "I think you and Mr. Hines are on a great fishing expedition, and you're bound and determined to snare Michelle in this whole fiasco."

"Ms. Ferrell—"

"Let me finish," she snapped, rising from her chair. "This institution lost my sister. Most likely, Michelle stole someone's badge and walked out of here. I have no idea who or why someone killed a doctor here—maybe it was a random act of violence, maybe the doctor was into something shady. I don't know, and I doubt that you know either because you're too busy trying to place the blame on my sister."

"I'm not blaming Ms. Andrews for anything."

"Could have fooled me." She headed toward the door. "Sorry I couldn't be any more help, but I have a sister to find."

Ming sat back as she watched the angry woman storm out of the room. "Wow. What a bitch."

William made himself a pot of coffee after languishing in the sweet, love-filled memories of Paris. Despite so many years of trying to forget, it astounded him how clearly those images came back to him. The sights, the smells, and the sounds stirred up a lot of painful memories. Yet he knew if he had the chance to go back, he would in a heartbeat.

During the three months he spent in Paris, he'd hardly left Josie's side. He didn't know exactly when she fell in love with him, but he was pretty much smitten that first night.

He smiled to himself as he reached for the powdered creamer from one of the cupboards. Just as quickly, his mood shifted. He wasn't out of the woods yet. There was still a high chance for his colleague, Dr. Bancroft, to finger him as a possible suspect in Michelle Andrews's disappearance.

William took the first sip of his coffee as he reviewed his last visit to Meredith's office . . .

"I'm telling you I know this girl," William insisted, as he closed the door to Meredith's office.

Meredith settled behind her polished mahogany desk and looked at him with her kind, chocolate-colored eyes. "Maybe you do, Dr. Hayes, but it doesn't change the fact that Ms. Andrews is a very sick woman."

William shook his head while he paced in front of her. "That's just it. Her name isn't Andrews."

"According to her chart it is." Meredith crossed her arms. "She has a long history of mental illness and has been in and out of trouble with the law for most of her life. It started off with petty theft and cruelty to animals. Before long she was a full-fledged menace to society. By fifteen her adoptive mother had had enough and kicked her out onto the streets."

He shook his head and rejected everything Meredith said. "It's a lie. The woman I met—"

"Isn't it possible that this woman just simply looks like the person you're referring to? I'm told that she has a sister—"

"I'm not wrong about this." William slammed his hands down on her desk.

Meredith blinked and calmly stared up at him. "I don't know what this is all about, Dr. Hayes, but this conversation is over."

He closed his eyes and drew a deep breath. "I'm sorry. I didn't mean to snap at you like that."

She didn't respond.

He drew himself upright and took another calming breath before he started again. "Can we at least lower her medication so that she's not so sedated? I'm sure that she'll be able to tell us who she is."

"I already know who she is."

William's temper threatened to explode again.

"Dr. Hayes, did you happen to notice the slashes across Ms. Andrews's wrists?"

The question deflated his anger.

"No? I did. They were slashed pretty badly by Ms. Andrews herself. Do you want to know who else wants to talk to Ms. Andrews?"

William now lowered his weight into the vacant chair across from Meredith's desk as her words punched him hard.

"The police," she answered for him. "She's a suspect in her boyfriend's homicide." Meredith stood, then walked around to the front of her desk and leaned against it. "Do you see why I won't let you go in there and talk to her?"

"No," William said, truthfully. "This is a case of mistaken identity."

"On your part, yes." Meredith crossed her arms. "If you go in there filling her head that she's someone else, trust me, she's going to agree with you. She's going to tell you whatever you want to hear so she can get out of this place."

"That's not true."

"Sure it is," Meredith said. "Andrews is the smoothest liar you'll ever meet. She's not only a danger to herself, but to those around her as well."

"And all of this is in her chart?"

"Most of it. The rest is from personal experience." Meredith nodded. "This is not the first time Andrews has been here at Keystone. I've treated her before."

The phone rang, and William returned to the present. He sloshed coffee over the rim of his cup and burned his hand. "Christ!" Clumsily, he sat the cup back on the counter and waved his hand around as he made his way over to the phone.

"Hello."

"Ah, Dr. Hayes. You're there." Ecaterina's thick Romanian accent came over the line.

"Good morning, Cat," he said. "You got my message."

"Yes. I would've called back sooner, but Nicolae and I had a few errands to run this morning."

William chuckled. "No need to explain. I understand."

"I just don't understand why you need me to go all the way out to Pine Mountain."

"I'm taking care of, uh, one of Sheila's cousins." William rubbed at his temples as he recited the lie he'd practiced. "She's pretty out of it, so she shouldn't be too much trouble."

"You're such a good brother-in-law," Cat praised. "Taking care of Larry's extended family like this."

William's guilt multiplied. His behavior in the last twenty-four hours was akin to an out-of-body experience. Kidnapping, lying—what would come next?

"I'll be happy to come out there Monday and do what I can," she said cheerfully. "Anything for you, Dr. Hayes."

William thanked her and hurried off the phone.

A headache immediately bloomed in William's temples. He reviewed his plan to leave Josie with his trusted housekeeper. The risk was high, but it was also a necessity.

He was already scheduled off for the weekend, but if he took any more time off from the Institute right on the heels of a disapperance, surely he'd raise more than a few eyebrows. Speaking of which, he thought, grabbing his cup again, he should see if anything was on the news.

He strode into the living room and clicked on the television. On Channel 2, news anchor Warren Savage stared back at him. Keystone's emblem and a digital graphic of a white-chalked body projected from the corner of the screen.

"Police were called to Keystone Mental Institute early this morning when a prominent doctor at the facility was found dead in the trunk of her car. Minutes later, the institute discovered a patient was missing. Authorities are trying to piece together whether the two incidents are connected. The name of the doctor as well as the missing patient has yet to be released at this time."

William pressed the mute button on the remote. *Dead? Found in the trunk of a car. Murdered?* He stared at the reporter for a few frantic heartbeats before bolting to the kitchen to retrieve the phone. Upon picking up the receiver, he quickly hung up. Who was he going to call, and what was he going to say?

"The truth," he thought. He would say he saw everything on the news. He nodded, telling himself it sounded good, and grabbed the phone again.

While he waited for the line to connect, the words to his prepared speech jumbled inside his head. On the fifth ring, the line was transferred to Marcus Hines's voice mail.

William hung up without leaving a message.

But his mind raced over the previous night's events, and he couldn't stop obsessing over what the hell had happened and who was murdered. Slowly the rest of the reporter's words sank in: ". . . authorities are trying to piece together whether the two incidents are connected."

"If I'm caught, they're going to think I'm a murderer."

To help combat Josie's withdrawal symptoms, William decided to administer methadone injections twice a day. The drug was a narcotic pain reliever, similar to morphine. It was commonly used for drug addiction detoxification and maintenance programs.

For most of Saturday, William helped his patient through fits of delirium, heavy sweating, vomiting, and manic outbursts. He found all of these to be good signs.

The day flew by, and, as night descended, William was exhausted. When Josie fell into a deep slumber, he could no longer ignore his own needs. First thing being first, he sated his hunger with a large bowl of pasta and a bottle of Heineken.

Outside, he heard the rain return and pound the windows and roof as though it had a vicious vendetta against the house.

William moved into the living room and settled into an armchair juxtaposed to a plaid sofa and in front of the television. He should check the news again, he rationalized, but he had no idea what he would do if the news broadcast his picture as the latest member on the most wanted list.

He punched the power button on the remote control, and the screen came alive with snowy static. William grunted and scanned the other channels. They all showed the same thing.

Great. The cable was out. He stood up from the chair and crossed over to the television. He checked the cable box and the other cords and connections. Everything appeared to be fine.

A power line must be down, he concluded.

A brilliant flash of lightning illuminated the wall of windows and the house lights flickered as a mild threat.

He huffed a tired breath and went in search of gas lamps, flashlights, and candles.

He lit the fireplaces in the living room and master bedroom. From the upstairs linen closet, he gathered extra blankets and comforters. When he put everything in place, there was a mighty thunderclap overhead, and the lights went out.

He returned to Josie's bedside and changed her IV bag, mopped the sweat from her fevered brow, then settled back into the chair across from the bed and watched her.

His thoughts wrestled with how she came to be admitted to a psychiatric ward under a false name. Could it truly be a case of mistaken identity? How likely was it that the hospital had gotten her mixed up with another patient?

Slim to none.

However, sixteen years was a long time. He'd lived another life since then and was sure that she had, too.

His gaze fell away from the bed and slid to the medical chart on the vanity table next to him. He picked up the chart and flipped through it once again. All the while, the square box refused to cram into the small triangle.

William set the chart aside. With everything he had attended to that day, he didn't have much time to call Marcus Hines again. The cable was still out, and there was no way for him to know who was murdered. Had the murder happened while he was on the premises? Did he leave any clues to *his* criminal actions?

Scientists say there are always clues, but he prayed that, in his case, it wasn't true.

What if this woman was really Michelle Andrews?

He cleared his head of this train of thought. He had been over it numerous times before he concocted his plan to steal Josie away. He wasn't mad, and he hadn't taken the wrong woman.

An ear-piercing scream followed by a loud crash propelled William to his feet.

From the bed, Josie flailed about like a madwoman. Her jumbled words were incomprehensible, but it was clear that she no longer wanted the IV in her arm.

"No, no, Josie." He rushed over to her and struggled to restrain her. At her surge of superhuman strength, William climbed onto the bed and pinned her hands down.

In response, Josie bucked, thrashed, and, as a last desperate attempt, sank her teeth into his arm.

He clenched his jaw shut. No matter what, he refused to release his hold on her, and after what seemed like an eternity, she gave up and drew away from his arm.

Seconds later, the fight left her body, and she fell limp beneath him.

Panting heavily, William held firm, suspicious of her abrupt surrender. Finally, as his adrenaline waned and Josie's breathing became slow and even, he sighed with relief and released his grip.

Immediately, Josie came up with a left hook that literally stunned him but didn't knock him off of her.

"Josie, stop. It's me, William. I'm trying to help you."

She got another good blow across the high part of his left cheek before he was able to pin her back down.

"No. No! Let me out!" she screamed.

William's heart raced while he debated whether to give her a sedative. In the end, to do so would be counterproductive.

Josie's threats diminished to low grumbles.

It was a long time before William relaxed. When he did, he was fairly confident that she was sound asleep. At least he prayed she was. He couldn't take another blow to the head.

He climbed off her and exhaled in a long, tired breath. He definitely had his work cut out for him, and he expected more outbursts before daybreak.

After he checked Josie's IV tube, he righted the stand and spotted an old porcelain basin across the room. He stood up from the bed and walked over to retrieve it.

Minutes later, he'd filled the basin with iced water and gathered a few towels. He settled back beside the bed and dipped a towel into the water, wrung it out, and pressed it against her face.

She sighed softly in her sleep as if it was the very thing she needed.

The first seventy-two hours of detox were usually the hardest. He would do all he could to help her through it, even if it included being her punching bag.

When he finished cooling her off, he put everything away and returned to the armchair. The rain continued outside. Instead of drifting off to sleep, he heard a light plopping sound.

He eased out of the chair again and quickly found the spot in the room where there was a small leak in the ceiling.

He rushed back downstairs and found a bucket to set under the drip. After a quick look through the house, he found two other places where he had to set pots.

Once he was through, he returned to the room and settled back into the armchair. But before he was able to close his eyes, Josie started up again.

It was going to be a long night.

First thing Sunday morning, the rain finally stopped, and William found himself on the roof of the house. As a man who loved working with his hands, he found repairing the roof almost therapeutic.

Once he was through, he checked on his patient before heading back out to chop firewood. With him returning to work the next day, he now worried about the atmosphere at Keystone. The electricity and cable were still out, so he had no idea what was being reported on the news. At one point, his curiosity led him to sit in the car for news snippet, but he heard nothing. Because of that, he shied away from calling other colleagues to pick their brains on what was going on.

He also had the added worry of leaving Josie with Ecaterina. If her condition didn't improve, there was no way he could leave her with a sixty-eight-year-old woman.

The heavy exertion turned out to be just the stress reliever he needed. By the time he finished wielding a heavy ax and carrying the logs inside, he was ready for a hot shower and a nap.

The nap never came.

Instead he made mashed potatoes over a gas stove. The food would be soft enough for Josie to eat and easy on her stomach. From the cabinet, he retrieved a packet of instant apple cider and prepared that as well.

Josie remained curled in her favorite position with all the covers tucked beneath her.

He couldn't help but smile as he moved over to the bed. He set down the tray and pressed a hand against Josie's forehead to check for a fever. It was still slightly elevated, but nothing life-threatening.

"Josie, I'm going to sit you up now," he said, but he might as well be talking to a rag doll.

Concerned, he checked the dilation of her eyes and again found nothing to be worried about.

"Well, let's see if I can get you to eat something." He propped her up against the bed pillows and reached for the bowl.

He apportioned a small amount of potatoes onto a spoon, but couldn't get Josie to eat. After about a half hour of coaxing, he gave up and put the food aside.

Two hours later, he tried again and still had no success.

As the day sped along, William struggled not to be alarmed by Josie's behavior. It had been forty-two hours since he'd taken her from the institute, and by his calculations, she should be responding to the methadone and coming out of her fog.

With a frustrated sigh, he took the dishes back downstairs. He prepared himself another bowl of pasta and grabbed a warm beer from the fridge. He hoped the electricity would be back on before Ecaterina showed up Monday.

"Tomorrow," he moaned. He would have to act as if nothing had happened. He frowned as he remembered Saturday's news report. He really should try to call Hines again, but should he be worried? When he returned to work, would it be a trap?

He drew in a tired breath. He wasn't at all comfortable with lying, but, at this point, what choice did he have?

He grabbed a second beer and after achieving a good buzz was able to set his fears aside.

The day passed with no violent outbursts from Josie. It was close to midnight before he was able to get her to eat anything, and she was still unaware of her surroundings.

He tucked her back into bed before he settled in for another night in the armchair. But he couldn't sleep. He couldn't stop wondering what was going to happen when Josie finally woke up—when she was finally able to recognize him.

He imagined that she wouldn't be too happy.

Lowering his gaze, he contemplated grabbing another beer. He needed something to numb his growing anxiety—not that it was entirely aimed at Josie, but more toward himself for letting her go in the first place.

As the night ticked on, William was content to listen to Josie's steady breathing. Hours later, exhaustion finally claimed him. However, he didn't sleep long before the sun's early-morning rays sliced through the blinds and warmed his face.

It was time to face the day. Time to return to the scene of the crime. He glanced at his Timex and saw he had less than an hour before Ecaterina arrived.

Standing, he stretched and popped his aching bones. A painful cramp lingered in his neck, but it was undoubtedly a direct result of his sleeping arrangements.

He walked over to the bed.

Josie was still out of it.

How could he leave her like this? What would he tell Cat now?

"Okay. Pull yourself together," he said. After

giving himself a moment to think everything over, he realized that he didn't have a choice but to follow his original plan. He couldn't call in sick, and he was pretty sure Josie's violent episodes were over. Heck, at this rate, there was a good chance that she would still be knocked out when he returned.

Exhaling, he reached into the drawer for a new hypodermic needle, gave Josie her morning injection, and changed her IV bag.

Afterward, he rushed to get himself ready for work. While he dressed he wondered if he should change his story with Ecaterina. How much should he tell her? If she'd seen the news reports about Keystone, would she put two and two together?

A new wave of anxiety gripped him. He had expected Josie to be conscious by now, and he would have convinced her to play along with having a simple flu bug. Now, the only thing he could do was pray—pray that Josie slept until he returned from work.

A loud knock on the front door jerked William from his private reverie. It was time.

Another knock accompanied the visitor's persistent ringing of the doorbell.

William rushed down, peeked through the peephole, and smiled as he welcomed his long-time friend and housekeeper into the house.

"Good morning, Cat."

"Morning." She breezed through the door. "Traffic was crazy." She peeled off her coat and tossed it up on a gold hook behind him. "So where is she?"

He closed the door. "She's upstairs in the master bedroom. Sleeping."

"It's so nice of you to do this for your sister-in-law," Cat said, and removed her scarf. "Then again, you've always been such a kind person. Are there any special instructions?"

"Yeah. Uh." He pinched the bridge of his nose and tried to think where he wrote everything down. "I think it's all upstairs. I'll go get it. I need to finish changing anyway." He walked over and gave her a quick kiss on the cheek. "The electricity is out from the storm the other night. Is that going to be a problem?"

"Nah. I'm a tough old bird. I can handle it. What happened to your head?"

William touched the bruise above his eye. "Just me being clumsy." He smiled. "I owe you big for doing this."

"Yeah, yeah. Place a dozen roses on my grave when I'm gone, and we can call it square."

William smiled. "Tell you what, I'll buy them sooner than that."

"Even better." She winked, then headed into the kitchen. "You better hurry up. You're already running late."

He nodded and rushed up the stairs. He was suddenly confident in his decision to ask Cat to watch Josie.

Opening the bedroom door, William's mind was awhirl with all the things he needed to do and what might be waiting for him when he arrived at work. He walked over to the bed and gazed down at Josie.

He didn't want to leave, but he didn't have a choice. "I'll be back," he whispered, but it was a statement of hope rather than a promise. He had no idea what awaited him at Keystone.

Turning, he quickly grabbed everything he needed and headed out of the room.

At the soft click of the door, Josie opened her eyes.

An hour later, in record time, William arrived at Keystone. Despite his preparation in the car, his heart skipped a beat at the sight of police cars and news vans monopolizing the employee parking deck.

He rubbernecked to see what was going on as he scanned his parking card. When the mechanical arm lifted, he rolled inside.

The moment he saw the yellow crime tape surrounding a black BMW, a wave of nausea hit him.

"Meredith," he whispered, recognizing the car.

A horn blared, and William slammed on his brakes just in time to avoid ramming a silver Mercedes that had suddenly backed up in front of him.

While his heart pounded against his chest, he saw heads from the crime scene swivel in his direction.

"So much for keeping a low profile," he chastised himself under his breath.

When the silver Mercedes pulled out of its parking space, William recognized the flaming mane of Dr. Ambrose Turner and gave him a quick wave of apology.

As a matter of convenience, William whipped his Navigator into the vacated spot. "Keep it together. Keep it together," he coached. Everything rode on his being cool. No one should suspect him in Michelle Andrews's disappearance. After all, she wasn't even his patient.

Climbing out of the car, he grabbed his things and headed toward the building.

"Sir!" Someone shouted.

William kept moving.

"Hey, you!" the voice thundered again.

It finally dawned on William that the person was talking to him. He turned around and when he caught the wave of an approaching police officer, his stomach dropped somewhere between his knees.

"You must be in your own world," the baby-faced cop commented, flashing him a quick smile.

"Can I help you?" William said.

The cop's thumb stabbed back at a line of cars. "Your lights. You left your lights on."

"My lights?" A second passed before the man's words sank in, and for William to react. He faced his car again just as the headlights automatically shut off.

"Oh, look at that," the cop said. "I guess you didn't need my help after all."

William only managed a benign smile. "Guess not."

The cop shrugged and turned away.

Relieved, William continued toward the building, all the while his nerves rattling. He hadn't made it inside yet, and he was already a wreck.

During his short trek to the building his mind wandered to what could have happened to Meredith Bancroft. The doctor's kind face surfaced from his memory, and the nausea returned. He hadn't known her long, as he'd only been working at the institute six weeks. However, he'd been impressed not only by the physician's intelligence, but also by her sharp wit and easy disposition.

Strolling through the doors of the institute, William dragged himself out of his melancholy thoughts just as Dr. Rae Coleman nearly bumped into him.

"Oh, good morning," she said, gushing up at him. "Just got off the graveyard shift. I haven't seen you around. What happened to your head?"

He relied on his previous explanation. "Just me being clumsy."

"You should be careful. Can you believe what's going on around here?"

"Actually, I don't know much about it," he said. "But that is Meredith's car taped off, isn't it?"

"I'm afraid so." Rae abruptly changed her course toward the exit to backtrack and follow William through the hallways. "Dr. Bancroft was found dead in the trunk of her car."

He stopped. Hearing the words aloud brought the tragedy home.

"I know," she said. "We're all upset about the news. But you should have seen poor Brian Bancroft. He said that he knew something was wrong when Meredith hadn't made it home early Saturday morning. Said he just knew in his gut that something bad had happened."

William imagined the man's heartbreak. "My prayers go out to him." He resumed walking with a heavy heart. "Where is Mr. Bancroft now?"

"Grady Hospital."

He frowned at Rae as he pressed the UP button for an elevator.

"Heart attack," she added. "This is just horrible all around."

Stunned, William blinked. "Is he going to be okay?"

"We don't know yet," she said remorsefully. "Marcus is supposed to keep us posted."

A bell chimed, and an elevator door slid open.

William stepped inside, hoping for a clean escape, but Rae followed him.

"And guess what else," Rae continued.

"There's more?" He swallowed while his stomach twisted into knots.

"Yeah. We're missing a patient—Michelle Andrews."

"What?" he asked with dramatic incredulity. Hopefully, he wasn't overdoing it.

"Hospital break, kidnapped, or just plain wandered off—we don't know yet. I just know that the patient's sister has been here and raised holy hell with Marcus."

"Sister?"

Rae rolled her eyes. "Oh. Consider yourself lucky you've never had to deal with that one. First time she came by to visit, Andrews attacked her. I swear it was like an old episode of *Dynasty*. Andrews gave her a black eye and everything. After that, we had to keep Andrews heavily sedated—for her safety as well as the staff's."

"Sister?" he asked again, feeling a prick of unease.

"Yeah, and a real piece of work, too. If you ever see her around, stay clear. But I have a feeling she's going to be around a lot. Marcus is afraid that she's going to file a lawsuit against the institution."

William struggled to keep up with the conversation. "That shouldn't be a problem," he said with a weak smile. "I wouldn't know who she was anyway."

"It's kind of hard not to." Rae laughed.

"Why is that?"

She shrugged. "Because she's a dead ringer for Michelle Andrews. Twins."

He could feel his panic morph into a full-blown anxiety attack. Instead of climbing to the twelfth floor, William felt as if the elevator was plummeting to the ground. Luckily, his feelings didn't come across in his expression because Rae ranted on.

"Frankly, I think someone took her. The last time I checked on Andrews, she was too sedated to go anywhere, let alone muster the strength to steal a badge and escape on her own."

William swallowed. "About this twin sister."

"What about her?"

The elevator stopped. "You wouldn't happen to know her name, would you?"

"Sure." She shrugged as the door opened. "Josephine Ferrell."

Numb, William stepped out of the elevator while Rae dogged his heels. Another vision of prison bars flashed in his mind, this time with the added image of himself dressed in a bright orange suit.

"Kind of wild, isn't it?" Rae asked.

"Yeah, it's a lot to take in," he said, making his way to his office.

"Marcus will keep us abreast of any funeral arrangements. Of course, with Brian in the hospital—"

"Dr. Coleman, I really have to start my rounds. Maybe we can play catch-up later," he said, exchanging his coat for a white lab jacket. He rushed to his desk and retrieved his digital recorder for dictation.

"Of course we can. I guess I got carried away since I hardly ever see you around. Different shifts and all."

William nodded, then waited for her to leave. After a pregnant pause, it finally dawned on her that she was holding him up, and a blush of embarrassment stained her cheeks.

"Well, I better go," she said, backing out of his office. "I'll see you around?"

He nodded again and watched her leave. Instead of getting right to work, he closed the door and laid his head against the frame. "Stupid, stupid, stupid."

The severity of his reactions was making him physically ill. At the same time, if he didn't pull himself together, he was going to draw unwanted attention.

"Twins," he whispered, and backed away from the door.

Josephine had never mentioned that she had a sister. It had been more than sixteen years since he'd seen her, but he was pretty sure he was right about that.

If he was wrong, he had just kidnapped a schizophrenic patient and left her alone with Ecaterina. He walked over to his desk and grabbed the phone.

A quick rap on the door interrupted him. He turned as an agitated Geena, one of the institute's older RNs, entered the office with her pudgy hands clamped on her plump waist.

"There you are. Your eight o'clock family counseling session just left. Mrs. Banks said their time is just as valuable as yours and they would come back when you remember how to tell time." She pushed up the wire-frame glasses on her button nose. "Can't say that I blame her."

"I deserved that one. But Geena, I'd appreciate it if you could leave the attitude at home."

She straightened. "Will do." Geena turned with a sly smile and left his office.

William picked up his phone again and called Ecaterina. After he counted fifteen rings, he hung up, fearing the worst.

The patient had a splitting headache.

At the moment, all she could do was lie still and hope the room would stop spinning. After a while, she grew tired and closed her eyes. A second later, she heard a door open.

"All right now. The electricity is back on, and it's time for something warm to eat," a woman's heavily accented voice said.

Frowning, the patient struggled to open her eyes.

"I'm glad you're awake," the elderly woman

said, smiling down at her. "William thought you'd be out of it for most of the day."

William?

"Let's get you feeling better," the woman said, easing the patient back against the pillows. "I told him you'd probably be hungry before he came back. I know how these flu bugs can be. You'll need plenty of fluids, so I made you some chicken noodle soup."

"W-where . . . ?" the patient forced the question out of her parched lips and winced when her throat burned from the effort.

"Ooh. You really *are* out of it," the woman chuckled then spoon-fed soup into the patient's mouth.

After a few sips, the patient relished her new-found warmth. However, the older woman's slow feeding became an agitation and she grabbed the spoon and shoveled the hot soup greedily into her mouth.

"My, you're hungry."

She ignored the woman and concentrated on emptying the bowl. After a while, she did away with the spoon and simply lifted the bowl and drained the remaining contents.

"O-okay." The older woman said, reaching for the empty bowl. "Maybe I should get you some more."

The patient nodded and wiped her hand along

her mouth and struggled to focus on her host. "Who . . . ?"

The woman fluttered a blue-veined hand across her chest, then flattered the patient with a belated smile.

"Of course you don't know who I am. What was I thinking?" She patted the patient's arm. "My name is Ecaterina. I work for your cousin Sheila's brother-in-law—I think." She laughed at herself. "I get confused whenever I try to decipher things like that." She chuckled again. "I'll just run and get you some more soup."

The patient frowned and eased back against the pillows. *Cousin?* She struggled to think, but her head ached.

"S-sick," she groaned, pulling at the covers. However, she couldn't seem to untangle her feet from the bedding. The spinning grew worse while the soup seemed to slosh around in her stomach. "B-bathroom," she whined as she teetered on the edge of the bed.

"Dear Lord." Ecaterina reappeared and rushed toward her. However, she didn't reach the bed in time and the patient toppled out and hit the floor. Stars danced behind her eyes while her stomach threatened to repel her lunch.

"Oh, dear," Ecaterina said. "Let me help you."

They made it to the toilet bowl just as her stomach relinquished what she'd eaten. After that, she dry heaved until her stomach muscles cramped.

Ecaterina made a cool compress at the bathroom sink and did her best to help clean the patient up. "You poor thing. How long have you been sick like this?"

The patient gave a slow shake of her head. She didn't want to talk; she wanted the compress to take away her headache. When it appeared it wasn't working, she tried being as still as possible.

"Goodness. Maybe I shouldn't have tried to put something in your belly like that. I guess that's why William is the doctor, and I'm just a housekeeper." Ecaterina pressed another compress against the patient's forehead. "Come on, Josie. I'll help you get back into bed."

The patient's eyes fluttered open again. "What?"

"I said I'd help you get back into bed."

"No. My name. What did you call me?"

Ecaterina frowned. "Josie. That is your name, isn't it?"

Detectives Delaney and Simmons stopped by their favorite Chinese restaurant, the Emerald Dragon, for takeout before heading back to the office. They walked through the doors of the dark restaurant exhausted from their long day at Keystone.

Xiang Zhu, a petite Asian woman greeted them from behind the checkout nook. "Ah. Back again?"

"Are you kidding?" Tyrese smiled as he leaned against the counter. "This is our home away from home." He winked.

Ming rolled her eyes, then flashed Xiang a polite smile. "I'll have my usual."

"One sesame chicken; and what about you, Detective Simmons?"

"How about this time you give me your number?" he asked cheekily. "I would love to take you away from all of this."

Xiang gave him a sweet smile. "My family owns this restaurant. I would never want to leave them. But how about I order you your usual as well?"

Tyrese sighed and straightened up. "I guess that's going to have to do then."

"All right. I'll be right back," she said, and walked toward the kitchen.

"Another crash and burn." Tyrese chuckled.

Ming smacked him on the back. "The story of your life."

"Tell me about it." He sucked in a deep breath and looked down at his partner. "So do you suppose Dr. Bancroft's husband knows who wanted to kill his wife?"

"No clue, but I have every intention of asking him once he's stabilized." She eased out of the way as more customers entered the establishment. "Are you thinking he might have something to do with his wife's murder?"

"It wouldn't be the first time."

"True." She nodded, then thought it over for a moment. "But then we would be looking at one hell of a coincidence. A murder happening at the same time someone kidnaps a patient."

"If she was kidnapped," Tyrese interjected.

Ming rolled her eyes. "Please don't tell me you're buying into Ms. Ferrell's whole wandered-off theory."

"We can't ignore it."

"Hey, maybe Andrews stole the badge and killed her doctor on the way out," Ming added sarcastically. "Of course, I don't know where she would've acquired a gun unless she's been keeping one beneath her bedpan for the past six weeks."

Tyrese chuckled. "Anything is possible. Maybe one of her doctors hypnotized her to commit the murder, gave her a weapon and everything."

Ming stared at him. "You really ought to watch something else other than the Sci-Fi Channel."

He shrugged. "Like I said, anything is possible."

Ming grew thoughtful. "I guess. Right now my gut is telling me to learn all I can about the sister. That Josephine character—something about her just doesn't sit right with me."

* * *

It was close to five o'clock when Josephine returned to Keystone in a limousine with a team of attorneys. Hines spotted her from his office window on the third floor and grumbled under his breath. Maybe if he ran, he could get out of there before Ms. Ferrell made it to his office.

"Wishful thinking." He turned away from the window and pinched the bridge of his nose. Dealing with lawyers, cops, news crews, and an antsy staff, Hines was thankful the day was finally drawing to a close.

At the brief rap on his door, he marveled at how fast Ferrell made it up to his office. "Come in," he called out.

William poked in his head. "I just got a message that you wanted to see me?"

Hines exhaled and flashed the tall, handsome doctor a brief smile. "Ah, yes. Come on in."

William entered the office and closed the door behind him. "I meant to stop by earlier, but I arrived a little late this morning."

Hines nodded. "I doubt if I would've had time to talk with you. It's been one thing after another today. I'm sure you've heard about Meredith and our missing patient?"

"Yes. Dr. Coleman filled me in. Any news on Brian?"

"Looks like he's going to pull through. Thank

God. It's the only good news of the day." Hines took the seat behind his desk. "I know you're new, but trust me this sort of thing doesn't normally happen around here."

William nodded but was mindful to mask his emotions, especially when so many bubbled just below the surface. "I know this is a trying time for the staff."

"Tell me about it. I've had calls from most of the women on third shift fearful about returning to work. With there being such a shortage of nurses in the state, that's the last thing I want to hear."

Again, William nodded and waited.

Hines sighed. "I've talked to some of the other doctors and because of this recent tragedy, we're going to be a little shorthanded. Is there any way you can move your vacation from next month to this week?"

"Excuse me?"

"Well, Meredith would have been on vacation this week and next week. But she would have been here when you took yours next month. Actually, we have quite a few people who requested time off in November. Bottom line is that I rather spare you now instead of later. Dr. Turner and Dr. Coleman have agreed to share your appointments if you could do this for us."

William blinked and recognized the gift horse for what it was. "Sure. That wouldn't be a problem."

Marcus sighed and visibly relaxed. "Great. So after you wrap up today, then we'll just see you back in two weeks."

"Two weeks?"

"I know it's short notice," Hines went on. "But you'll be doing me a great favor."

"Then consider it done." William relaxed and forced a smile.

At the sudden loud pounding on the door behind him, William jumped.

"Ah, that must be Ms. Ferrell." Marcus's shoulders slumped. "I wish *I* was going on vacation. Can you please let her in?"

Blood drained from William's face. "Ms. Ferrell?"

Hines straightened his tie. "Yeah. She's . . . something else. Of course, you probably already heard about her by now." He sighed. "But I better go ahead and get this over with. Go ahead and let her in."

Slowly, William turned. A combination of fear and anticipation swelled within him as he took a deep breath and opened the door.

"**G**ood. Y'all are still here." Josephine breezed into Hines's office while a strong trail of heavy perfume wafted in her wake. "I brought you your damn papers."

She brushed past William without sparing him the slightest glance.

Josie. Air rushed from William's body as his gaze followed the immaculately dressed caramel beauty. Diamonds clung to her ears, neck, and wrists while a magnificent fur coat was draped around her slim shoulders. She was stunning.

William's attention was so focused on the woman from his past that it took him a while to notice the four men dressed in black suits behind her.

He should leave, he realized, but couldn't manage to move. Instead, he wanted her to look at him—to recognize him.

"Dr. Hayes," Marcus said.

William's gaze shifted toward Marcus. "Yes?"

"I don't think you've had the pleasure to meet Ms. Ferrell. Ms. Ferrell, Dr. William Hayes. He's one of our new physicians at Keystone."

"Are you one of the jerks responsible for losing my sister?"

He flinched as his brows furrowed. "No. But you must be the sister Michelle gave a black eye. I see that it's healed rather nicely."

Marcus coughed, but William suspected it was to mask a snicker.

Slowly Josephine's lips curled. "Funny." Her gaze swept over him. "You sure are handsome. I'll give you that much. Dead ringer for that actor." She snapped her fingers as if trying to recall. "George something or another."

William forced a smile. "George Clooney," he said. "I get that a lot."

"I bet you do." Her smile brightened as her eyes twinkled.

He felt nothing as he stared at her. Nothing at all. "I better get going. Someone is waiting for me."

"Thank you, Dr. Hayes," Marcus said, smiling. "Have a nice vacation."

William nodded and turned toward the door.

"Sure hope I see you around," Josephine called after him. A hint of a Southern accent clung to her words.

William glanced back and failed to manage a smile. He didn't know what the hell was going on, but he did know that this woman was *not* Josie.

"Y-yes. You know my name." Tears splashed down Josie's face as she grabbed Ecaterina in a bear hug.

"Now, now, honey." Ecaterina awkwardly patted her on the back. "There's no reason to cry."

Josie squeezed tighter and sobbed uncontrollably.

The older woman consoled her the best she could and even helped Josie back into bed.

The crying session only worsened Josie's headache, and she begged Ecaterina for relief. A half hour after she downed two Tylenol capsules, the room finally stopped spinning, but her head still felt as if it was going to explode at any moment. All the same, she wondered what was going on and how she came to be in this house.

She was disturbed by the lack of control over her body. One minute she was burning up, and in the next she was freezing. She needed something, wanted something, but had no idea what.

Though she was grateful to the kindly older woman who took care of her, she wasn't sure whether she could trust her. She didn't even know if she could trust herself—as silly as that sounded.

Josie's gaze slid to a photograph on the nightstand next to the bed, and out of curiosity, she reached for it.

"They're a beautiful couple, aren't they?" Ecaterina said, breezing into the room. "You and your cousin Sheila don't, uh, share too many features." She smiled awkwardly. "Are you two first or second cousins?"

Josie stared at the blond woman in the picture. "Sheila?"

"Yes. That's your cousin Sheila."

Frowning, Josie concentrated on the stunning and photogenic woman, but only drew a blank. She couldn't remember ever having a white cousin. "I don't know." She exhaled with disappointment. "I don't remember her."

Slowly her gaze traveled to the man in the photograph and something sparked within her. "He looks sort of familiar," she whispered.

"Well, I should say so," Ecaterina chuckled. "He's married to your cousin."

Josie took in the man's dark hair and blue eyes, but his features weren't quite right. They seemed wrong somehow. She stared at his eyes. They were the right shade, but they, too, were wrong.

When she realized she wasn't making any

sense, she lowered the picture and touched the bruise above her eye. It throbbed as she struggled to remember how she had gotten it. The harder she tried, the more frustrated she became.

"Open up," Ecaterina instructed.

Josie obeyed and was rewarded by having a thermometer shoved under her tongue.

"I was supposed to give you a shot a few hours ago," Ecaterina commented as she looked over a list of some kind.

"No shot," Josie mumbled, shaking her head.

"Oh, I'm sure it's not going to hurt." The older woman said. "William said it's supposed to relax you." She picked up a small vial.

Josie kept shaking her head.

Ecaterina ripped open a small packet and revealed a new hypodermic needle.

Josie yanked the thermometer out of her mouth. "*No!*"

Ecaterina jumped from the bed and stared into Josie's combative gaze with incredulity. "Look. I am only trying to help."

"I didn't ask for your help," Josie snapped, and tossed back the covers. She struggled to get out of bed, but her show of defiance ended when her wobbly legs failed to support her.

The next thing she knew, she hit the floor with a yelp and a loud thud.

Once again, Ecaterina came to her aid. "Sweetheart, you're going to end up killing yourself at this rate."

Embarrassed and humiliated, Josie accepted the woman's offered help and after a few minutes managed to get back into bed. "No shot," Josie declared stubbornly. "No drugs."

"You just took Tylenol," Ecaterina reminded her. "Come now, William wouldn't prescribe something that would harm you. But if you don't want the shot, I'm not going to make you take it."

"Who's William? I don't know any William." The moment she said it, she realized it wasn't true.

The older woman tsked under her breath and placed her hand to Josie's forehead. "What did we do with that thermometer?"

"I don't have a fever."

"You thought you could stand up, too," Ecaterina countered. She searched around the bed and found what she was looking for. "Now say 'ah.'"

Josie relaxed a little bit and did what she was told. A minute later, she discovered she was wrong again. She did have a fever.

"You're sicker than you think. Why don't you reconsider taking that shot?"

"No." She inched away from the woman and rubbed at her head again. When she pulled her hand away, her gaze narrowed on the jagged welt across her wrist.

Her heartbeat accelerated at the sight of it. Tears welled in her eyes as a memory struggled to surface. Despite her fever, Josie suddenly felt cold and scared, but she couldn't think of a reason why.

"Josie?"

A strange haze swirled around a faded image in Josie's mind. The next moment, her head exploded with pain. Josie reeled back, then slumped against the pile of pillows behind her.

In no time the pain consumed her.

Ecaterina didn't know what to make of the young woman's strange behavior. One minute she seemed fine and in the next seemed to suffer from some type of epileptic fit. Her gaze darted to the small vial and hypodermic needle. Maybe she did need this shot.

"Make it . . . stop," Josie pleaded.

That was all it took, and Ecaterina gave her the shot. Minutes later, Josie calmed down.

For the first time, Ecaterina wondered about what type of flu bug this woman had. And what happened to her wrists? Ecaterina frowned, then covered the woman while she slept.

Josie, however, dreamed of another pair of blue eyes. A pair that deepened with concern, twinkled with laughter, and glowed with love. She knew those eyes well and had dreamed of them often.

"William," she murmured. Warmth radiated throughout her body. As the pain evaporated, she welcomed the memories of an old love—a forbidden love.

It had been a time of freedom, exhilaration, and self-discovery. She had found the man of her dreams, her soul mate.

However, her feeling of euphoria soon crashed beneath a tidal wave of heartbreak.

"Shh. There's no need for tears."

She wanted to cry. She had to cry.

"Josie, it's all right. I'm here now."

She drew comfort from the man's gentle voice and quieted down.

"Shh," he said. "I'm going to take care of you," the voice promised.

Josie believed him. Something warm brushed against her face, and she sighed with contentment.

Soon a question nagged at the back of her mind. *Who* was promising to take care of her and why should she trust him?

You can never trust anyone again, she warned herself.

She struggled to open her eyes. It was hard; her eyelids were so heavy. Her lashes flickered, and she was able to make out something in the blurry light.

A shadowy figure hovered above her. Through sheer determination, she brought the image into focus. Within seconds, a familiar pair of deep blue eyes crystallized.

Josie sucked in a startled gasp of surprise. "William?"

A wide smile curved onto his handsome face. "Yes, Josie. It's me."

J osie studied the man above her and struggled to make sense of this apparition. It couldn't be, she reasoned, and squeezed her eyes shut. Her mind had to be playing tricks on her. It wouldn't have been the first time, she reasoned, but this was too cruel to be true.

The cold returned. She shivered and grasped for the covers though it was like grabbing a block of ice to keep warm.

"It's all right, Josie," William said. "Your body is going through withdrawal. You're going to be okay."

She clamped her jaws tight and trembled violently.

"It's going to come and go, but you'll be all right."

Josie didn't feel all right. In fact, she was nauseous.

"You want to throw up?" he asked gently.

She nodded and was instantly scooped out of the bed. Seconds later, she was hanging over the toilet bowl and emptying her stomach. When she finished, her abdomen ached, and her head spun.

As before, a cool compress was placed against her head and a geyser of gratitude erupted inside of her and flowed from her lips.

"Calm down. It's okay. It's okay." William cleaned her up.

Josie desperately wanted to believe that, but wasn't at all sure he was who he claimed. A lot had happened since the loss of her career: the death of her father, Michelle, and her emotional breakdown.

In such a short time, she went from being a strong independent woman to someone who was afraid of her own shadow.

And then there was the accident. She curled into a fetal position against the bathroom's cold tile.

Splashes of a memory teased her from behind her closed eyes. She was knee deep in water while trying to scrub blood from her hands. And there was laughter. Who was laughing?

"What have you done, Michelle?" a woman's voice had asked.

Josie continued to scrub at her hands. "I didn't do anything."

"How can you say that, Michelle? You just killed Daniel!"

Josie shook her head. No, she didn't. She couldn't have.

Quivering, she remembered a flood of lights blinding her. "I didn't kill him," she croaked. "I didn't."

Josie clawed her way out of the gloomy memory, desperate to seek refuge from the heinous accusation and confusion. She woke with a start and found herself back in bed and surrounded by darkness.

"William?" Josie sat up.

"I'm still here."

His voice drifted from her right, and she swiveled toward it. Her eyes grew wide as she struggled to make out his outline.

With a soft click, a low glow of light revealed the impossible.

"This isn't happening," she whispered, and clutched a hand to her chest. Her gaze roamed over him. "I don't understand."

He waited until their gazes locked before he took a deep breath, and replied, "That makes two of us."

She frowned and glanced around the room again. "Where's Ecaterina, or did I imagine her?"

"She went home hours ago." He crossed his arms. "You gave her quite a scare. Of course that's my fault," he admitted. "I didn't tell her the truth about you."

She drew in a breath, then proceeded with trepidation. "The truth?"

He hesitated while he probed her gaze. "I kidnapped you."

Josie blinked, not certain she heard or understood him; but before she could question him, a collage of snapshot images flashed in her head. "The hospital."

"A mental institution," he clarified.

Her heart leapt as more pictures spun through her mind. Pressing a hand against her throbbing temple, she rejected his words. Why would she be in a mental institution?

"How can you say that, Michelle? You just killed Daniel!"

"I'm not Michelle!" Josie shook the voice from her head. "My name is Josephine!"

William smiled. "I know."

"It's Josephine," she repeated.

"I know," he said, draping an arm around her shoulders. It was awkward comforting her. Now that she was conscious, his heart struggled to protect itself.

Josie eased out of his arms. "So you believe me?"

"Of course I do." William pretended her withdrawal didn't bother him and stood up from the bed.

"Thank you," she said softly. "I'm surprised that you helped after . . . ?"

Their eyes met again.

William couldn't ignore the pain and uncertainty reflected in them. "You needed my help."

Her gaze fluttered down to her hands. "No one would listen to me. They just kept drugging me to the point where I couldn't think."

William watched her as she fidgeted with her hands.

"They were stealing my life."

His mind immediately jumped to the Josephine Ferrell he'd met earlier. "Your sister?"

More tears splashed down her face. "Everyone."

He frowned. "I met your sister today," he began slowly. "She was introduced to me as Josephine Ferrell—as you."

Josie closed her eyes at this news and took a long while to compose herself. "She's evil."

William drew a deep breath. "I still don't quite understand what's going on."

Josie sighed. "I don't know what to tell you. A lot of this doesn't make much sense to me either." Her eyes opened, then captured his gaze. "But thank you."

William folded his arms. "I had to do some-thing."

"But this is going to cause you a lot of trouble."

"Potentially," he agreed. "If I'm found out, but I don't plan for that to happen. Right now, the au-thorities don't know if your disappearance is a kid-napping or if you left voluntarily. Once we get you back on your feet, it should be a breeze to convince the authorities you're the real Josephine Ferrell.

"After that you can have your sister arrested for fraud and probably a wealth of other charges for the things she's done to you. If we play our cards right, no one will ever need to know I took you from Keystone. Maybe we can keep that secret be-tween us?"

"Deal." Josie agreed with his logic, but the plan was too simplistic to be trusted. "So it will be my word against Michelle's?"

"No." He frowned as he moved over to the arm-chair across from the bed. "We should be able to find plenty of people to corroborate your story: friends, family—"

"Significant others?" she supplied softly.

William paused. "Yes, uh, those, him, one of those could help."

She studied him while the corners of her lips softened. "There might be a slight problem with that. I don't have any family or friends here in the States. My father was all I had, and he's dead."

"My condolences. I didn't know. When?"

"A year ago, I think. What's today's date?"

"October 15."

"It was just April . . ." Her mouth fell open as if the information floored her.

"Surely, there are aunts, uncles, nieces, nephews, or even distant cousins?"

Josie sighed. "I couldn't pick out a cousin from a police lineup. I hardly know anything about my parents' families. I was never around them. Surely, if I don't know them, they're not going to be able to tell the difference between me and Michelle."

"Wasn't your father a wealthy businessman?"

She fell back among the bed's pillows. "My father left me a sizable inheritance."

"Which I'm guessing is what Michelle just stole from you," he said, then watched as a cloud of despair settled over her features. "Sorry."

Josie shook her head. "You have nothing to be sorry for," she said with a long measure of remorse. "You were the only one willing to help me."

"I was the only one who knew who you were." He paused before continuing. "I guess that leaves medical records. We can get on the phone and order a copy of your medical and dental records."

"That's right," she perked up. "I've been seeing the same physicians in France for years."

"See, there you go. We'll be able to prove your

identity in no time," he encouraged. "Of course, you could always just sing for them," he joked. "You're Josephine Ferrell, the great jazz and blues singer."

Her gaze refused to meet his. "I can't," she whispered.

"Why not?"

Josie raked her hands through her hair. "I need to get some more rest," she said suddenly. "I'm very tired, and my head hurts."

William frowned. "Are you feeling nauseous again? Do you need me to help you to the bathroom?"

"No," she said, curling beneath the covers. "I just need to rest. We can call my doctors first thing in the morning."

"Of course we can."

The silence between them grew tense, and Josie hoped William wouldn't ask her any more questions. She truly wasn't up to it. Everything overwhelmed her at that moment. Maybe tomorrow she would be able to make better sense of it all.

"All right." William clicked off the light. "Get yourself some rest."

"William?"

"Yes?"

She hesitated, then decided that she couldn't ask. Not now, anyway.

"Don't worry," he said, when she didn't respond. "I'll still be here when you wake up in the morning."

"Promise?"

"I promise."

The moment Josie closed her eyes she spiraled down a twister of disjointed memories. She tried to scream, but the velocity at which she fell swallowed her voice.

She was frightened and certain she'd never reach the bottom of the spinning vortex. Having never been a religious woman, she felt awkward in her prayer for help. Suddenly, everything stopped when she landed in a memory.

She was lying on something soft while tears were blanketing her face. Her heart pounded as she struggled to stifle her tears. Slowly she became aware of voices. Someone was in the room with her. The chore was difficult, but she managed to lift her head and pry her eyes open.

Her dear friend, Calvin Anderson, took her into his arms. "It's going to be all right, Josie. You'll see."

"This can't be happening," Josie heard herself say. "I just talked to my father this morning. His plane was supposed to—"

"I know, sweetheart." His arms squeezed around her. "Sometimes, these things happen without warning. He's in a better place now."

"He's all I have." She buried her head against his chest. "He can't be gone. He just can't."

As suddenly as she'd arrived at the painful memory, a powerful force gripped her soul and pulled her into another one.

She sat solemnly in the front pew of the First Baptist Church as she listened to a beautiful rendition of "His Eye Is on the Sparrow." Though the song reflected hope, Josie felt everything but the elusive emotion.

After the song ended, an endless parade of her father's business associates and their bejeweled socialite wives took the podium to recount funny, happy, and bittersweet stories of Charles Ferrell.

Josie didn't know how much longer she could sit in her prim-and-proper pose and listen to a bunch of strangers just go through the motions. It was disheartening how impersonal a funeral could really be.

Her gaze strayed from the podium's latest speaker to dance among the multitude of flower arrangements. Even that kind gesture seemed to be a warped competition among the rich. Who can show they cared the most?

As an only child, Josie was uncomfortable at the amount of attention directed at her. She shot covert glances at other mourners in the church and could almost hear the question on everyone's mind. How much money did she inherit?

But Josie would give every penny of the money back if God would just return her father.

Fresh tears spilled down her face. She dabbed at her eyes with her father's old handkerchief, then caressed the thin material's embroidered initials.

Josie had lost her adoptive mother at the age of eight. Her father, unsure about raising a little girl on his own, shipped her off to the finest boarding schools in France. Despite growing up in another country, Josie and her father had developed a unique and strong bond, one she couldn't believe was over so soon.

Within a blink of an eye, the service ended and Josie took center stage while strangers either shook her hand or enfolded her in cold embraces. Quite suddenly, she stood in front of her mirror image.

Josie blinked, convinced that her eyes were playing a trick on her.

The woman smiled. "You're not going crazy. I'm real."

Josie pulled back her veil as her gaze slowly raked the woman, but she was unnerved by the fact that not only did their hairstyles match, but they also wore the same black dress and shoes.

"I meant to introduce myself before the service, but I arrived late." The woman jutted out a hand. "Michelle Andrews."

Josie's hand slid into Michelle's while she continued to stare. "Are we cousins or something?" she asked.

Michelle held firm to her smile, but added a light chuckle. "We're an 'or something.'"

Josie's mouth carved a deep frown.

"We're twins," Michelle announced, with a bubbly flare.

Before Josie could recall her response, she was once again yanked from the memory and propelled fast-forward.

After meeting Michelle, Josie didn't return to her life in Paris, but instead decided to stay in Georgia in order to get to know her new sister.

Together they took it upon themselves to research their adoptions. However, after months of digging, they unearthed no real answers to why they were separated.

It was perhaps out of pity that Josie allowed her indigent sister to move into the Ferrell estate, but it wasn't long before Josie realized that she'd made a mistake.

Here was where her memories clouded and meshed together. She controlled nothing, let alone her own mind. Through it all, Josie remained by her side . . . no, Michelle stood by her.

When had she started confusing their identity?

She struggled to concentrate while pictures blurred at an alarming rate. In no time at all, she was back in a blood-filled room with her wrist throbbing painfully at her side.

"Josie, Josie. Wake up."

Josie lifted her hands and saw the deep slashes in her wrists and screamed.

"Josie, baby. Please wake up."

Wrenched from the memory, Josie bolted upright in bed. An ear-piercing scream reverberated off the walls and boomed back at her to snap her out of her trauma.

"It's okay, it's okay. I'm here. It was just a dream."

Josie blinked her dilated eyes and focused on the man in front of her. "William," she said, with a relieved sigh.

However, her heartbeat threatened to crack her breastbone, and her temples were a few pulses away from explosion.

He folded his arms around her, and, like a wilted violet, she shrank away.

"My head," she moaned. "I need something for my head."

William hesitated, then sprang from the bed,

only to return a minute later with two capsules and a glass of water. "Normally, it's not a good idea to take any kind of drug during detox."

She greedily swallowed the capsules and chased them down with the water. "Thank you."

"What were you dreaming about?" he asked, and brushed a few strands of hair away from her face.

"It wasn't a dream," she answered, but was careful to avoid his gaze.

"Then what were you remembering?"

Josie shook her head.

William huffed an impatient breath. "I've perched myself on a very slim limb, Josie. You can trust me."

The edginess of his tone is what drew her direct gaze. When she probed his azure eyes, she was blindsided by a jolt of electricity that crackled clear down to her toes.

"Sorry." A voice in her head demanded she look away, but she could no more do that than stop her own heart. "I was remembering things that had happened in the past year. Things I wish I could forget."

"For example?"

"Meeting my sister."

William folded his arms. "What is the story between you two? I could have sworn you didn't have any siblings."

"I didn't." Finally, her gaze fell. "We met at my

father's funeral." The silence grew to a deafening crescendo before Josie chanced another look at him.

His compassionate stare met hers unblinkingly. "I'm sure it was a vulnerable time for you," he said finally.

"Undoubtedly a calculated move on her part." Josie rubbed at her neck to relax her tense muscles. "I'm still not sure how . . ."

The sentence was left suspended in the air for a full minute before William prodded gently, "Do you remember your suicide attempt?"

She closed her eyes, but a vision of blood-splattered hands forced them to spring open again. "I can't do this right now." Her voice trembled. "I'm sorry."

William nodded and smiled. "I understand. We can talk about it at another time."

Josie swallowed. She preferred never to talk about it, but knew that was impossible.

"Do you think you'll be able to get back to sleep?" he inquired. "Maybe I can prepare you some warm milk or something."

"I'm not sure if I want to." She palmed her forehead and massaged the small wrinkles across it. "I'm hot, and I feel dirty."

"How about a warm bath?"

She loved the idea of a bath, the hotter the water the better.

"I bought plenty of nightgowns for you."

She managed a small laugh. "I hope it's not the only thing you brought."

"No." He laughed along with her. "I grabbed a few other things." He rose from the bed. "One warm bubble bath coming up."

"Bubble bath?"

"Lavender, right?"

Her lips softened at it edges. "You remembered."

"How could I ever forget?"

Another crackle of electricity buzzed through her. However, this time she was able to break her trance. "A lavender bubble bath would be wonderful. Thank you."

"Don't mention it."

The moment he turned away, Josie released the entrapped air in her lungs. Her gaze followed his tall figure as he disappeared into the en suite bathroom.

At the sound of running water, she slumped back against her pillows and compared this William Hayes to the hopeless romantic she had met and fallen in love with so long ago. He was still slender, though his chest was broader, more muscular than she remembered. His once-smooth baby face held subtle character lines around his mouth and eyes.

His eyes, however, were unquestionably the same. The same intensity radiated in their depths.

Despite the fact that he was being a very kind care-giver, a strange coldness permeated him—a wall of some kind.

Over the past sixteen years, she had thought about him often. The light scent of lavender wafted from the bathroom. She closed her eyes and inhaled the relaxing fragrance. This time there were no horror images flashing from her memory, but there were a few memories of her and William kissing in the rain near the Eiffel Tower.

His soft sensual lips made him an exceptional kisser. She had always loved how his fingertips made circles around the small of her back while their tongues mated in an ancient dance.

"The water is ready," William announced.

Her eyelids popped open as he returned to the room. She couldn't suppress the heat of embarrassment as it crept up her face.

He frowned. "What is it?"

"N-nothing." Logically, she knew he couldn't see the visions playing in her head, though she couldn't help but feel as though he had.

His brows furrowed above his disbelieving expression. "Are you sure?"

"Positive." Josie drew a deep breath and pushed back the covers.

"Careful now." He rushed to the bedside to aid her as she stood.

"That's all right." The moment she was on her feet, she experienced a strong case of vertigo. "I think I . . ." She collapsed against him.

"I've got you." William's arms closed around her. "Walking is a little trickier than it seems," he joked.

"You're telling me." She laughed, feeling foolish.

He helped her to the fragrant bathroom, where a tub of cloudlike bubbles awaited her.

Josie was suddenly hit with a dilemma. How was she going to get into the tub?

"Here. Lean against the wall for me," William instructed.

She obeyed, but then panicked when his hands reached for the hem of her nightgown. "Wait!"

"What is it?" He sprang away from the gown as if the material had transformed into fire.

Her chest heaved as though she'd just completed a marathon. "You were about to undress me."

His face scrunched into confusion before a flicker of understanding dawned in his eyes. A soft rumble of laughter bounced off the acoustic tiles. "There's no need to be modest. I've already . . ." At her face's darkening color, William abandoned the direction he was headed and cleared his throat.

"As a doctor, I can assure you that I can be completely professional about this."

She shook her head. How could she stand

naked before William and view him simply as a doctor? The notion seemed impossible.

"Or I can try not to look," he offered.

Josie perked at the idea, then frowned at the thought of his "seeing" her with his hands instead. "Maybe I should do this another time."

He looked wounded. "You don't trust me?"

"It's not a matter of trust."

His frown deepened. "No? Then what is it?"

She scrambled for an explanation but drew a blank.

"Look, if you don't want to do this, I understand."

Josie's shoulders slumped with relief; however, guilt soon perched upon them. Given what he'd already done for her, he probably viewed her behavior as a slap in the face.

"No." She fluttered a weak smile. "I'm being silly."

A mild surprise lifted his brows. "Are you sure?"

"Yeah, but I don't know how much longer I can lean against this wall." She laughed.

William hesitated.

She reached a hand out to him. "I appreciate your help."

His eyes probed hers, undoubtedly in search of sincerity. Finally, he smiled, then reached for the hem of her nightgown.

Time ticked slowly while Josie watched William lift her nightgown. She studied his expression with great intensity when he exposed her bare legs. When there was no reaction, she couldn't decide on whether she was relieved or disappointed.

She closed her eyes as the material passed her panties and midriff.

"Can you lift your arms for me?" William asked. "Here, just lean back against me, and I'll help you."

Josie did as he instructed, then sucked in a sharp breath at the unexpected surge of electricity when her body pressed against his.

Finally, the gown cleared her head, and, for a

fraction of a second, their gazes locked before her hair cascaded like a curtain over her eyes.

William cleared his throat. "That wasn't so bad, now was it?"

A weak smile fluttered at her lips while she fought not to be embarrassed about her state of undress.

"Here, let me help you turn around," he said.

When the soft whirl of heat radiating from the bathroom vents kissed her sensitive breasts, it was all she could do not to melt in his arms.

However, there was one last article of clothing yet to be removed.

William's hand glided like a feather down the curve of her hip as he slipped off her cotton briefs. While the process seemed to take forever, Josie's eyes fluttered open to see him reveal her triangular nest of black curls.

William showed no reaction or visible signs of emotion, and disappointment pierced Josie's pride.

Her panties skimmed past her knees, and she stepped out of them.

With one arm around her waist, William stood and met her eyes. "Okay, let's get you into the tub."

She managed another weak smile as he helped her sink into the warm water. Thick, scented bubbles surrounded her and covered her nudity. After drawing a deep breath, she sighed and relaxed.

"Ah, this feels good." She leaned back and discovered an inflated plastic pillow. "I could stay in here forever."

William looked as if he wanted to say something, but apparently thought better of it. "Let me get you some soap and towels." He stood up and retrieved everything she needed from the bathroom linen closet.

"That should take care of everything." He clapped and rubbed his hands together as his gaze roamed over everything he'd set by the tub. "Just holler if you need anything else."

William walked backward toward the door. "Even if you need help with your back or something. I, uh, will just be in the other room."

Josie smiled. He wasn't made of stone after all.

"I think I can handle everything from here. Thanks."

He nodded, then swiveled around in time to clip the doorframe.

Josie stifled a giggle.

William glanced back at her as he rubbed his forehead. "Oops." He hurried out.

She held on to her smile and shook her head as she sank deeper into the tub. Playfully, she lifted a handful of bubbles and blew them into the air.

She stretched a trembling leg above a mountain of bubbles and watched as water and suds slid from her ankle down along her calf. As she reached for the bar of purple soap, Josie noticed the slight tremor in her arm and hand.

All playfulness disappeared while she studied her grip on the soap. The harder she tried to control her muscles, the worse it became.

Out of frustration, she tossed down the soap and cupped her face in her hand. *What in the hell is wrong with me?*

Helplessness wasn't an emotion she'd ever allowed herself to wallow in, but it was one that had visited her often in the past year.

William's voice floated in from the bedroom. "Are you all right in there?"

She unburied her face and rolled off another lie. "Yes. I-I'm fine." She wiped at a tear before it had a chance to fall. Somehow she had to muster the strength to win back control of her life. This time when she lifted her shaky hand, anger and determination roared through her veins. Within seconds, her hand steadied.

Triumphant, Josie's smile returned.

She reclaimed the lavender soap from the bottom of the tub and scrubbed her skin until it tingled. Without a scrub brush, she scooted up to the center of the tub and struggled to reach the middle of her back.

While deliberating whether to call William for help, his voice drifted toward her once again. "Need any help in there?"

She hesitated, and, as a result, William poked his head around the door.

"Josie?"

"Yeah, uh, maybe you could help me with my back?"

"Not a problem." His heavy footsteps padded onto the tiled floor as he moved farther into the bathroom.

At the return of his tall, brawny figure, Josie's heart skipped a beat, but she pretended not to notice.

"You wouldn't happen to have some hairpins or a clip for my hair?"

He turned toward the long, L-shaped countertop and pulled open a series of drawers. "Sheila should have something around—aha! Here we go: a monster of a hairclip. It sort of looks like a crab, doesn't it?" He handed it to her.

"I see why you would call it that." She piled her hair at the top of her head. "I need to wash this mess, too."

"I can do that for you."

She smiled up at him. "You're kind of taking this role as a knight in shining armor rather seriously, aren't you?"

"You know me. I don't like to do things halfway." He glanced up at the shower caddy. "It looks like Larry and Sheila are an Herbal Essence couple. Will that do?"

"At this point, I'll take anything. But won't it be a little difficult to wash my hair while I'm sitting in the tub? It's not like there's a whole lot of room in here."

"How about we finish the bath, then wash your hair at the sink? There's a vanity table in the bedroom. We can use the chair for you to sit on."

"That will work," she said, but didn't like being a charity case.

William lowered himself onto his knees and gently took the soap and washcloth from her hands.

The tremors returned, but this time Josie swore they came from the sudden swarm of butterflies in her stomach.

His hand dipped into the water, by her calculation a mere inch from her behind, before he placed the soapy towel against her back and washed it in slow, deliberate circles.

Josie's breath thinned in her lungs.

"I'm experiencing a strong sense of déjà vu," William said.

The observation was an awkward one. There were numerous times when she and William had shared a shower or bubble bath. All she needed now was for him to climb in and for two flutes of champagne to appear mysteriously.

"I just put my foot in my mouth, didn't I?" he said at her silence.

"No, it's okay." She glanced down at the depleting bubbles and reached out to pull an armful of them back toward her. "But it was a long time ago."

William's hand dipped back into the water, and this time his knuckles brushed against her butt. She gasped and grew still.

He stopped. "Is something wrong?"

Say something and end this torture. "N-no. I'm fine." Her words echoed with a strange hollowness. If William noticed, he was kind enough to pretend otherwise. As Josie steeled herself against the pleasure of William's gentle strokes, a strained silence enveloped the former lovers.

She was dying to know what he was thinking but couldn't muster up the nerve to ask.

He glided the soap over her shoulder blades, then abruptly stopped. "This is new."

"What?"

"A tattoo."

Josie froze. She had forgotten about it.

"It's Chinese, isn't it? What does it say?"

There was no way she was going to tell him the Chinese characters spelled his name. She squeezed her eyes tight and came up with another lie. "Love."

"Humph." He started scrubbing again. "I never figured you to be the tattoo type."

"I guess you don't know me as well as you think."

"I don't know." He chuckled. "I know you pretty well. And it's a good thing, too, or you'd still be at Keystone."

She nodded. "Good point."

The small talk ended, and the heavy silence returned.

William washed the back of her neck, between her shoulder blades, and worked a trail down her spine. Everywhere his hand went her skin tingled in its wake, and it was growing harder to pretend to be unaffected.

"Okay. That ought to do it." He placed the soap in its dish on the accessory deck, dipped the cloth into the water several times, and rinsed off her back.

"Thanks," she said. Her gaze remained downcast while he climbed back onto his feet.

"You don't have to keep thanking me, Josie. I'm glad to be able to help." He grabbed a large body towel.

"Hold on while I go get that chair before we get you out of there." He disappeared into the bedroom, but returned quickly.

However, getting into the tub was nothing compared to getting out, and Josie's embarrassment deepened at the amount of water she splashed on him. Through it all, he remained gracious.

After successfully being transported to a small wrought-iron chair with her towel draped around her, William set out a robe close to her and gave her a few minutes alone to dry herself and apply the supplied bottles of lotions and creams.

Though William was out of sight, Josie suspected he remained close in case she experienced some sort of episode. She appreciated and hated it at the same time.

She sighed, confused about her mixed emotions. How many years had she wished that their paths would cross again? Now, through some truly bizarre happenstance, here he was.

In her dreams, she'd envisioned he would spot her at a CD signing or promotional gig. She would boast about her successful career and her wonderful marriage.

But her life hadn't gone as planned—nowhere near it. Because of a series of polyps on her vocal cords, her singing career was over before it really began. After three moderately successful CD releases, Josephine Ferrell's singing career had ended.

Her music never garnered the big crossover audience in America, but she was close. She was sure of that. And Etienne—she didn't want to think about it.

"How are we doing in there?" he called out from the bedroom.

"So far so good." She injected pleasantness into her voice and hurried to finish massaging lotion onto her elbows. A few minutes later, garbed in a large, fluffy robe, Josie gave William the okay to rejoin her.

"All righty, then. Let's get this thing started." He flashed her a smile as he entered with a pitcher, then gathered more towels.

His return immediately wrecked Josie's calm reserve. In retrospect, he'd always had that effect on her—and she had always enjoyed it.

William positioned her and the chair in front of the sink and gave it enough room so she could comfortably lean her head back over the sink. Since she couldn't get her entire head under the immobile faucet, William filled the pitcher with water, then used it to wet the areas that wouldn't reach.

"Seems like you've done this before," Josie commented. She closed her eyes and loved the feel of his strong fingers as they massaged her scalp.

The sound of his light chuckle washed lazily over her. "I guess you can call me a veteran."

Josie instantly thought of his wife, and as a result her feelings of euphoria ended. "Your wife is a lucky woman," she said before she could stop herself.

William's fingers froze for an eternal second and then resumed. "I used to do this with my *ex-wife*. I'm not married anymore."

"Sorry. I didn't know." There was no denying

the rush of relief she experienced after his confession, but now a series of questions strolled through her head.

"No way you could've, I guess." He reached for the bottle of shampoo. "It's been almost two years."

She detected sorrow in his voice, and a low level of jealousy stirred within her.

They fell silent while his fingers worked up a good lather. It was nearly impossible for Josie to stop her toes from curling or prevent the soft moans from escaping her lips.

"Glad you're enjoying this," he commented, with another chuckle.

"How can I not?" she said. A lazy smile curled her lips. "You have great hands."

"I think you might have told me that before."

"Oh, yeah." An embarrassed Josie remembered. "How could I have forgotten?"

"Beats me." William chuckled.

She smiled but couldn't combat the sudden chill that crept from her toes and slowly transformed her body into a giant glacier.

"Josie, are you all right?"

She heard him, but couldn't get her teeth to stop chattering long enough to answer.

"It's okay. It's okay." He shut off the water, wrapped a towel around her head, and helped her to lean forward.

Her shivers turned into violent convulsions, but Josie felt William's arms slide beneath her, and she was aware of him taking her back into the bedroom. When he placed her on the bed, she thought her soul was being lifted from her body. The experience frightened her.

William quickly piled blankets on her. All the while, he whispered words of comfort in her ear. "Just ride it out, Josie. I'm here for you."

His words filled Josie's head. Hope fluttered inside her chest, but another part of her was too afraid to believe him. *Trust no one.*

However, the eighteen-year-old Josie, the part that still fantasized about that one magical summer in Paris, railed against her defensive mantra.

This was William, after all. He hurt her once, and he could do it again.

A feathery kiss brushed against Ming's cheek, and she woke with a soft moan.

Her husband, Conan, smiled down at her. "Why don't you come to bed? I want something warm beside me tonight."

Ming sat up and stretched out her arms as she let loose a wide yawn. "What time is it?"

"Three o'clock." Conan placed his large hands against her shoulders and began an impromptu massage.

"Ah, you're looking to have sex." Ming chuckled and closed the case notes she'd fallen asleep on. "I should've known."

"Yeah. It's about that time of year." Conan leaned down and pressed a kiss against her forehead. "One of these days I'm going to get you to leave your work at the office."

"I think better at home."

"All right then. Maybe we should start having sex at the police station."

Ming laughed as she stood and looped her arms around his neck and gave him a quick peck. "Definitely not one of your better ideas."

"Oh, I have some ideas." He captured her lips in a tantalizing kiss as he slid his hands down her backside and gave her butt a gentle squeeze.

Ming sighed and wiggled her rump playfully against him before she came up for air. "If you were going to kidnap a person from a mental institution, how would you do it?"

"What?" Conan frowned at the question thrown in from left field. "What are you talking about?"

"This case I'm working on." She turned from him and sat back down at the table to reopen her notes. "Whoever took Michelle Andrews from Keystone had to be either the luckiest bastard in Georgia or the smartest. They were able to get in, take a body, and leave without anyone seeing a thing. What are the chances of that?"

"Work? I was squeezing your butt and grinding against you, and you were thinking about work?"

"Sorry, honey," she said, scanning over her last entry. "But after three days on the Andrews case, I don't think we're getting anywhere. It's as if this woman just disappeared into thin air, and that's just not possible."

Conan huffed out a frustrated sigh. "I'll go make some coffee."

"Oh, thanks, honey."

"Don't mention it."

"It has to be someone working on the inside." She shook her head and turned the pages. "A dead doctor, a missing patient . . . and a missing medical chart. That alone is odd."

"Fascinating," Conan called from the kitchen. "Do you want fresh ground, or are we celebrating the moments of our lives?"

"You pick, honey." Ming drummed her fingers on the table while she willed for something to jump out at her, but nothing happened. The department had already ordered cross-references for Keystone employees with names from the Daniel Thornton murder case and come up with nothing.

They'd also delved into Andrews's background and Ming had no doubts that the missing patient had a few enemies of her own. However, everyone they'd interviewed turned into dead ends.

"You murder a doctor and take a patient," she whispered to herself. "Why?"

Conan returned to the table and set a coffee mug beside his wife. "Anything I can help you with?" He pulled out a chair beside her and made himself comfortable. "You know I've been able to put together a few jigsaw puzzles in my time."

"This is a little more complicated than a puzzle, honey." She flashed him a smile, but didn't pull her gaze from her paperwork.

He popped open a bottle of beer. "Since I'm not having sex tonight, and I've had more than my fair share of cold showers this month, I can at least lend my genius to my government to help crack their most difficult cases."

Ming laughed and rolled her eyes.

"Ha-ha." He took a swig of beer, then challenged, "Try me."

She settled back in her chair and crossed her arms. "Okay, smarty-pants. Where do I start?"

"From the beginning. I would hate to think that you're setting me up for failure." He winked and took another swig.

"All right. I have two murders and a missing person. Murder number one, Daniel Thornton, a five-year member of our prestigious most-wanted list, is discovered dead in a public park beneath a tree. Cause of death: He drowned."

"But doesn't that close your case?"

"Technically, but the drowning—"

"Please don't tell me you're forsaking my sex life to work on a closed case."

Ming sighed. "Murder number two, Dr. Meredith Bancroft—seemingly a different case; however, she is the doctor of murder victim number one's girlfriend. Then we mosey on inside and we discover that, lo and behold, the girlfriend, Michelle Andrews, is missing from the mental institution. Now Andrews isn't exactly Sandra Dee. She has a rap sheet a mile long."

"Uh-huh." Conan bobbed his head as he listened.

"So, what do you think so far?"

He turned up his bottle and took a deep gulp. "Is there a butler in this story?"

She leaned over and popped him on the arm. "Come on, genius. This isn't Clue. I want to hear your fresh prospective."

"Well, tell me a little bit more."

Ming shrugged. "There are a few other characters. Andrews's twin sister for one—talk about a cold bitch."

"Twin?" Conan frowned.

"Yeah. I did some digging, pushed a few envelopes, and peeked inside their adoption records. Apparently, this sister, Josephine Ferrell, was adopted by some well-to-do family and lived most of her life overseas. She was even a jazz slash blues singer for a couple of years. All in all, she's just some rich kid who inherited a ton of money about a year ago when her father was killed in a plane crash."

"I take it this Andrews wasn't so lucky?"

"She wasn't adopted by a rich family, but a pretty good suburbanite family took on the challenge . . . and failed. When Tyrese and I went to talk with Michelle's adoptive mother, she made it pretty clear that she'd severed all ties with Michelle sometime ago. She didn't show the least bit of interest in her daughter's disappearance."

"Ouch."

"You're telling me." Ming thought about it for a moment. "This Josephine has a clean record, but she's definitely a handful. I didn't care for her." She paused. "Actually, something about her made my skin crawl."

"All right, all right." He set his beer down, braided his fingers, and cracked his knuckles as a stalling tactic. "Okay, how about this. This Andrews chick killed her boyfriend or had him killed—I don't know—maybe he slapped her around one too many times, then she entered the mental institution to cover her butt. So if she's arrested or found guilty, she can say that she was crazy at the time."

"And the doctor?"

Conan shrugged. "I don't know. I usually think better after sex."

Ming shook her head. "No dice. You're supposed to offer a fresh look at this. You didn't fulfill your end of the bargain."

"You mean if I come up with something that you haven't thought of, I get to have sex?"

"You got it."

Excited, Conan turned up his bottle and drained the rest of its contents. "All right. Something you haven't thought of . . . okay. I think I got it. Michelle killed her boyfriend—"

"You said that already."

He held up his hand. "Let me finish. She killed her boyfriend, then convinced someone at the institution to help her escape. The doctor stumbled onto their escape, so they killed her, then she went on to kill her twin sister so she could take her place."

"Wait a minute. That's three murders. Who said anything about three murders?"

Conan got to his feet, then pulled Ming to hers. "Hey, have you ever seen the two sisters side by side?"

She blinked. "Well, no. But the staff at Keystone—"

"Saw them before the patient disappeared," he reminded her. "How do you know that there isn't another body out there to be discovered?" He began to rock against her. "Did I tell you about this fantasy I had of you the other day? You never took off your gun."

"Switch places?" Ming said, frowning.

"Yep." He nuzzled her neck. "You're wearing my favorite cologne."

"It's Ivory soap."

"Still my favorite." He worked his way down her collarbone.

"How *did* they meet?"

"Who cares?" He slid open her top button. "Boy, your skin sure is soft."

"Josephine lived most of her life in Paris," she mused. "She's rich, has everything going for her . . . how *does* Michelle fit in the picture?"

Conan worked his magic on a few more buttons.

"Someone like Michelle wouldn't be too happy that her twin sister received the better end of the stick."

"Mm-hmm."

He slid off her shirt and fumbled with the hooks of her bra.

"That would mean I met Michelle, not Josephine." She thought it over, then shook her head. "Nothing in my notes supports your theory," she continued. "I mean, this is pretty thin."

"Thin is good." He tried tugging. "Was this thing so difficult last time?"

Ming wiggled away. "Baby, stop. I think I better

call Tyrese." She grabbed her shirt from the floor.

"But—"

"We've looked at everything else, it won't hurt to check this out." She gave him a quick peck on the cheek, then rushed off to find the cordless phone.

"But—"

"Thanks, honey," she called out over her shoulder. "I owe you one."

"But . . ." Conan hunched his shoulders and slumped back in his chair at the table. "I want to have sex."

"What do you mean, you 'can't find her'?" Michelle Andrews seethed as she paced the great room inside the Ferrell Estate. "Josephine couldn't have walked out of that hospital on her own." Her eyes flashed, then narrowed. "If I didn't know any better, I'd think that *you* had something to do with her escape."

"You're being ridiculous." Dr. Ambrose Turner retreated in the midst of her growing anger and took a nervous sip from his Scotch on the rocks.

"Am I?" her voice dripped with venom. She closed in on him, then circled as if contemplating to attack. "Then how come my guy couldn't find her when he went upstairs to her room?"

"We've been over this a thousand times." Ambrose slammed his glass down on a nearby table. "I *don't* know."

Disbelief blanketed her face.

"I do know that you never mentioned killing Dr. Bancroft," he snapped.

Finally, Michelle's intense expression relaxed with a sinister smile. "I don't like loose ends." Their gazes clashed, while she added, "You should know that."

Ambrose's heart skipped a beat.

Michelle shrugged. "She saw my face."

"And who is this D'Angelo? How do we know that we can trust him?"

"Don't worry about D'Angelo. He's a good friend of mine. Besides, it's not like I could have gone in there myself. I could've been recognized, and you were too chicken to do the job."

He stared at her and felt, once again, that he was in way over his head. However, it wasn't easy untangling from Michelle's finely spun web—a few had died trying.

Michelle drew a deep breath and settled into a plush couch across the room. Her long shapely legs crossed seductively, and Ambrose felt his anger ebb away.

"I still have a major problem," she announced in a pout. "I need to know whether you're still on board or whether you need some further coaxing."

Ambrose swallowed the hard lump lodged in his throat.

Michelle's smile widened. "You know I haven't asked you how Trisha was doing lately."

The mere mention of his wife's name caused a trickle of fear to slither down his spine. For a fleeting moment, he thought about lashing out, but wondered how close to a weapon Michelle hovered. He knew perhaps more than anyone that Michelle was not a woman to cross, and she was most certainly always prepared for the unexpected.

"Of course, I'm on board," he said, with a tight smile and an erratic pulse.

"Good." She winked. "Then you'll have no problem finding who helped Josie out of that hospital." She uncrossed her legs and stood once again.

As she closed the gap between them, Ambrose hated to admit even to himself that he was more turned on than he had ever been in his life. This was how it was always like between them—a dangerous attraction.

"You'll help me find her, won't you?" she asked, pressing her body against his.

He couldn't think when she did that.

She leaned forward until her lips were just inches away from his. "We'll find her and kill her."

Ambrose sealed the deal with a kiss.

* * *

Josie sighed and stretched out her body as far as she could, then snapped back into her tried-and-true fetal position beneath the many piles of blankets William had supplied. She drew a deep, cleansing breath and smiled lazily.

She felt good, damn good, in fact.

Slowly, she became aware of a light snoring. Was that her? Couldn't be, she concluded, and opened her eyes.

The room's popcorn ceiling was the first thing that came into focus before her gaze slid down teal-colored walls. Oil paintings of luminous lighthouses and cobblestone churches hung from the walls.

The snoring continued from her right side. She turned her head and was startled by the close proximity of William's handsome but sleeping face.

Belatedly, she realized that one of his arms was draped across her waist. He must have fallen asleep comforting her last night.

Josie smiled.

He was so adorable when he slept. The small wrinkles and character lines she'd noticed the previous night were now smoothed and relaxed. He deceptively looked as though he didn't have a care in the world.

"I still can't believe you're here," she whispered, then stretched out her hand to brush her finger lightly against the petals of his lips.

He stirred, but didn't wake.

For the moment, Josie watched him. Lord knows, she had never thought she would have this opportunity again.

She had spent more than a decade regretting the day she'd met the man, and, suddenly, here he was, playing the role of her knight in shining armor. It didn't make sense.

Josie turned away and gently pried his arm from around her waist.

When she sat up, she expected to be woozy, but was pleasantly surprised that she felt fine. Glancing down at herself, she repositioned her robe and tightened the belt before she chanced standing up from the bed.

There was a slight tremor to her legs, but it was nothing she couldn't handle. A towel fell from her head, and her damp hair spilled down against her neck and face. She pushed it from her eyes and hooked it behind her ears.

Unsure whether she should risk walking on her own, Josie stood beside the bed a long time before she inched one foot forward, then the other. Successful, she permitted herself a small smile.

Before long she had made her way across the room to the door. She left William sleeping in bed while curiosity led her to explore the house.

The cold surprised her, and she wished she'd thought to put something on her bare feet as she moved around on the hardwood floors. Josie took her time checking out the other unoccupied rooms. Everything had a country deco feel. That was interesting. It wasn't quite her taste, but it was interesting.

Back in the hall, she discovered a wall leading down the staircase covered with family pictures. Josie recognized the couple smiling back at her.

Sheila. They were definitely not cousins. Her gaze drifted to Sheila's husband, and now she knew why his eyes were so familiar. *Larry.* He was William's older brother.

Studying the man's face, she was struck by the brothers' differences. Larry's features were broader, his dimple cheeks pinchable, but where William was tall and muscular, Larry was shorter—stockier.

Overall, she was convinced that her William was the better-looking of the two.

Smiling, she grabbed hold of the banister and descended the stairs one step at a time. Once she reached the bottom, she noted that the cold was nearly unbearable, and she wondered if the heat was working.

There were two other bedrooms and a full bath on the bottom floor, not to mention a large kitchen that paid homage to wooden roosters and ceramic cows. It was cute in a strange way.

The refrigerator was packed with food. She

grabbed a bottle of water and took an apple that was nestled in a fruit bowl.

The living room revealed more pictures and an interesting set of plaid furniture. *Are these people related to Jed Clampett?*

The room also displayed three floor-to-ceiling windows, which gave a panoramic view of a forest of some kind. Where was she?

She moved closer to one of the windows and smiled at the deer congregating around the house.

She was at peace watching them and the occasional squirrel darting off a tree. As a result, she stood there a long time drinking water and eating her apple.

However, peace never lasts long, for fear has a way of embedding itself in one's heart and thoughts. At that moment, Michelle terrified her. She didn't know how Michelle got the better of her or even how she pulled off the impossible.

Josie glanced down at her scarred wrist and, in her mind's eye an image of them covered in blood weakened her knees.

She quickly closed her eyes in remorse and turned away from the window. The chill in the house seemed to seep into her bones.

During her roaming, she had discovered a den equipped with blue-and-white-plaid furniture, a fireplace, and an upright piano. Her heart immediately lightened at the sight of the polished instrument, and she crossed the room toward it as if hypnotized.

Before she sat down on the small bench, her eyes were drawn to the photographs placed on cute little doilies on top of the piano. These pictures weren't of Sheila and Larry, but of William and a stunning brunette.

Josie set down her water and picked up one of the pictures and realized it was of a wedding: William's wedding.

Air rushed from her lungs as she lowered herself onto the bench. She took in every detail of the woman's smile to the glittering diamond on her finger and the bulge of her belly.

Unexpected tears seeped from her eyes as the pain from that distant heartbreak returned.

Tossing her apple away in a plastic wastebasket beneath an end table, she opened the piano's wooden cover and lightly walked her fingers down the ivory keys. Pleasantly surprised to find it in tune, Josie straightened her posture and began to play.

Immediately, her mood lightened as her hands danced over the keys. Once upon a time, music was her passion—her life.

Her hands slowed.

She couldn't remember a time when music wasn't a part of her. Her parents were supportive and did all they could by sending her to the best schools. It had always been a fair conclusion that she would be a famous musician.

One of her hands fumbled over a key as her eyes misted.

Before she had met William, she had everything figured out. She was happy and engaged to the perfect man—or so she thought. Up until that point, she thought she knew what she wanted and knew how to get it.

But it was all a lie.

Josie stopped playing as her mind drifted back to her and William's emotional good-bye . . .

"You love me!" William shouted, gripping her arms and pulling her close. Her bedroom walls vibrated with the force of his anger. "You know you do."

Josie struggled against him. "I'm engaged, William. Last night was a mistake. It should never have happened."

"How can you say that?"

He released her with such force that she staggered backward. When she glanced up into his eyes, her heart felt as if it was being ripped out of her chest. "I'm sorry, William. I never meant to hurt you, but—"

"Don't say it." He reached for her again. "You're making a mistake. *We* belong together."

She shook her head. "No. There are too many differences. You know it, and I know it."

His face darkened. "What—because you're black and I'm white? Is that what you're telling me?"

She swallowed her shock and outrage. "Of course that's not what I meant."

His eyes narrowed as if he didn't believe her.

"We're from two different worlds. We want different things out of life," she insisted. "Etienne and I are cut from the same cloth."

William's gaze drifted to the man in the photograph beside her bed, and a mask of utter loathing covered his features. "You mean you're from the same social class."

"Why are you refusing to *hear* what I'm saying?"

"Because it not the truth," he snapped, and succeeded in drawing her back into his arms. "You can study music back in the States. There are just as many opportunities there, if not more."

"Why do I have to give up *my* life?"

"Fine. I'll move here. I don't care where I practice medicine. I just want us to be together."

"And what about Etienne?"

"What about him?"

Again, she extracted herself from William's grasp. "I can't just break my promise to him."

"But I'm the one you want," he insisted.

She said nothing as her lower lip trembled, and her eyes brimmed with tears.

Doubt crept into his eyes. "You *do* love me," he said, but it sounded more like a question. "Josie?"

She stepped back, while her gaze lowered to the hardwood floor. In an instant, William's strong fingers directed her chin up. "I'll leave if you can look me in the eye and tell me that you don't love me."

Her gaze met his sharp blue eyes, and a painful lump swelled in the center of her throat. As much as she wanted to give in to this man, she couldn't completely ignore her promise to another.

"Josie," he urged again.

"I'm sorry, William, but I don't love you . . ."

"Why did you stop playing?"

Josie jumped and looked up to see William smiling from the den's entryway. "I'm sorry. Did I wake you?"

"Frightened me is more like it." He crossed his arms. "But it's good to see you up and about. How do you feel?"

"Good. I'm still a little shaky, but overall, I feel a lot better." She met his steady gaze and gave him a wobbly smile. "I don't know how I'll ever repay you."

"You don't owe me anything. I'm just glad I could help."

Josie's gaze fell.

He moved away from the archway and over to the piano. "Mind if I join you?"

"Not at all." She scooted over on the bench to make room.

William sat beside her. "You know it's been a long time since we've sung together." He played a few bars of "Willow Weep for Me." "Remember that one?"

Josie smiled but felt the sting of tears behind her eyes. "How could I ever forget?"

"I always thought that you were the next Billie Holiday."

She shifted uncomfortably in her seat.

William abruptly changed the music and sang, "I'm a fool to want you."

She closed her eyes and remembered their first night onstage. "To want a love that can't be true." Her voice trembled so badly that she lowered her head in shame.

He stopped playing. "What's wrong?"

She shook her head and refused to look up at him.

He draped an arm around her shoulders and pulled her trembling body against his. "You can tell me," he encouraged.

His attentiveness deepened her embarrassment mainly because she knew that she was being silly for crying, but damn if she could stop herself.

"Josie?" he asked, giving her an affectionate squeeze. "I know that I'm not the best singer, but I've never caused anyone to start crying before."

She laughed.

"There. That's much better." He kissed the top of her head.

Shocked, Josie lifted her head and met his gaze again. The air in the room thinned while her heart thudded against her chest. When a magnetic force pulled them together, a voice in her head warned her to resist, but it was no more than a whisper.

Her gaze fell to his lips when his warm breath brushed against her face. Butterflies she had long forgotten began their wild flutter seconds before William's soft lips pressed against hers.

The familiar taste of him was the sweetest homecoming she could have ever imagined. While her mind filled with exploding fireworks, her resistance melted like wax. There was no harm in stealing this one moment in time, she convinced herself.

Josie pressed closer and opened her mouth to his probing tongue. Everything about him and this kiss felt right despite the fact that she knew it was wrong.

As abruptly as their kiss began, it ended.

"Sorry," William said, breaking away. "I shouldn't have done that."

Disappointment stabbed her heart as humiliation burned her face. "What did I do?"

"Nothing." William stood from the bench and the room chilled. "It's not you. It's me. I . . . don't worry. It won't happen again," he said.

Before Josie had a chance to reply, William turned on his heel and left her alone in the room.

For that she was grateful. It meant that he never saw the tears that slipped from her eyes.

It was another chilly morning as Detectives Delaney and Simmons huddled together while they watched a pair of paramedics lift a gurney into a waiting ambulance.

"Well, you were right. There was another body," Tyrese said, sipping his morning coffee.

"Just not the one we were looking for," she said. As she crossed her arms, her gaze swept across the accident scene. Only the rear end of a silver Mercedes stuck out of the lake—an odd place for a car.

"Any theories?" Ming asked.

"Not yet, but check with me after the caffeine kicks in."

"Murder?"

"Always a possibility. Not too many people decide to take a drive into a lake. No one I know anyway."

Frustrated, Ming turned and faced her partner. "I give up. Why did you drag me down here? The is Gwinett County—out of our jurisdiction."

Wearily, he nodded toward the vehicle. "Look at the bumper. See anything familiar?"

Sighing, she turned back around and scanned the car's back bumper, however nothing jumped out at her. She shrugged. "What?"

"Don't tell me you're losing your touch," Tyrese snickered.

And then she saw it. A silver sticker that read, KEYSTONE M.D.

"Bingo." He patted her on the back. "Sorry, I'm all out of door prizes though."

Ming started toward the ambulance. "Who is it?"

"Ambrose Turner, according to the driver's license. Police detective Cathy Lansing called our department when she saw the sticker. Said that she remembered seeing something on the news about our investigation at Keystone."

Ming nodded. "So is this our baby?"

"Not officially, but it probably will be before the day is out."

"Two Keystone doctors," she whispered to herself. "What the hell is going on here?"

"I don't know. Maybe we're off the mark thinking the Keystone murder is tied in to the Thornton case," Tyrese said.

"And Conan's twin theory?"

He chuckled. "Even farther off the mark."

She folded her arms as she watched a team arrive to recover the sinking Mercedes. "Maybe it was just an accident."

"The bullet in the back of his head says otherwise."

Exasperated, Ming turned on him. "None of this crap makes any sense."

He held up his cup. "No yelling. I'm still waiting for the caffeine to kick in."

Ming shook her head and stormed past her partner. "We're going to start over."

"Meaning?" Tyrese's long strides struggled to keep up with hers.

"I want another interview with everyone we talked to in the Thornton case. All of this is related somehow. I just know it."

"We're supposed to be looking for Michelle Andrews, remember?"

"We are." She continued to their car. "As a matter of fact, I think it's time we paid a visit to the Ferrell Estate."

"I'm sorry, Ms. Ferrell, but your passport has expired," Rhonda, according to her Delta name tag, said politely.

"What do you mean?" Michelle pressed down on the rim of her sunglasses to glare at the smiling woman.

"It says so right here." Rhonda pointed to a line in the little blue book. "It expired six months ago."

Michelle's eyes followed the woman's finger, and her heart sank at the printed expiration date. "Well, can't you just renew it?" she asked irritably. "My flight leaves in thirty minutes."

Rhonda's smile lost a little of its luster. "We don't renew passports, Ms. Ferrell. We're not a government agency. We do have a concierge service that might be of assistance to you. You may not be able to get your passport today, but with the proper paperwork, they could probably express a renewal within five to seven days."

"Five to seven days," Michelle thundered. "I don't have five to seven days. I have a plane to catch in thirty minutes."

"I'm sorry, ma'am. But there's nothing else I can do. Your passport has expired." Rhonda handed the small book to her.

Angry, Michelle snatched the passport. "Thanks for nothing," she seethed, and crammed everything back into her purse. She leaned down, grabbed her carry-on bag, and stormed out of line.

"What now?" she asked herself.

Minutes later, while she was scrounging around for the airport's concierge, she realized that her luggage had boarded the plane. "I don't believe this." She stomped her foot and stifled a scream.

When she finally found the concierge and gave him a blast of her temper, she received the same information Rhonda had imparted.

"What *exactly* is considered the proper identification?" Michelle asked.

"You just need to bring a certified birth certificate and a current, valid driver's license," a smiling Ned said.

Michelle's heart sank to her knees. "I have a valid driver's license." She reached into her purse for the stolen license she'd lifted from Josephine.

"You'll still need a birth certificate," he insisted. "You *are* a US citizen, aren't you?"

"Yes, but—"

"Then you'll need a birth certificate to leave the country."

Michelle clenched her jaw and fought the urge to snatch the short man from over the counter.

Once again, she turned in a huff and stormed off. An hour later, she was back at the Ferrell Estate. However, she was surprised when her taxi rolled up next to a Buick Regal.

"That will be fifty-eight twenty-five," the cab driver informed her.

Michelle reached for her purse but her attention was drawn to the two figures at her doorstep.

"Fifty-eight twenty-five," the irate man said again.

"Just a second, Mohammed," she snapped.

"It's Rasheed."

"Whatever." She paid her tab and opened her door. When she stood, she finally recognized the tall Asian woman waiting for her.

Trouble.

Michelle drew a deep breath and raised her chin. She slid both her purse and her carry-on bag over her shoulder and closed her cab door.

Delaney smiled as she folded her arms across her chest. "Been on a trip?"

"I don't see how that's any business of yours." Michelle joined the two blue suits and slid her key into the lock. "It's not my birthday, so to what do I owe this pleasure?"

"Humph. I would've thought you'd asked whether we've found your sister," Delaney said.

Michelle opened her door. "You don't look like the bearer of good news." She stepped inside and left the door open so her uninvited guess could follow her.

"Wow," Delaney said. "Nice place you have here."

"Thanks," Michelle droned in a bored voice. She set her bags on the foyer's table.

"And empty," Delaney added. "I always figured

a place like this would be crawling with servants."

"I'm in the middle of hiring a new staff," Michelle lied. "Does your shadow speak, or is he just arm candy?"

Delaney gave her a thin wry smile. "I forgot you two haven't been introduced. This is my partner, Detective Tyrese Simmons. Simmons, Ms. Andrews."

Michelle's stomach muscles tensed. "It's Ferrell," she corrected.

Delaney's smile disappeared. "My mistake."

A strained silence lapsed among the three parties, distinctly giving Michelle the sense that she was in the middle of a life-size chess game.

"I'm still waiting to hear what brings you here," Michelle said.

"We wanted to ask you a few questions regarding you and . . . Michelle," Simmons answered. "Specifically, how you two met."

"And what is the relevancy of that?"

"Well, it's just a big hole in the puzzle. Given the difference in your upbringing, we're just curious."

Michelle weighed whether she should answer the question, then decided that it was a harmless inquiry. "We met at my father's funeral."

"What—she just showed up?"

Michelle shrugged. "Yes. So?"

"She just crashed a funeral?" Simmons asked.

"Something like that."

"That didn't strike you as odd," Delaney challenged.

Michelle didn't answer. She was almost certain that Abbott and Costello here were leading her toward a trapdoor. "As much as I'm enjoying this little chitchat, I have other things to attend to, and I believe that you two have a missing person to find."

"Actually"—Delaney finally closed the front door—"we were a little concerned about your welfare."

Michelle's brows dipped together. "Come again?"

"Well, it's pretty clear to me that . . . Michelle had some help leaving Keystone. According to the staff, she was pretty much out of it through most of her stay. Now whether she was kidnapped or she convinced someone to help her is what remains to be seen. If the latter is the case, then there's no real crime that's been committed unless she and her partner murdered Dr. Bancroft."

"Get to the point," Michelle snapped.

"See, you're probably not aware of your sister's extensive criminal record, and I'm thinking that someone as unstable as Michelle can't be too happy that her twin sister was adopted by such a wealthy family while she wasn't quite so lucky." Delaney paused for dramatic effect.

Michelle shifted her weight. "I'm still waiting."

"Isn't it obvious?" Simmons said.

"Apparently not," she said tightly.

Delaney walked across the foyer and stopped within inches of Michelle. "Andrews never does something for nothing. She approached you for a reason." Delaney took her time and glanced around the large home before she continued. "I'm guessing that she wants her piece of the money pie."

The silence returned while the women's gazes battled.

Finally, Michelle stepped away and mulled this latest development over but decided it was best to toss their theory back in their faces. "I don't believe you."

"That's your choice."

Michelle grew bolder. "I think that you two are grasping at straws again, and you're wasting my time. So I would like for you to leave. *¿Comprende?*"

Delaney and Simmons glanced at each other.

Michelle glided over to the front door and opened it. "Now."

Simmons walked out the door with a grave expression while Delaney smiled.

Michelle glared.

"Make sure that you stay in town. I have a feeling that we'll be back." At the door's threshold, Delaney stopped. *"Nous connaissons la vérité et nous allant vous attraper."*

Michelle's eyes narrowed.

Delaney blinked, gave her a cracked smile, then cleared the threshold. "*Au revoir.*"

Michelle slammed the door.

Tyrese smiled and shook his head as he headed over to their car. "That went well. What did you say to her?"

"That we knew the truth and we're going to catch her." Delaney followed him.

"You're kidding?"

Delaney opened the passenger door and slid into the seat. "Conan was right."

Tyrese closed his door and turned to look at her. "Excuse me?"

"She didn't understand me." Ming's jaw set determinedly. "I don't know how she did it, but that woman in there is *not* Josephine Ferrell."

J osie was beginning to feel like a human being again. With assistance, she was able to blow-dry her hair and get dressed in something other than a nightgown. William had purchased her some clothes and underwear, so she selected a pair of jeans, an Atlanta Falcons jersey, and a very comfortable pair of Nikes. To her surprise everything fit perfectly.

Drawing a deep breath, she brushed off all thoughts of her embarrassing episode with William that morning.

Besides, she had a hell of a lot of other problems to deal with at that moment.

She needed to get her hands on her address book. The book could help her get in contact with friends, doctors, dentists; whomever she needed to help her with proving her identity.

Tired of her thoughts chasing each other, Josie turned off the light and walked out of the bathroom. She quickly moved over to the phone on one of the nightstand tables. In no time she'd reached France's information line and requested the number for her longtime physician, Dr. Dumas. However, she was disappointed when she reached the practice's automated voice mail.

"Bonjour. Ceci est Josephine Ferrell. J'appelle pour demander une copier de mes rapports médicaux." What's the address?

"Je rappellerai avec ma nouvelle adresse et mon nouveau numéro de telephone." She hung up and rolled her eyes at her absentmindedness.

She rushed out of the bedroom and was greeted by wonderful aromas of bacon and coffee. Her stomach churned and growled with anticipation.

Within minutes, she joined William in the kitchen. "It smells like heaven in here," she declared, peeking around him to see what was on the stove.

"Thanks," he said.

Josie's sense of smell hadn't deceived her. There were bacon, sausage, and eggs. On a griddle were perfectly shaped pancakes and in a bowl on the counter were diced cantaloupe and honeydew.

"It looks like you went to an awful lot of trouble."

"Nah. It's no trouble at all." William moved from the stove top to the oven, where he removed golden brown biscuits.

He moved around the kitchen like a seasoned chef. It was an unexpected turn-on, and Josie found herself watching him with great fascination.

"Did I miss something, or are you expecting an army?" she chuckled.

"No. I just figured you'd be hungry. You haven't had much in the past few days." He turned his attention to the pancakes.

Josie sensed he was trying his best to avoid eye contact. She stepped back so she could stay out of his way, but she couldn't help but ask, "Is something wrong?"

A long pause ensued before he answered, "No."

It was an obvious lie, but the tension between them was too thick for her to call him on it. She changed the subject. "I called my doctor's office to request my medical records."

William stopped what he was doing. "You did?"

"Yeah. Well, I reached their voice mail, and I didn't have an address to tell them where to mail the records."

"Oh, yeah. I can, uh, write that down for you," he said.

She glanced over and tried to read him, but she

was unsuccessful. She didn't understand his cold demeanor. Especially, since he was so attentive last night, but after their kiss . . .

Josie shook the direction of her thoughts out of her head. "Can I help with something?"

He glanced around. "No. I have everything under control." He moved to the refrigerator. "Would you like orange juice or grapefruit juice?"

Something was obviously wrong, and she rolled her eyes at his lame attempt at avoidance.

"Josie?" He turned to look at her. However, when their eyes met, he quickly dropped his gaze. "Orange or grapefruit?"

"Orange."

He grabbed the appropriate carton.

"Look, William. About this morning—"

"It's already forgotten."

She blinked at his continued coldness.

William took a few platters of food over to the kitchen table and returned. "How many pancakes do you want?" he asked.

Josie crossed her arms. "I don't know, two or three." Her stomach growled. "Better make it four."

His lips finally curled upward. "You got it."

Quite suddenly, Josie felt light-headed and wavered on her feet.

William rushed to her side. "Josie, are you all right?"

She nodded even though she wasn't sure.

He helped her to the table so she could sit and catch her breath.

"Look at me," he instructed, while he lifted the lids of her eyes. "Come on, Josie. Look at me."

She struggled to do just that. When she met his gaze, it was like looking at the calm blue of the ocean. She loved how they sparkled, how they made her feel at peace.

"You're doing good," he encouraged.

Just as suddenly as the spell came on, it was over. However, her heart raced, and her throat was drier than the Sahara.

"I think I'll have that juice now," she panted.

"Sure." William hopped up and went to get it for her.

Meanwhile, Josie calmed down and gathered herself. "Do you know how much longer I'm going to have to put up with this?" she asked, just as he returned.

"Well, it's different for everyone."

She accepted the glass and drained nearly the whole thing in one gulp.

"I better get you some more." He left and returned with the whole carton. "I have you on methadone right now," he said. "I'll give you another shot after breakfast."

She reached for the carton.

"I'll pour it for you," he said.

"I can do it," she snapped.

William held up his hands in surrender as she refilled her glass. She immediately felt silly. "I'm sorry."

"It's not a problem."

After she'd quenched her thirst, she asked the most prominent question that came to mind. "What is methadone?"

"A narcotic pain reliever." William grabbed a chair and set it next to her. "It's generally used for maintenance for drug detox. Your body developed a dependency to the narcotics that were pumped into your system. The pain you're experiencing is your body's way of demanding the drugs. Methadone helps you with that pain."

Narcotics? "What exactly were they giving me at that place?"

"At Keystone you were given pretty high doses of lithium. Your last toxicology reports also showed Tegretol and Depakote, which are used when a person shows resistance to lithium. Before you were admitted to Keystone blood tests showed traces of Prozac, heroin, you name it. You were a walking time bomb."

"What?" Her jaw slackened. "Why in hell were they giving me all of that? I don't recognize half of those drugs."

He hesitated. "The lithium was still being administered because they thought you were Michelle."

Josie lowered her gaze.

William braided his hands together. "What do you know about your sister?"

Josie sighed. "The question is what do I know about Michelle that's *true*."

"Okay, let's start there. Lithium is usually prescribed to patients for a wide range of things: bipolar disorders, manic depression, and even those with chemical imbalances." He gave her a few seconds for the information to sink in. "It's too bad you don't know anything about your biological parents. A lot of times, these things are genetic."

"So Michelle . . ."

". . . has a long history of mental illness." He stood and went to the kitchen.

Josie wiped a stray tear from her eyes. "Just because someone struggles with mental illness doesn't mean they're evil."

William returned and placed all he'd prepared onto the table. "Michelle might be the exception to the rule. I've been reading Michelle's medical chart, and it isn't pretty. Given the circumstances, you're more than welcome to read it for yourself. My big question is how she managed to pull off this whole switcharoo."

Josie placed her elbows on the table and lowered her head into the palms of her hands. "I'm getting a migraine."

"You still get those?"

She gave him a sad laugh. "As far back as I can remember."

"Well, let's get something into your stomach. Who knows, maybe you're just hungry."

She nodded and was grateful when plates were brought to the table. Minutes later, she had a little bit of everything piled in front of her. She undoubtedly looked like a pig, but she was way past caring. It had to be the best meal she'd ever tasted.

Josie moaned in ecstasy with each bite while she started to believe that she could quite possibly devour everything he'd set on the table.

William, however, leaned back in his chair and sipped coffee. "As flattered as I am about you enjoying the meal, I'd feel better if you'd slow down and take your time."

She nodded, but couldn't do it.

"How about we talk about Michelle some more," he said, seeking to slow her down through conversation. "How long did she stay with you until . . . ?"

"Until I lost my mind?" she finished for him.

"That's one way of putting it."

"It's the only way to put it." She leaned back and took a slow sip of her orange juice. "My father's funeral was June 20 of last year. That was the first time I'd ever laid eyes on my sister."

"How did she find you?"

Josie set her glass down and drew a deep breath. "She said that about a month before my father's death, a friend of hers brought her an old jazz CD of mine and commented how much we looked alike. From there she claimed that she did some research on the Internet and was able to find my bio."

"Your biography mentioned your parents?"

She nodded. "And where I was from. So later when my father's death made one of the papers, she figured it was the best opportunity to meet me."

"It just fell into her lap—how convenient." Disgust dripped from his voice.

"It seemed innocent enough, plus I'd just lost the last family member I had, so I guess I leapt at the possibility of discovering another one." Josie shrugged as her gaze fell to her empty plate. "No one wants to be alone."

An uncomfortable silence fell over the table, and Josie regretted sharing so much.

When he, at last, reached across the table and took her hand, she was surprised by the comfort his touch gave. So much so that she was humbled by it.

"Don't beat yourself up," he said gently. "You did what anyone in your position would have done."

She wasn't sure if she agreed.

"Okay, so you met her at the funeral and then what?"

Josie removed her hand from his to reach for more bacon. "Well, both of us always knew that we were adopted, but had no idea that we were twins or had been separated, so we tried to research our adoptions." She shrugged again. "Who knows, maybe there were other siblings."

William studied her over the rim of his coffee mug and pretended that his heart didn't tug at her forlorn expression. "Were there?"

"Our adoption records are sealed." She reached for the biscuits. "Apparently our biological parents don't want to be found."

He lowered his cup. "I'm sorry."

She refused to meet his eyes.

"Josie, you know you didn't do anything wrong?"

She grew still—too still.

William's gaze narrowed. *Was there something she wasn't telling him?* The silence became deafening before he probed gently. "Josie?"

A tear raced from her lashes, but she quickly wiped it away.

"I know you," he said. "You're not to blame for any of this. You have to know that."

"I've got to take something for my head," she moaned.

He sighed with relief. She wasn't keeping something from him; it was another migraine. "Let's get you that shot first. It should also help with your headaches."

Josie shook her head. "I need some Tylenol or morphine—something. I don't feel too good."

He rushed back to her side. "Are you feeling nauseous?"

Josie frowned and clutched her stomach again. "Yes . . . no . . . I don't know. I-I think I just need to lie down."

"Sounds like you're still experiencing withdrawal symptoms. If you let me, I'll help you upstairs."

She nodded and allowed him to loop an arm around her.

Minutes later, Josie sat still while William administered the methadone, then instructed her to lie down. When she was finally alone, guilt churned in her belly. She had to get out of there . . . and soon.

Images she had long tried to suppress sharpened into focus. She saw Michelle's boyfriend, Daniel, and could still feel the weight of a gun in her hand.

He never looked at her—never knew what she was about to do.

Josie lifted the gun as if she was in a trance, aimed, and fired a single shot in the center of his chest.

"Oh my God," Josie turned and sobbed into her pillow. "What have I done?"

Michelle spent the rest of the day tearing through boxes at the Ferrell Estate and looking for Josephine's birth certificate or adoption papers. However, after eight hours of digging all she had for her efforts was a splitting headache.

"I'm never going to find that damn thing," she huffed, and stood up from the floor of what had once been Josephine's old bedroom. "It's probably in France somewhere." She kicked a box in frustration.

Her anger quickly reached the boiling point. "This is all Ambrose's fault," she seethed. All his gifts and confessions of love meant nothing. She asked him to do one little thing—like *kill* her sister, and he couldn't even do that.

Michelle kicked another box, but then smiled with satisfaction. "I hope you rot at the bottom of that damn lake."

Her thoughts raced to Detective Delaney, who was turning into a major pain in her backside.

They're going to get you.

"They can't prove a thing." Her eyes darted to the room's elegant splendor. "I'm not giving all this up without a fight." She moved away from the boxes and paced along the plush carpet. "I need a new plan."

It doesn't matter. They're going to get you.

"Not if I have something to say about it."

What can you do? You let Josephine slip through your fingers.

She ground her teeth.

If Josephine were out of the picture, then you wouldn't have to leave town.

"But where in the hell is she?" Again, Michelle cursed Ambrose. If he'd just done what he was supposed to, she wouldn't be in this situation.

You had a chance to kill her, too, you know.

"She was supposed to kill herself," she corrected, then wondered again how Josie survived after losing so much blood. "Those slashes were deep. I saw them."

The memory of Josephine lying so still in the sauna and staring at her slashed wrists flashed through Michelle's head. Josie's expression had looked amazingly composed and serene; but in her eyes, Michelle read horror.

At the time, Michelle laughed. It had been so simple, she thought. Well, with Daniel's help, anyway.

"I'm going to miss dear Danny," she mused. "Having him around did have its benefits. After all, it'd been his idea to slip Michelle's lithium to her twin sister. It sounded impossible until Michelle noticed Josie's frequent migraines. Danny, in his infinite genius, had the lithium pills made to resemble Josie's beloved Excedrin tablets.

However, the lithium had little to no effect. So, they upped the ante. The next pills they transformed were Prozac and OxyContin.

They'd struck the jackpot.

Since all the pills were mixed together in Josie's bottle and could be taken in any combination, Josie was putty in their hands.

Michelle was amazed how receptive Josie was to suggestion. But whereas Daniel wanted to simply extort money from Josie, Michelle wanted it all—and without splitting it down the center with him.

Even that plan almost blew up in your face.

"I handled it," she retaliated, as she stormed out of the bedroom and down the long hall to the staircase.

It was still a close call.

"Close only counts in horseshoes and hand

grenades." She chuckled while she descended the spiral staircase. Minutes later, she reached the bar in the study and made herself a drink.

For the umpteenth time that day, she regretted having let go of the hired help. Of course, it was the third crew she'd fired since she'd been there.

Since Josie had initially returned to Georgia to bury her father and settle the estate, she'd given his employees a sizable severance package. She had no intentions of staying Stateside for long.

Michelle changed all of that.

She glanced around her opulent surroundings and snickered. "It's like taking candy from a baby."

Josie is still out there somewhere.

Michelle rolled her eyes, but conceded that the voice had a good point. "I have to find her."

She'll go to the police before you find her, then it'll all be over.

Seething, Michelle turned to exit the room, but instead her attention was drawn to the stacks of paper crumpled under her feet. She started to kick them aside, but her gaze zeroed in on the title Deed of Property.

"Well, what do we have here?" she asked, kneeling. She scanned the paper. "More property," she said under her breath and shook her head. "The rich just keep getting richer."

In the past few months, Michelle was stunned to learn just how much land Josephine's adoptive parents had owned in Georgia alone. There was the estate in which she was currently residing in Alpharetta, a cabin at Lake Lanier, a high-rise in Buckhead, and now this house in Pine Mountain.

Plenty of places to hide.

Michelle frowned as she stared at the deed. Could Josie be hiding out at one of these places? "I think its time I paid a visit to these properties . . . including this Pine Mountain."

Trisha Turner sobbed endlessly as she sat in an interrogation room. In her mind, she couldn't stop replaying the memory of seeing her husband off to work that morning.

The door finally swung open. A tall Asian woman and an even larger, broad-shouldered black man strolled into the room. Something about their severe expressions had a sobering effect on her.

"Sorry to have kept you waiting," the woman said. "I'm Detective Ming Delaney and this is my partner, Detective Tyrese Simmons."

Trisha nodded her greeting but wiped at her tears.

Both detectives took seats on the other side of the table.

"I don't understand why I was brought here."

Simmons's thick lips slid into a smile while he braided his fingers in front of him. "We think there might be a connection between your husband's murder and one of our cases."

"Murder?" Trisha's sniffles gradually diminished. "You don't think it was an accident?" Her eyes darted to each cop and her heartbeat accelerated at their hesitation.

"Mrs. Turner, your husband was shot in the back of the head." Delaney began in a soft lilt. "Do you know of anyone who might have wanted to cause your husband any harm?"

"Shot?" Trisha's hands crossed her heart. She couldn't believe the line of questioning. "Why, everyone loved Ambrose. He was a kind and brilliant psychiatrist."

"Yes, I'm sure he was," Delaney conceded, but her gaze locked on to Trisha's and wouldn't let go until it penetrated her soul. "But how was his behavior in the last week?"

Blinking, Trisha lowered her hands to her lap.

"What is it, Mrs. Turner?" Simmons asked.

She shrugged as she thought about it. "Well, he'd been a little distracted—but I'm sure it was just because he'd lost a close and dear colleague at the institute this past weekend."

"Distracted how?" Delaney asked.

Trisha struggled with how to describe what she meant. "Ambrose is . . . was sort of anal about schedules. He woke up every morning at five-thirty. He jogged, he expected meals served at a certain time—you could set your watch by him." She twisted her hands. "But lately . . ."

Silence stretched as the agents waited for her to continue.

"It's been longer than just these last few days. He had trouble sleeping and occasionally would go out for long drives. So I assumed that . . ." She couldn't hold it together any longer and buried her face in her hands.

Neither officer consoled her, but they gave her all the time she needed to pull herself together.

When she at last quieted down, Delaney asked, "What did you assume?"

"That he was seeing *her* again." Trisha glanced up to see the agents' stoic expressions.

"Your husband was having an affair?" Simmons asked.

Shame blanketed her body. "I'm not sure, but possibly."

"You said 'again.' Did he have one in the past?" Delaney asked.

"He . . . used to have a mistress." Her voice lowered to a whisper. "But he swore he . . . had ended it sometime ago."

Ming watched as tears slid down the widow's face. She couldn't help but imagine how distraught she would be if anything ever happened to Conan. But she did know what she would do if he ever cheated on her.

"Did you believe him?" Tyrese pressed.

Trisha hesitated.

Ming read that she was weighing whether to tell the truth or let sleeping dogs lie. "Let's just say that he didn't end it. Do you think this woman might want to cause him harm?"

An awkward laugh burst from her chest. "Why? Ambrose is harmless."

Ming and Tyrese didn't answer.

"What?" Trisha asked. "You know something I don't?"

"We'll ask the questions." Ming knew by the way the woman's body jerked that she'd inadvertently ruffled Trisha's feathers.

Simmons took the reins. "Where was your husband going this morning, Mrs. Turner?"

"To work."

"Does he always go to work with a packed suitcase and an airline ticket to Brazil?"

Trisha blinked.

"His flight was at ten o'clock this morning," Ming added gently. "He wasn't on his way to work."

The widow's tears dried instantly as her shoulders drooped. "That bastard."

Ming leaned forward. "Can you still not think of anyone who might want to harm your husband?"

"He was probably with her that night," Trisha said, as if she hadn't heard Delaney.

"With whom?" Tyrese and Ming asked in unison.

"I should have left him a long time ago," Trisha rambled. "But he was such a good provider. I've been out of the work force for over twenty years, and what would all my friends think if I couldn't hold my marriage together?"

Ming frowned and was momentarily thrown for a loop by such a Dark Ages comment. "Let's slow down, Mrs. Turner. What night was he with someone else?"

Trisha crossed her arms. Anger radiated from her. "Friday night," she said in a sharp clipped tone. "I heard him leave the house around midnight. He was only gone for a couple of hours. He probably thought I wouldn't wake up."

Dr. Bancroft was murdered early Saturday morning. Ming glanced over at her partner to see if the same suspicion had crept into his thoughts.

"What time did he return home?"

"Three o'clock. I remember because I read the clock on the nightstand."

Tyrese reached inside his jacket for his small notepad. "But you suspect that he was with his mistress?"

"Most likely." Trisha's lower lip trembled, a sign that a battle still raged inside of her.

"Do you know who she is or where we might be able to find her?"

"A few years ago I hired a private detective to follow him around. I thought if my suspicions were correct, that I could leave him with a clear conscience. But I never did."

Delaney and Simmons waited patiently.

"I have a file on the affair at home if you want to see it." Trisha blew her nose and struggled to pull herself together. "Do I know who she is? How can a woman ever forget the name of the whore who'd made a mockery of her marriage?"

Ming fought the urge to comfort the distraught woman, but she encouraged her to take her time.

Trisha nodded, gathered herself, then finally responded. "Her name is Michelle . . . Michelle Andrews."

Despite its being a convenient way to avoid William, Josie grew restless from lying in bed. She needed to come up with a plan. She couldn't just let Michelle steal her life. She sat up and watched the fading sunlight slide through the blinds.

How on earth had she allowed someone to do this to her? Just as quickly, she realized that she hadn't *allowed* anything.

At the soft rap on the door, she turned to see William ease into the room. His magnetic eyes captured her attention, but when he smiled his lips triggered a memory—one when she and William lay naked in front of a fireplace while his lips kissed every inch of her body.

"How are you feeling?" he asked, bursting her memory bubble.

Josie glanced away. "Better."

The room was filled with too many atoms or something because it was suddenly hard to breathe and even more difficult to keep her eyes averted.

"Well, I thought you might want to get out of the house—stretch your legs for a while."

She perked up at the possibility. "You mean I can actually be a part of the world again?"

He clapped and rubbed his hands together, and his dimpled cheeks made an appearance. "I figured you deserved it. Fresh air along with my company—you're a lucky girl."

Josie laughed and got up from the bed. "Nothing's going to attack us out there, is it?"

William touched the fading scratches on his face. "Just the occasional tree branch." He chuckled. "We're nestled against a national park. Generally, there're no campers out here this time of year, so the most we'll run up against are deer."

"Then I'm game."

Josie didn't respond to his barb, but instead smiled secretively to herself. If Larry was anything like his brother, she knew exactly what Sheila saw in him.

The moment Josie stepped out the front door and into the cool breeze of autumn her spirits lifted to wondrous new heights. The kiss of the fading sun and the wind's gentle caress welcomed her back to the land of the living.

"It's beautiful out here," she commented as her gaze darted around a world blanketed with red and gold leaves.

"Yeah, it's nice." He led the way across the long wooden porch, then helped her down the small stairs that deposited them onto a paved cul-de-sac next to the garage.

Despite the light sweater, Josie reacted to William's touch as if it were pressed against bare flesh. It seemed the longer they were around each other, the stronger the attraction. She met his azure gaze and was almost certain the same emotions flowed through him.

Once they reached the graveled road, she glanced around, and asked, "So where are we going?"

"I figure we can cut through here," he said, pointing to a wall of trees. "A few feet up, there's a hiking trail. We can walk along it for a while."

She nodded, but then her eyes darted in the opposite direction. "Where does the road lead?"

"At the bottom of the hill is state highway 354."

"And the main interstate?" A memory teased her.

William shrugged. "We're about twenty minutes from I-185. Why?"

"What else is near here?"

"Well, there's Callaway Gardens."

"Callaway Gardens?" she perked.

"Yes. It's a—"

"Then we're in Pine Mountain?"

"You know the area?"

"My father played golf at Callaway all the time. He has a little place not too far from it. Maybe we can check it out?"

William blinked, then shrugged. "I don't see why not."

Josie flashed him a smile and reached for his hand as though it was the most natural thing to do. It felt like sliding on an old dress and marveling at how well it fit.

They fit; they always had.

"Sorry." She released his hand.

"Don't be," he said, reclaiming her hand. "It's all right."

Her breath hitched in her throat as her heart skipped a beat. The man could still affect her like no other.

For the first few minutes of their walk, the only sound came from the crunching of leaves beneath their feet. After a while, she cast long side glances at the man beside her and wondered what he was thinking.

The hiking trail wasn't so bad; at most, it was a curvy, paved walkway around a mountaintop. Before long, they reached an overlook with a picturesque landscape of the setting sun.

"It's magnificent," she whispered. Her gaze danced off the myriad colors splashed against the sky. "Have you ever seen anything this beautiful?"

"Of course. I'm looking at her."

Surprised, she turned and met his sincere gaze. In an instant, her emotions tangled into a large mass within her chest. She found herself wishing he would gather her into his arms and kiss her senseless, but such an act would be like opening a can of worms.

He brushed his hand along the side of her face. "It's good to see you back on your feet again."

The way he looked at her made it impossible for her to hold on to a string of conscious thought. "I never thought I would ever see you again. I've missed you." The words were out of her mouth before she had the chance to censor them.

William's hand lowered to his side.

"I'm sorry," she said, glancing away to stare back at the sunset.

"There's no need to apologize," he said softly. "The past is the past. I just want to help you through this, then you can be on your way."

Tears stung the backs of her eyes, but she kept her gaze focused on the dying sun.

After a long silence, his voice drifted lightly on the wind. "Mind if I ask you a personal question?"

Josie hesitated. "Sure." She straightened her back and braced herself for the question she feared he would ask. "What ever happened to you and Etienne?"

"Oh, well . . ."

"Never mind," he said suddenly. "It's none of my business."

"William, I'm not exactly proud of how I ended things between us." Against her will, her gaze darted to his, and a hollow ache throbbed within her heart. She needed to tell him the truth. She needed to tell him why she never married Etienne, but where should she draw the line? Should she also tell him how she raced to Georgia to find him only to learn that he had married someone else?

It wasn't fair. She hated this man. He broke her heart; but yet, at this very moment she would give everything to slide into the comfort of his arms and erase the past sixteen years.

Leaves crunched underfoot as William shifted his weight. It was clear that he was uncomfortable with the direction of their conversation.

"Until recently, I've tried hard to forget about the last time we saw each other . . . or rather the day I made a complete ass out of myself."

Josie would had to have been deaf not to hear the pain that haunted his voice.

"It's always hard for a man to get over his first true love."

Josie squeezed her eyes closed and struggled like hell not to break down. She had been stunned by how quickly he returned home from Paris and married someone else. It couldn't have been more than two weeks. *Two weeks.* Not only that, he'd managed to stay married for fourteen years.

If he was so in love with her, how could he have married someone else? She couldn't.

"Maybe we should talk about something else," William said. "I was hoping the walk would relax you."

"I'm fine," she said absently, and waved him away. However, holding back her bitterness was damn near impossible. "Seems you weren't lonely for too long," she said with healthy dose of sarcasm.

Their gazes clashed in an instant duel.

"What difference does it make? You'd made your choice," he said coolly. "You had your beloved Etienne."

His words stabbed her like daggers, and silenced any angry retort she might have.

"Besides, I didn't marry Sammy because I was in love with her. I married her because she was pregnant."

Josie flinched as though he'd struck her. "He wasn't mine," he clarified. "Sammy was in trouble and needed help. I guess I clung to the idea that someone needed me."

Tears glossed Josie's eyes as words deserted her.

"Sammy and I broke up just before my trip to Paris—before I met you." The fading light caught the shimmer in his eyes. "She had gotten involved with someone who had turned out to be a sort of hit-and-run—a friend of mine. She didn't want to tell her parents that she had gotten pregnant and might have to drop out of school. I became a shoulder to cry on, then later a solution to a problem."

"You got married to help out a friend?"

"I've known people to get married for stranger reasons. At least we had a solid friendship going into the marriage. Sammy and I never had what *we* had, but it was a decent marriage—for a while.

"It didn't work out, but I have a wonderful son out of the deal. His name is Christopher. You'd like him. Of course he lives in Phoenix with his mother right now, but I have him six months out of the year."

Tell him. "I didn't know," she said finally.

"No. I wouldn't suppose you did."

A gentle breeze swirled around them. The evening suddenly turned cold, while the rustle of leaves became music.

Tell him. "We should head back." She lifted her chin. "It's going to be dark soon."

William's shoulders slumped disappointedly as a shadow fell across his handsome features.

Josie knew at once he was erecting an invisible wall between them, and she immediately started doing the same.

They turned together and walked back toward the house. They were more than halfway home when Josie surroundings suddenly seemed familiar.

William slowed down. "What is it?"

Josie glanced around and spotted another trail. "I know where I am." She headed across a thicket of leaves toward the new trail.

"Wait. Where are you going?"

"My father's mountain home is this way. I'm sure of it." She started down the trail again.

"You want to go *now*?" he asked.

She didn't answer him. Instead, her footsteps quickened.

Left with little choice, he followed.

Darkness descended quickly, and the temperature plummeted. What William thought would be a short stroll soon turned into a laborious hike.

"Are you sure you know where you're going?" he asked, glancing over his shoulder and seeing nothing.

"Well, I've only been down this trail a couple of times, but I'm pretty sure it's just over the hill."

"A couple of times," he mumbled under his breath. He was fairly certain there weren't any bears in the area, but he wasn't willing to stake his life on it. "Maybe we should do this in the morning, Josie. At the very least, it should be safer."

"Don't tell me you're afraid of the dark."

"It's not the dark, but what lurks in it."

Her light chuckle danced on the cool air and transformed her into a spirited nymph that was well out of his reach. The thought brought on a fresh wave of sadness.

Suddenly, there was a light off in the distance,

and he was finally able to see her clearly once again.

"There it is." Josie stopped and turned to face him.

He glanced up and was blown away by the three-story sprawling mansion. "That's your father's *little* place?"

A smile bloomed across her face. "Gosh. I haven't been here in ages." She raced toward the house.

William caught up with her and wrapped his strong arms around her waist. "Something is not right," he warned.

She pried herself out of his grip. "What do you mean?"

"The lights, Josie. Why are the lights on?"

"Are you sure no one has been there?" Michelle asked the man on her cell phone. She was pleased that her old running mate and partner-in-crime, D'Angelo, had loaned her a few of his men to help search for her missing sister. Thus far, no one had been able to find anything. And that worried her.

"The place is empty."

"Well, check again. She has to be somewhere, and no one is going to rest until we find her." Michelle sneered, and disconnected the call.

"What she say, Chuck?"

Chuck, a mammoth of a man, pocketed his cell phone and heaved a long frustrated breath. "We have to go back."

"Why? We tore the place up. No one's there."

"Then it won't hurt for us to double-check." He started up the black Escalade. "I don't get paid enough for this crap."

His partner laughed. "You better not let D'Angelo hear you say that."

"Whatever. Let's just go check this place out again."

"What are we supposed to do if we do find this chick anyway?"

"Do you really have to ask?"

With serious trepidation, William and Josie peeked through various windows to her father's mountain hideaway. It was a shock to see overturned furniture and broken glass everywhere.

"We should get out of here," William said, shaking his head and tugging Josie on the arm.

"Everything is destroyed," she whispered. "Who—?" The question died in her throat. She knew exactly who would do such a thing.

Snatching her arm away from William, she bolted from the cabin's window and headed straight for the front door.

"Josie, no."

She ignored him and entered the house. Tears sprang to her eyes as she saw a few of her father's treasured items completely ruined. "How did she even know about this place?" she whispered when William reached her side.

"I think we should leave just in case whoever did this comes back."

"C'mon." Her gaze sliced over to him. "We both know who did this."

He exhaled a long breath and took another glance around. "She's looking for you."

"That would be my first guess." She inched farther into the house and picked up small items that had survived. A few shattered picture frames caught her attention, and she gravitated toward them.

At the sight of her father's bright smile, Josie felt as if the sun had finally broken through the dark clouds of her depression.

She traced a finger across his handsome face and fought back a new wave of tears.

William knelt beside her and studied the picture from over her shoulder. "Your father?"

Unable to trust herself to speak, Josie nodded.

However, William's attention drifted from the distinguished-looking gentleman and over to the cute little girl that sat on the man's lap. Her blinding smile and twinkling gaze shouted to the world that this was one of the happiest days of her life.

"You two look good together," he finally commented.

Josie emitted a soft laugh and glanced at him. "He always told me that I was his favorite girl."

"I can see that." William's gaze softened as it roamed over her heart-shaped face. With each flutter of her long lashes, William felt his heart squeeze just a little tighter. "Do you think your father would've liked me?" he asked, before he had the chance to stop himself.

She drew in a long breath as her lips trembled upward. "I think my father would've loved you."

Their eyes locked for an eternal moment. Each fought the urge to lean forward for a kiss, but secretly desired that the other would give in to the temptation.

Headlights arced through the house as tires crunched on the gravel outside and jarred the former lovers' private world.

"Ohmigosh." Josie scrambled to her feet, but was at a loss to what she should do—where she should go.

William jumped to his feet, wrapped an arm around her waist, and practically dragged her toward the back of the house. "Hide."

Where? Josie thought. Judging by the condition of the cabin, Michelle had left no stone unturned.

"In here." William dashed into a dark cupboard beneath the stairs.

"I'm telling you, Chuck," a man's voice drifted into the house. "This is just a waste of time. Nobody is here."

"I know, I know, but we were sent to do a job. If you have a problem with that, take it up with D'Angelo."

William and Josie held their breath, as the men's voices grew louder.

"Hey, Chuck. Did you get a box of Cabanas Belvederes from Mitch for attending his bachelor party?"

"Nah, man. I can't stand the taste of cigars. You know that."

The other man laughed. "What are you, a punk or something?"

"Do I look like a punk?"

William felt Josie trembling against him; in an attempt to give some type of comfort, he slid an arm around her waist and held her. Despite the swell of danger, he was still very aware of her full breasts pressed against him.

The voices drew closer. "I'm just saying that you need to give these stogies a try. You'll be big pimpin'."

"Whatever."

William held his breath as the men stopped in front of the cupboard. Weaponless, he didn't

know what he was going to do if the men opened
the door. One thing for sure, he was going to try
his best to protect Josie.

"You know there's a lot of nice stuff in this
place. Maybe we should help ourselves a little before we head out."

"I don't think so. That Josephine chick doesn't
sound like a lady to cross. This is her place. She
probably has everything inventoried. I know the
type."

"Well, I'm just saying. If she doesn't mind the
place ransacked, then surely she wouldn't—"

"No. We're looking for her sister. We find her,
we kill her, then we can go home."

At Josie's gasp, William's eyes widened in
alarm.

"Chuck, did you hear something?"

"Shh."

Everyone fell silent.

Josie was convinced her actions had just sealed
their fate. Her head instantly filled with horrify-
ing images of them being tortured to death. But
there was no way out. They were trapped.

"I don't hear anything," Chuck finally growled.
"But let's check out the back to make sure. "The
faster we get this whole thing over, the better."

The men's heavy footsteps led away from the
door, and still Josie was too afraid to move. After

several heartbeats had passed, William leaned in so close his warm breath tickled the shell of her ear.

"We need to get out of here," he whispered.

"Okay," she said, shaking her head; but when she heard his hand settle on the door knob, she stopped him. "Right now?"

"We can't stay in here. They'll find us."

His take-charge tone did calm her; however, she wasn't convinced that this moment was the time for them to make a break for it. He turned the knob, and once again, she stopped him.

"What if they catch us?" she asked in a frantic whisper. "I mean they probably have guns. We don't have a weapon and—"

William silenced her with a kiss. The shock of such an action blew her away, but she returned the kiss with fervor. Her body relaxed and melted against him. When he pulled his lips away, she was calm.

"I need you to focus," he whispered. "We can do this."

She wasn't so sure.

"We're not going to let Michelle win."

Those words made something click inside of her. Her head filled with the sound of Michelle's high, sinister cackle. *The world would be a better place without you. All you have to do is just slice.*

Josie's wrists ached.

"Are you ready?" William asked.

She nodded though she knew he couldn't see her in the dark.

"I'm going to count to three," he warned.

"Okay." She mentally prepared herself, but could feel her body begin to tremble again. *Dear God, not now.*

"One . . ."

Josie's temples throbbed.

"Two . . ."

Her stomach tightened and threatened to expel the remaining contents.

"Three." William gently pushed the door open.

It took everything in Josie's body not to tug him back into the cupboard when he poked out his head. When he took the first tentative step out, he reached for her.

Drawing a deep breath, she slid her hand into his and crept out of their hiding place. The stillness of the cabin unnerved her and heightened her paranoia. Where had the men gone? Were they watching them right now?

William pressed a finger against his lips and led her around the staircase, then through the living room.

Josie's vertigo worsened to the point that she was wobbling on unsteady legs. "Will," she whispered, pitching forward.

He caught her, but not without crushing a picture frame underfoot. The cabin's silence was broken.

Doors crashed from someplace within the cabin.

William swooped Josie into his arms and high-tailed out the front door. He ignored the pressure of her deadweight and willed his body to perform the task of getting them the hell out of there.

They'd actually made it into the woods before the sound of gunfire filled the night. But as darkness welcomed them into its folds, he feared that it wasn't enough to protect them from harm.

"Did you see who it was?" A man's voice rang out. "Was it the girl?"

"I didn't see anything! I thought you saw something. You were shooting!"

"Quiet. I think hear something!"

William stopped. With the forest floor covered in leaves, he knew it was suicide to race through them. Not to mention, Josie seemed to grow heavier by the second.

Which way, he wondered. He had no clue. He couldn't see a thing. He turned to his right and was surprised the ground had disappeared.

They were falling.

Stunned, he hit earth, but tumbled down a deep slope. He'd lost his hold on Josie, but he could feel her rolling next to him. It seemed like they would never stop when at last they did. It took a moment to catch his breath, but then he frantically searched around with his hands.

"Josie?" His hands brushed against her still form. Fear exploded in his chest. Was she all right? Was she dead?

William quickly found her pulse and nearly collapsed with relief.

A man's startled wail caught his attention. At the sound of another body slamming into the hill, William quickly gathered Josie in his arms and tried to make a run for it.

"Will?"

"Shh." He struggled to keep his hold on her. At the moment, he could only pray that she was okay. There was no time to check. Once again, he was concerned about the crunching of leaves beneath his feet. It was like a homing device on his movements. He stopped at a large tree and slumped down beside it.

He struggled, but finally managed to control his labored breathing. The sound of rustling leaves reached his ears.

A hunter was on the prowl.

Josie reached for him, and he placed a silencing finger against her lips.

"I know you're out there," the man's menacing voice called out. "Is that you, Michelle?"

William felt her body tremble, but she was being

a good girl and remaining quiet. He needed a weapon.

The footsteps grew closer.

William gently felt around him. Maybe there was a stick or a fallen tree branch he could use.

"Why don't you just give yourself up, Michelle?" the man continued to taunt. "We just want to talk to you."

He was inches from them now. Finally, his hand found the very thing he needed: a large rock.

"Come out, come out, wherever you are," the man's devilish voice singsonged.

The predator stepped around the tree and William came up swinging. There was an eerie crunch when the rock connected with the man's skull.

A shot rang out seconds before the man hit the ground. More leaves rustled, and William knew the man was still a threat. He followed the sound of the leaves and swung the rock a second time.

At long last, all was quiet.

"I think I can walk now," Josie whispered in the darkness. She could feel the strain in William's corded muscles slowly ebb away.

He sloshed through the forest of fallen leaves as though he hadn't heard her.

"Really, William. You can put me down now."

"It can't be much farther," he said, in an exhausted pant.

Through the weak glimmer of moonlight, she made out his tensed features and noted how he went out of his way to avoid making eye contact. Her guilt increased tenfold. This was all her fault. She had nearly gotten them killed. "Put me down," she insisted gently.

William drew a deep breath and finally came to a stop.

"Please," she added.

Bending forward, he lowered her feet to the ground.

Her limbs trembled, but they were able to support her weight.

Meanwhile, William used the brief downtime to draw in a few extra gulps of air.

"Are you all right?" she asked.

He didn't answer.

"Will—"

"Can we talk about this later?" he snapped. "I want to get out of these damn woods."

Josie swallowed the rest of her question and gave him a moment to collect himself. She knew what was eating at him—the possibility of having killed a man.

"It's not your fault."

"Please," he begged. "Just help me find a way out of this place. I feel like I'm about to go mad."

She glanced around, unable to make out anything more than a few inches in front of her nose.

"Anything look familiar to you?"

"No," her voice croaked. Tears burned the backs of her eyes. They were lost. He knew it, and she knew it.

Glancing up at the starless sky, Josie believed

that even the heavens were against helping them find their way back to Larry and Sheila's home. A light drizzle sprinkled across her upturned face and blended with her tears.

"We'll just keep going straight," he decided.

She nodded, seeing no point in arguing.

As it turned out, it was a wise decision. Minutes later, they emerged from a final thicket of trees to stand in front of the dark house.

Josie wanted to sink to her knees and have a good cry. But she didn't dare, especially since the cold wind was delivering the rain in hard, slanted sheets.

Silently, William slid an arm around her waist and directed her toward the house. When they entered, a strange awkwardness settled on them.

So many thoughts ran through Josie's head, and she was too nervous to put a voice to any of them.

"I'll start a fire," he said, pulling off his jacket, while heading toward the living room.

"Do you think that's a wise idea?" she asked, following him. "I mean, what if the smoke draws attention?"

"We're not the only house on the mountain."

"But what if they come here?"

"They won't."

"But how can you be so sure?"

"Look, Josie," William barked. He raced his

hand through his hair and drew in a deep breath. "I don't know anything. I don't know who those men are, but I doubt that they're crazy enough to draw so much attention to themselves by systematically searching each house on the mountain. Besides, we don't know if one of them . . ."

She stepped forward to console him. "He got what he deserved."

William's sharp gaze sliced toward her. "No one deserves to die, Josie. No one."

She stopped, feeling her insides go cold.

He turned away again and finished removing his jacket. "First thing in the morning, we're going to the police."

Stunned, she watched him disappear into the living room. "And tell them what?"

"The truth," he shouted. "The whole damn truth."

"And what the hell do you think is going to happen? "You'll lose your job. They'll arrest you."

"We'll still be *alive*," he retaliated. "I've done all I can for you. I got you out of the hospital; but I don't know a damn thing about dodging bullets. Those were trained killers."

"And we escaped," she reasoned.

"Barely—by the skin of our teeth. And no offense"—he paced—"but you weren't much help out there."

"Oh, so it's my fault?"

"You were the one who wanted to take a trip up to Daddy's old cabin. I should have known that was a bad idea."

"Well, you didn't, and neither did I," she yelled back. "Nor did I suspect I would have another 'spell' and nearly get us killed."

"Great, then we agree. We don't know what we're doing. We should go to the police."

"They aren't going to believe us," Josie yelled. "They think I'm crazy, or did you miss the whole point of my being locked in a mental institution?"

"Josie—"

"We go to them now without proof, I'll be back in a hospital before you can bat an eye. How long do you think it will take before Michelle and her goons get to me then? The only way I can stay alive right now is to stay invisible until I can get proof."

William shook his head as if he was unconvinced.

"I'm talking about a couple of days at best. I'll get someone on the phone in the morning and have the records sent overnight." She was desperate for the extra time and not entirely for the reasons she argued. She needed more time to come up with a good plan to get out of Georgia.

Now more than ever, she knew that she couldn't tell him about Daniel. William wouldn't understand. If he'd killed that man tonight, no one would argue it wasn't self-defense.

Josie's case would be a different story.

William finally looked as if he was wavering, but his words were like a slap in the face. "We have to do what's right."

Heat rushed up her neck and inflamed her face. "Then you'll have to do it *without* me," she seethed, and spun on her heels.

"Wait." William rushed to catch up with her. "Where are you going?"

"I'm leaving." She brushed her wet hair from her face as she stormed toward the front door.

"What? That's crazy!" He grabbed her arm and spun her around "You can't leave."

She snatched back her arm. "Watch me." Turning, she jerked open the front door.

Lightning flashed and lit up the night sky. However, it didn't stop Josie from bolting out into the rain. In an instant, her clothes were plastered to her skin. The cold wind chilled her to the bone but did little to cool her anger.

"Josie, stop being ridiculous! You don't have anywhere to go!" He ran after her, then spun her around again and was startled when her open hand struck his face.

"I didn't ask for your help. I can take care of myself!"

"You're not in any type of condition—"

"No." She backed away from him. "You do what you have to do, and I'll do the same."

"You're talking crazy!"

"I'm *not* crazy! Don't you dare say that." Her hands balled at her sides.

"Fine. You're sane. Screaming out in the middle of a storm is perfectly normal. *Now* can we go back in the house?"

"Just go to hell." She turned and stalked off.

With his own anger mounting, William followed her and grasped her arm, but this time he was prepared when she attacked. Dodging a blow, he quickly seized her hands and pinned them to her sides. "I'm trying to help you."

"I don't want it." Josie struggled to wrench her hands free. "Since I nearly got you killed, you should be happy to get me out of your life."

"I never said that."

"You didn't have to," she shouted above the loud wind. "It's painfully obvious. Dump me at the police station and let me be *their* problem."

"That's not what I meant."

She squirmed violently, trying to get away from him. "Let me go!"

"Not until you calm down."

"I'm not going to the police!" She fought, and belatedly realized that she'd been lifted off her feet. "Put me down."

"No." He pulled her back into the house and kicked the door shut.

William's curt reply further aggravated her. Here was someone else who was trying to control her life, and she was going to have none of it. At last, she freed her arms and swung in every direction.

"Josie, stop it." He set her back on her feet and struggled to pin her arms down again.

"It's my life. I can make my own decisions," she screamed repeatedly.

Another blow landed across his left cheek, but he shook away the stars and locked her arms down at her sides.

"It's my life," she wailed.

"I know," he whispered close to her ear. "I know."

The fight left her body, and she slumped against him. Together, they sank to the floor, where her silent cries became heart-wrenching sobs.

"It's going to be all right," he comforted. "You're not going have to do anything you don't want to. I promise." He held her, stoked her hair, then rained small kisses against her temples.

She leaned closer and slowly turned her head so that his soft lips pressed against the side of her face, her cheeks, and finally her lips.

At first the kiss was so light that she could barely feel his lips, but stars spun around Josie's head at a dizzying rate.

His arms tightened possessively around her waist and within seconds she felt his hands make those tiny circles she loved so much against the small of her back.

Slowly, she slid her arms up his chest and locked them behind his neck. The kiss deepened, but Josie couldn't seem to get close enough. She desperately wanted to fuse with his heat. Fire surged through her veins, sharpened her senses, and made her pulse race.

Intoxicated by the taste of him, she moaned during the passionate tango their tongues performed.

Her melodic moans, as well as her soft breasts pressed against him, seduced William. He loved how her body responded to his slightest touch and how her breathing came fast and light.

A caldera of emotions broke inside him, and he was scorched by fire. Finally, he deserted her lips to blaze a trail down to the crook of her neck.

She sighed and lifted her chin high to give him better access. "Will . . ."

It had been an eternity since he'd heard his name spill with such passion from her lips. A part of him still wasn't sure whether all of this was just a dream, yet she felt too good and tasted even better to be a figment of his imagination.

An ache buried in the core of Josie began to pulse out of control. God help her, she wanted—

needed—to make love to William despite the residue of fear.

She tugged at his wet shirt, then broke away from his lips to pull the garment over his head.

William stood up and held out his hand.

They stared at each other for an eternal moment, then came together again in a storm of passion and desire.

"I want you," she panted. "I want you now."

That was all William needed to hear before he swept her into his arms and carried her up to bed.

Heaven was indeed a place on earth; and to William and Josie's surprise, it also existed outside of the borders of Paris, France. Once the old lovers entered the bedroom and stood facing one another, both seemed to have made an unspoken pact to take their time and savor each movement and moment.

Josie gave William the honor of peeling off her sweater, then removing her top. The beautiful contrast of their skin tones was highlighted by the thin slivers of moonlight that filtered through the blinds.

Seconds later, they were pressed together for another tantalizing kiss. Each became addicted to the taste of the other and was consumed with a passion that left them quaking.

Josie's fingertips explored his chest, and she quickly discovered that his heartbeat pounded at the same rate as her own. The knowledge filled her with a new sense of power.

His big, strong, and possessive hands returned to their usual spot and began making slow and seductive circles while she enjoyed the sweet invasion of his tongue. And just when she couldn't take any more of his intoxicating kisses, his lips deserted hers to glide down the column of her neck and settle on a taut nipple.

Instantly, her knees weakened as she gasped for breath and dug her fingers through his silky hair. His gentle suckle unraveled her world and pitched her onto lofty clouds of splendor.

William swept her up into his arms again and gently placed her on the bed. He filled his hands with her soft breasts, then captured her gasp with a deep kiss.

She moaned as he lowered onto her and his rock-hard erection pressed insistently against her thigh. Her body rejoiced as if it recognized a missing part of itself.

He returned to her breasts and caressed her with his mouth, teeth, and tongue until she twitched wildly beneath him. William's hand floated like a feather down her body and brushed against the nest of curls between her legs.

Her anticipation heightened as he nudged her legs open, and the same feathery touch roamed her inner thighs. Josie closed her eyes, surprised by how much she trembled.

When his lean fingers finally dipped inside her, she nearly came unglued. At his slow, gentle strokes against her sensitive nub, her breath thinned to the tiniest of vapors.

Josie's repetitive moans filled the room like music, and they also served as an aphrodisiac for William.

After he'd thoroughly bathed her tanned nipples, his mouth traveled lower to explore other body parts. Seconds later, he locked his arms around her hips, and his tongue replaced his probing fingers.

At the intense pleasure, Josie thrust her hips up and tried to scramble away. Instead, she gave him better access to the very thing she was trying to withhold.

She gasped for breath, never seeming to get enough air into her lungs. The stars returned behind her closed eyelids, and she suddenly felt hot, then cold.

His talented tongue performed a series of erotic dances with the bud of her femininity, and she locked her legs around his neck. In no time, tremors of her first orgasm ripped away reality and created a new world where only pleasure existed.

William's plunder through her body's sweet honey only increased her struggle to break away from his hot mouth—but his grip remained firm.

Josie squealed with reckless abandonment as her next orgasm hit hard and fast.

However, William was relentless.

Breathing became a chore while she still fought to push his head away. The chant of his name slowly became cries for a mercy that never came. When her third orgasm slammed into her with the force of a locomotive, she was totally unaware of the mindless chatter that tumbled from her lips.

Granted a slight reprieve, Josie panted as though she'd just completed her first triathlon. A new world spun inside her head, while William temporarily left the bed.

She was just getting her bearings when he returned. She heard a rip and turned to see him opening a condom. Without murmuring a word, she reached for the packet. "Not yet," she whispered.

She leaned forward, kissed him tenderly, and began her own slow decline down his broad chest, past his rock-hard abs.

A low sigh of pleasure escaped William, while his strong hands glided through her black hair. She took her time rewarding him with the same intense pleasure he'd given her. And like her, he found himself repeating the Lord's name.

"I can't take it anymore," he said. His strength easily allowed him to extract Josie from her loving worship and place her on her back.

It took no more than a couple of seconds to slide on the condom; but before he bulldozed his way into her, he reminded himself to take his time—to extend the pleasure for as long as he could.

But he *wanted* to take her now.

While his needs and his wants warred within him, it was Josie who made the final decision.

"I need you," she whispered.

He thanked her by claiming her soft lips for another deep and intimate kiss . . . and, simultaneously, eased into her moist cave.

Josie tore her mouth away to gasp at just how well and perfect he fit. When he rocked slowly inside of her, she lifted and locked her legs around his hips. In no time, they found their own rhythm and lost themselves in the splendor of the other.

She was the first to utter a strangled exclamation as she was pulled into a vortex of euphoria.

Feeling her body tense around him, William picked up his tempo and coaxed her with erotic talk to give in to her building climax.

This time as she cried out her release, it felt as if she'd shattered into a million pieces, but then just as suddenly she was more whole than she had ever been.

Moments later, a strong force gripped William and extracted a roar from him that undoubtedly filled the entire house.

Josie wrapped her arms lovingly around him as if sensing his moment of vulnerability. For a few seconds, his body quaked with aftershocks while their hearts thundered against one another.

They held each other, enjoying their quiet intimacy and treasuring it like a precious jewel.

All too soon the real world, complete with its problems, started to creep back into Josie's thoughts. What in the hell was she doing?

As if he'd heard the question, William turned his head and peppered the side of her face with light kisses. Gradually, she became aware of the strain in her splayed thighs.

Lord, was she ready for another round?

Despite his growing erection, he seemed to be content to kiss, cuddle, and wipe every bad thought from her head.

And thank goodness, it was working.

In some strange way, Josie found that being in William's arms erased the past sixteen years. Their bodies welcomed each other home like the separation had been no longer than a few hours. Josie wondered how that was possible.

"I never thought I would have the chance to hold you like this again," William whispered. "You feel so good."

She said nothing as she fought off the threat of tears.

He leaned over onto an elbow. He stared down at her face, which was bathed in moonlight. "I know that look. It means trouble. Tell me what's wrong."

"Nothing," she denied feebly.

William frowned.

A slow smile wobbled across her lips. "I'm just wondering what the hell we're doing. What does any of this mean?" She watched as his forehead wrinkled with confusion.

"It means everything," he said gently. "There is still something between us. We can't deny that."

Her heart pounded wildly again as her gaze fell to the darkness that surrounded them. "And what about the past?"

His strong fingers directed her chin toward him so that their gazes met once again. "The past is the past. It can't hurt us."

That wasn't true, Josephine realized, and instantly reconnected to heartbreak she had experienced so long ago. But what were they supposed to do now? Making love was one thing, but opening her heart was another.

He kissed the lobe of her ear and chipped at the wall she was already beginning to rebuild. "We've always been good together," William whispered.

That was true. No man had ever made her feel the way William had.

She met his gaze and was propelled to a new level of defenselessness. She forced herself to look away, but could only do so for a few seconds before her gaze returned to his magnetic presence.

Slowly, his head descended. Both kept their eyes opened as their lips met.

Josie's heartbeat raced as her breathing became sporadic.

His soft lips lowered to a taut nipple.

She felt the playful flick of his tongue, and her insides melted instantly. She shook her head as tears swelled in her eyes.

William inched lower, igniting fires within as he went. "You feel so good, Josie," he whispered, and kissed her abdomen. "So good." He kissed her belly button.

He felt wonderful, too.

He nudged her legs open and kissed her inner thighs.

Tears slid from her eyes while her lips trembled.

"You'll always belong to me, Josie," he said, locking his arms around her hips and sinking his tongue deep within her.

She gasped as she arched her body and was once again thrown back into that new world of pleasure. For hours, William wore down her defenses, and she was mindless to everything else around her. By the time dawn approached, Josie feared that her heart had finally returned to its rightful owner.

Ming felt terrible that she'd fallen asleep during her husband's hot-oil body rub. Its dual purpose was to relax her and initiate foreplay. *Well, one out of two wasn't too bad*, she thought.

Like most mornings, she woke to the rich aroma of fresh-brewed coffee and the sizzle of turkey bacon. Lord, where would she be without her domestic husband?

Climbing out of bed, Ming shivered in the room's cool air. It would've been okay if she'd slept in her thermal underwear like she'd wanted to, but since she'd planned to have sex, she was stuck in some useless satin garb that made her colder than the room itself.

The things women do for men.

Once beneath the shower's blast of hot water, Ming's thoughts returned to her work—particularly to Michelle Andrews and how the woman had her hands in quite a few cookie jars.

Andrews was Daniel Thornton's last-known girlfriend and she was also a longtime mistress of Dr. Ambrose Turner. Both men were dead.

And where was the real Josephine Ferrell?

She probably needed to face the fact that there was a strong chance they wouldn't find Josephine. Ming exhaled and dipped her head into the steaming water.

So far, the likely scenario was that either Andrews or Dr. Turner killed Thornton, Bancroft, and Ferrell. With Ferrell gone, Andrews could switch identities with her reclusive sister without anyone being the wiser.

The plan had a few sparks of brilliance, but the execution was entirely too sloppy. Of course, at the moment, she couldn't prove any of it.

Ming reached for her half-empty bottle of Herbal Essence and wondered how she was going to piece this puzzle together. She squeezed a quarter of shampoo into her hand and gently worked her hair into a thick lather.

"Fingerprints," she whispered. Somehow, she needed to get Michelle's fingerprints. "Oh, that should be easy," she said sarcastically.

She wasn't crazy enough to think that Andrews would simply invite the police back into her home. Ming definitely wasn't going to convince her superiors to haul Michelle's butt in without any proof of her theory. She mulled everything over through her rinse cycle and was just applying conditioner when a new idea hit.

William woke up still joined to Josie. The fantasy of being able to do this every morning planted hope in his heart.

Gazing at her angelic face, he couldn't help but lean in and capture a kiss.

Carefully and with great reluctance, he withdrew from her and the bed. While he was in the shower, he couldn't help but relive the previous night's events.

Josie poked her head around the shower curtain. "Mind if I join you?"

A wide smile eased across William's face. "There's always room for you." He slid the curtain back and offered her a hand to step inside. "It's been a while since we've done this."

Boldly, she stood beneath the showerhead and pressed her nude body against his.

He kissed her and slid his wet, soapy hands down the curves of her butt. When he squeezed, she emitted a soft moan against his lips, and he loved its sound.

He deserted her mouth to make a trail of tiny, biting kisses down the column of her neck and against the curve of her shoulders.

Josie's moans turned into husky sighs, but it was the gentle way her breasts rubbed against his chest that destroyed his concentration. Her hands began their exploration, and he sucked in a shuddering breath when her soft fingers closed around his throbbing shaft.

He ached against her hand, tormented by a touch that was too light and too knowing. In retaliation, he drew one of her taut nipples through his teeth and licked it with lazy strokes of his tongue.

Josie gasped with pleasure. Nobody knew her body the way William did. He stroked, kissed, and loved her the right way.

It wasn't long before the lovers returned soaking wet to the bedroom, and Josie was lost in the rhythm of his caress.

Her hips soon moved against his hand with a sinuous demand that shredded his control. He needed to be inside of her. William slid on another condom and sank gently into her slick passage. When he moved, he did so with slow, deep strokes. It should be a crime for a woman to feel this good.

Josie moaned his name while she kneaded his back with her nails, and her hips matched his grind stroke for stroke. He wanted the moment to last forever, but then he felt his control ebb away.

He clasped her waist tightly and accelerated to a faster, wilder ride. William felt her body's orgasm a fraction before she cried out his name. The passion behind her cry was just enough to pitch him over the edge. His body tensed, then exploded in ecstasy. When they began, each was on a mission to explore new heights of passion . . . and they succeeded.

A few hours later, William woke up again and took another shower. He stole a kiss, then scrambled down to put on a fresh pot of coffee. However, no sooner had he entered the kitchen, than his cell phone rang from a charger off the kitchen counter.

When he scanned the name of the ID screen, he was surprised to read Marcus Hines's name. Immediately, his heart racked his chest as an endless series of possibilities scrolled through his head.

Finally, he shook them away, and answered. "Hello."

"Oh, thank goodness I found you." Relief filled Marcus's voice. "Please say that you're still in town."

William hesitated. "I haven't left the state, if that's what you mean."

"Perfect. I need another favor."

"Sure, if I can." It didn't sound like he was in any sort of trouble—at least Marcus hadn't started hurling accusations.

"We have another situation."

William frowned. "What do you mean?"

"Ambrose was killed yesterday. I need you to cut your vacation short and come back to work."

Stunned, William leaned back against the counter. "What? What happened?"

"I'm not sure. They found him and his car in some lake. He'd been shot."

"Shot?" William didn't understand. Two of their doctors murdered within a week?

"On top of that," Hines ambled on, "Bancroft's funeral is set for tomorrow, and most of the staff wants to attend; it's crazy around here. The only good news is that Brian Bancroft has been stabilized and returned home."

"That is good news, but back up. What do you mean Ambrose was found at the bottom of a lake?"

"No clue, but the police have been combing the place again."

William struggled to wrap his brain around this new development. "They think that someone at Keystone has something to do with it?"

"I don't know what they think. I just know two of our registered nurses have quit, and I had to convince four other staff members to not turn in their resignations. I'm on the edge of a heart attack trying to deal with all this. So, I'm hoping you're not going to bail on me. Can you come in?"

"Today?" He moved from the counter and paced the linoleum floor. How was he going to relay all of this to Josie?

"I *need* you, William."

He squeezed his eyes shut and drew a deep breath. "All right. I'll come in."

"Great. I need you to cover midshift. So I'll see you around noon?"

"You got it." William disconnected the call and cursed under his breath.

"Problem?" Josie's soft husky voice floated over to him.

He turned to see her wrapped in a white robe. Her angelic features were tight with concern.

"Hey, you." He faked a smile and returned the cell phone to the charger, then crossed over to her.

She slid tensely into his arms, and her lips landed warmly on his. Moaning, she glided her arms possessively around his neck and drew him closer.

When their lips at last parted, she remained locked in his embrace. "So who upset you on the phone?"

He hesitated. It suddenly occurred to William that he hadn't told Josie about the other events that happened the night he'd taken her from Key-

stone. He hadn't even told her how he'd orches-
trated her kidnapping.

"We need to talk." His arms fell away from her
body. "Maybe I should put on some coffee."

"O-okay." She frowned and followed him over
to the coffeemaker. "Something tells me I need to
sit down."

"That might be a good idea."

"That bad?"

He retrieved a red can of Folgers from the cabinet. "Yeah."

Suddenly cautious, Josie folded her arms and
stepped back. "All right. Let me hear it."

William glanced at her, drew in a breath, and
started from the beginning.

She listened, pleased to hear how he'd recognized her the moment he'd laid eyes on her in one
of Keystone's hospital beds. He recanted how he
approached a Dr. Bancroft with his suspicions.

"She told you that she'd treated Michelle before?"

"Yep. It's even in Michelle's chart, too, if you
still want to take a look at it."

Josie nodded, but urged him to continue.

"Well, I noticed one morning how the cleaning
crew seemed to move about the place without
drawing anyone's attention. It's like they're invisible to staff or something." He finished preparing
her coffee the way she liked it and handed it to her.

"Anyway, one day I had to take my SUV in for some minor repairs. One of the doctors recommended a shop not too far from the hospital. While I was there, I also noticed a few vans belonging to the same cleaning company that did our office. And just like that, I had an idea."

Josie sipped her coffee as she listened to the rest of the story. But then her heart dropped when she heard about what happened to Dr. Bancroft. "Murdered?"

"Yeah." He took the first sip of his coffee and exhaled. "I still can't believe it."

"It's kind of an eerie coincidence, don't you think?" She set down her cup and brushed at the tiny hairs of alarm on her arms. "And now another doctor is dead?"

He nodded. "Yeah."

"Do you think the deaths are connected?" she finally asked.

He hesitated again; he even entertained the thought of lying.

"I'm going to take that as a yes," she answered for him. "It has to be Michelle," she concluded sadly. "If this Dr. Bancroft knew the real Michelle, surely she knew it was just a matter of time before the doctor realized that I wasn't her."

"She seemed pretty convinced when I talked with her."

"Michelle wouldn't have known that."

"But where does Ambrose fit in all of this?"

Suddenly the scars on her wrists itched. "Those guys at the cabin," she said, meeting her eyes. "We know they were sent by Michelle."

"What is she going to do—systematically kill everyone that works at the institute? That's crazy."

"That's what we're dealing with."

He released a hard laugh, but it failed to sound genuine.

Josie didn't find it so funny. "Look what she's already done." She thrust out her wrists. "I'll sure as hell never underestimate her again."

The color drained from William's face. He took her hands and caressed her scars. "So, it wasn't a suicide attempt?"

"I might not have liked how my career turned out, but I've never been suicidal." She pulled back her hands.

"Then that settles it," William said, crossing his arms. "We're going to the police."

Ming kissed her husband, grabbed some toast and a cup of coffee, and raced out of the house. In her car, she dialed Tyrese and spilled the beans before he finished saying hello.

"Surveillance duty—you have to be kidding me?" Tyrese laughed.

"Afraid not." She shifted gears and adjusted her cell phone simultaneously. "We need proof that Andrews is masquerading as Josephine. After our visit yesterday, she's probably going to try to leave town. With Josephine's money it won't be too hard to do."

"Maybe you shouldn't have exposed your hand," he admonished. "I always said that women shouldn't play poker."

"No one likes a Monday morning quarterback," she retorted. "I need you on her tail to make sure she doesn't skip out."

"And what will you be working on while I'm doing all the grunt work?"

"A little entrapment project."

"Hey, hey. Careful with the E word," he warned. "The lines on these things aren't exactly secure, you know."

"Good point." Ming chuckled. "I have a few places I need to hit: Turner's residence and Keystone."

"Keystone again?"

"We need fingerprints," she said.

"Did I miss something?"

Realizing she'd left out vital information, she laughed again, then filled Tyrese in on her plan.

"The police?" Josie repeated. "We can't do that."

"Josie, we don't have a choice," William said gently. "If Michelle is behind three murders—"

"Three?"

"Well possibly three. Dr. Bancroft mentioned to me that the police wanted to question you . . . well, Michelle, regarding her boyfriend's homicide. I'm only guessing, here. But I don't think it's too far out of the realm of possibility."

Josie swallowed her surprise. "The police?"

"Yeah, but I don't know any details."

She fought a wave of panic. "Won't you get into a lot of trouble if we go to the authorities?"

"Initially . . . but they're not going to be able to pin Bancroft's murder on me. I don't even own a gun."

"I'm not going to the police," she said stubbornly. "We already went over that last night.

"And how do I prove it?" She held up her hands again. "How do I explain this?"

William frowned.

"Let's just wait until we receive my medical records—better yet, my dental records."

"Well, surely she's not fluent in French or can play the piano—?"

"What if she can? We have to have concrete proof, or they're going to think I've just pulled some con job on you. And then you'll be locked up for kidnapping, and I'll be headed back to Keystone in a straightjacket."

"Come on, Josie. That's just crazy talk. We both know who you are."

"Then why weren't you able to convince that Dr. Bancroft?"

William stalled.

"I'll tell you why. It's because you had no proof—and you still don't." She drew a deep breath and moved closer to him. "I'm just asking that we wait until we can get hold of my medical records. That's all."

She held his gaze, while his struggle with what they should do reflected in his expression.

Josie turned to reclaim her coffee but was disturbed by the visible tremor in her hand.

"Are you okay?" he asked.

She lowered the cup again and flashed him a weak smile. "I'm fine."

William glanced at his watch. "It's past time for your shot. I should go upstairs and get it."

She cringed at the thought of another injection. "How much longer will I have to take that stuff?"

While he crossed his arms and thought it over, Josie had no trouble picturing him in a white doctor's coat with a stethoscope around his neck.

"Given the amount of drugs everyone had pumped into your system, I'm guessing anywhere from thirty to sixty days," he said.

"That's a lot of shots."

He shrugged. "You could try going cold turkey; but I have to warn you, the convulsions, nausea, and migraines are usually severe. What you've experienced the last couple of days will seem like a trip to Disneyland compared to going cold turkey."

Josie's eyes widened. "If you're going to put it like that, then I'll take the shots."

"Good. I'll go upstairs—"

"I'll get it." Her smile trembled at the corners. "You write down the address for this place so I can call my doctors again."

William nodded. "All right."

She flattered him with a quick kiss. "I'll be right back." With that, she turned, and strolled out of the kitchen.

Once she was out of William's line of vision, she dropped her calm facade and leaned warily against the staircase's wooden rail. She had to do something fast. There was no way she was turning herself in to the police.

"I need a forged passport," Michelle informed her longtime buddy, D'Angelo. She moved farther into the cramped apartment and slid a hand lightly down his corded chest muscles.

He chuckled and blew a steady stream of cigar smoke into the air. "Is that all?"

"I'll make it worth your while." She pressed a kiss against his dark chocolate skin. "Like old times."

He fixed her with a hard glare. "Sort of how you did for old Danny boy?"

Michelle dropped her hand. "Danny was greedy."

"Never met a thief that wasn't." He looped an arm around her waist and pulled her close. "That includes you, my beautiful pet."

Her back grew stiff. "I assure you, I'm no man's pet."

"Is that right?" D'Angelo slid his free hand

boldly down her back, cupped her firm butt, and gave it a gentle squeeze. "Maybe I can change all of that." His eyes roamed over her best assets. "What can you offer for this passport?"

A smile returned to her tight lips. "Whatever you have in mind."

D'Angelo returned the cigar to his mouth and pinched one of her breasts through her navy chenille sweater. "You can always take the girl out of the ghetto, but you can't take the ghetto out the girl, huh?"

Michelle wrinkled her nose at him but held on to her smile. "Whatever you say, baby."

Their eyes locked and performed a seductive dance that blurred the line of who was conning whom.

Finally, D'Angelo shook his head and gave her a gruff laugh. "I have to be out of my mind to still be screwing around with you. Especially since your last two exes are six feet under. How about we talk cash?"

She relaxed her smile and pried his hand from her butt. "How much?"

"Well, you know these things aren't easy to get."

Annoyed, Michelle brushed off the front of her sweater. "Just throw out a figure."

He walked away from her and plopped down on a cheap leather couch. "Let's go over your tab. I got my boys to help you dump Danny's body."

"Yeah, God forbid they actually toss him in the woods or something. They planted him in a public park."

"What do you care? We got him out of that pool, didn't we?"

Michelle held her tongue. What was the point in arguing with him?

"I still have guys out combing Pine Mountain, Lake Lanier, and Buckhead for your sister. I would have taken care of her myself had she been in her room that night at the hospital." He smiled. "But I see you also got rid of your beloved Dr. Turner. Of course, I never knew what you saw in that white dude, nohow."

Her eyes narrowed as she straightened her shoulders. "I never told you my history with Ambrose."

D'Angelo blew her a kiss. "There's a lot I know about you." He winked. "And get it out of your head that you can take me out. I'm no punk."

Tension replaced the air in the room as Michelle sized up her old friend. In the end, she decided they knew an equal amount of dirt on each other. Plus, she needed him.

"How much?" she asked again.

"A hundred Gs and a piece of that sweet ass you promised me."

"What?"

"I think it's a bargain."

Given the circumstances, Michelle realized that she didn't have room or time to negotiate. "How soon can you get the passport?"

"After I get a photo maybe I can swing something in, say, forty-eight hours?"

She thought about it. "I'll need it under the name of Josephine Ferrell."

"Of course."

"How much more for a birth certificate?"

He cocked a brow.

"I might need it in the future."

When his gaze raked over her attire, Michelle could see his interest flare up again. "How about you give me a little sample now and I'll just throw in the birth certificate," he said, rubbing his hand down the front of his crotch.

Michelle smirked and settled her hands on her curvaceous hips. "Like what you see?"

"What can I say? Money looks good on you."

"Yeah." Slowly, she unbuttoned the front of her sweater and watched his eyes widened at the sight of her full breasts. "And I'm going to make sure I'll always have it."

Gathering her strength, Josephine climbed the stairs. Once she reached the master bedroom, she found William's duffel bag on the floor by the armchair. As she reached for it, her eyes landed on a set of keys lying on the small reading table.

There had to be a vehicle in the garage, she reasoned. She grabbed the keys. This was her chance. She could cut her losses and leave.

Her gaze slid over to the rumpled bed. Almost instantly, her body recalled the way William had made love to her . . . and how she'd responded to him.

It seemed like no matter what she did in life, fate kept dealing her a losing hand. She slumped into the armchair and allowed the weight of the world to settle on her shoulders.

How was it possible that she still cared for him after all these years? Once upon at time he'd come into her life and turned everything upside down. This time, he saved her . . . but for how long?

Her gaze lowered to the silver keys in her hand.

William wondered what was taking Josie so long. He glanced at his watch. He would have to leave in the next two hours if he was going to make it to Keystone by noon. Never a man to stand still, he decided to go out and grab a few more logs of firewood. As he waltzed out the back door and onto the wooden back deck, his mind tangled with what he was going to tell the police. He wasn't worried about a kidnapping charge so much as a murder charge.

It wasn't going to look good that he waited so long to come forward, he reasoned, lifting the ax

from the tree stump. Regardless, he would undoubtedly lose his job.

What was that? His ears perked at a rumbling
sound.

A few squirrels scattered about as if they were
frightened. Was someone there?

William strained his ears again and swore he
heard the crunch of gravel. *A car?*

With ax in hand, he rushed back to the house.
Surely, Larry and Sheila waren't returning early, he
thought. *They waren't due back until December.*

William bolted through the back door and
scrambled to the kitchen. Josie still hadn't come
down. He hurried to the front door and glanced
out the peephole, but his heart dropped at the
sight of the two menacing goons on the other side
of the door.

Ming and her team of police officers were welcomed to the Turner residence by the red-eyed widow. It was near noon, but Trisha answered the door wrapped in a pink robe and a pair of matching fuzzy house shoes. Despite the woman's swollen eyes and glowing nose, Ming thought the fortysomething socialite was still a striking woman.

"Morning, Mrs. Turner." Ming went through the formality of flashing her identification, but Trisha hardly spared it a glance.

"Come on in." Trisha stepped back and allowed Ming and her four companions entry. "Please excuse the mess, but I haven't had time to straighten up."

Ming moved into the foyer and glanced around. What was the woman talking about? The place was immaculate. "I know this is a hard time for you. We appreciate your help in this case."

Trisha shrugged, seemingly unaffected by the minispeech, then led the way to a handsome office. Three of the four lengthy walls were decked floor to ceiling with cherrywood bookcases. The shelves were packed tight with books bound in expensive leather, and the polished floor showcased the most beautiful Oriental rug Ming had ever seen.

"This is nice," Ming said, easing into the room. "This is where your husband worked?"

Again, Trisha shrugged. "He always said that he worked better in here than he did at Keystone," she said. "Fewer interruptions."

Ming noted that the widow's voice dripped with sarcasm. Moments like these were always difficult.

Ming's small entourage slid on latex gloves and promptly dispersed throughout the room.

Apparently, the sight of the police officers dismantling her husband's office proved too much for Trisha, as she turned and walked away.

Hesitant, Ming drew a deep breath and followed her. "Are you all right, Mrs. Turner?"

"Trisha. Please call me Trisha or by my maiden name Strauss."

The correction told Ming a great deal about the widow's state of mind. It also warned her to proceed with caution. "I hate to have to ask you—"

"You want the file." Trisha made a beeline to a bar in another spacious room decorated completely in white.

"Yes, ma'am. If it's not too much trouble." Rich people lived on a whole other level, Ming thought as she absorbed her surroundings.

"No trouble at all." Trisha slapped a thick manila folder onto the bar's counter, then promptly mixed herself a drink. "Can I get you anything?"

"Sorry. I'm on duty." Ming joined her at the counter and slid onto a wrought-iron barstool.

"Well, I *need* this." Trisha saluted her.

Ming nodded and opened the folder. The first thing to greet her were bold black-and-white photos of Andrews straddling Dr. Turner in the driver's seat of a shiny, silver Mercedes.

"I'm assuming they were parked," Trisha said, with a deep measure of disgust.

There were several more shots of the uninhibited lovers in the car, but those were soon replaced with ones of them making out by a pool.

"If you're wondering, that's our pool."

"He brought her here?" Ming asked before she could stop herself.

"A bold bastard, wasn't he?" Trisha took another sip of her drink. "And I stayed with him. How pathetic is that?"

Ming reached across the bar and gave the distraught woman's hand an affectionate squeeze. "Life isn't over. You'll get through this."

Trisha met Ming's stare as a new wave of tears brimmed her eyes. "Are you married, Detective Delaney?"

Lifting her hand, Ming flashed her modest wedding ring. "Three years this December."

"Hell, you're still newlyweds." A sardonic smile hugged Trisha's lips. "You're probably still having sex in every room of the house."

Ming nearly choked on her laughter. "I wouldn't say that, exactly."

One of Trisha's neatly manicured eyebrows rose. "Well, let me impart one thing I've learned in my disastrous marriage. Men are like houseplants."

Caught off guard, Ming's expression of interest collapsed into a frown. "Houseplants?"

Trisha allowed herself another smile. "They need constant attention, sunshine, water, and nurturing. You neglect any of those things, and they'll plant themselves in someone else's pot, if you know what I mean."

Ming's thoughts instantly flew to her often-busy schedule and her dwindling sex drive.

Hadn't she just fallen asleep on Conan the other night? "I'll try to keep that in mind."

Their conversation ended at the sound of approaching footsteps.

Detective Jorge Hernandez filled the room's entryway. "Delaney, may I speak with you for a minute?"

"Certainly." Ming hopped off the barstool and gathered everything back into the folder.

"Take it. I don't want it anymore," Trisha said, and continued to nurse her drink.

"Thanks." Ming left the bar and walked across a white plush carpet to join her colleague at the door. "Do we have something?"

Hernandez escorted her away from the door. "We found a .45 Para CCW hidden in a hollowed-out book."

"Bancroft was shot with the same type of weapon."

Hernandez nodded. "Figured you might want to take a look at it."

Ming dug her cell out of her pants pocket. "I better get the crime lab up here. We may have just found our murderer."

Michelle left D'Angelo more than satisfied; and by the time it was all said and done, she'd also bargained to have a few of his men for security.

Two large black males trailed behind her. Their presence elevated her confidence; not that it needed it, but she definitely felt that she was back on track.

In retrospect, she shouldn't have contacted D'Angelo, but who knows? Maybe she could think of a way to get rid of him before she left town. She hated loose ends.

Michelle smiled at the thought as she glided out of the back office and maneuvered through a busy boutique at Underground Atlanta. Minutes later, she slid behind the wheel of a red Jaguar and waited for her new security to show up before she pulled out.

From across the parkway, Detective Simmons returned to his own car and watched everything with keen interest.

"What are you up to, Andrews?" He grabbed his cell phone and quickly punched in Ming's number as he started up his car.

"You were my next call," Ming said, before Tyrese had the chance to speak.

"Well, you're always on my mind, too." Tyrese chuckled, but quickly grew serious again. "I think I have something."

"Same here. You first."

"Castellan's."

"What—the boutique store?"

"Yeah. You know who runs it, don't you?"

"A pain in the neck, D'Angelo."

"Bingo. Andrews just left his place and came out with a matching pair of goons."

Ming sighed. "We already interviewed him about the Thornton case. Him being Daniel's friend and all."

"Maybe we didn't ask the right questions."

"I'll get him back in for more questioning. Are you still following Andrews?"

"I'm on her like white on rice."

"Good. Now, it's my turn to tell you what I've found."

William only had a few seconds to make a decision. With wood burning in the fireplace and the Lincoln Navigator parked in the cul-de-sac, there was no point in pretending that no one was home.

One of the men pounded on the door and rang the bell simultaneously. From behind him, William heard footsteps on the stairs. He turned and met Josie's scared stare.

"It's okay," he mouthed quietly, then directed her to get out of sight with a curt nod.

She hesitated, then quickly rushed back up the stairs.

Another loud knock rattled the door and William, angrily, turned and jerked the partition open. "Yes, can I help you?" he barked at the two men.

Both men stepped back as their gazes lowered to the ax clutched in William's hand.

William's brow rose higher when neither man spoke. "Yes?" he asked again.

At last, one of the men stuttered out an explanation. "We, uh, out looking for a friend of ours."

The other goon, who was by then well past being afraid of the ax-wielding William, looked as though he was considering a quick quarrel to prove who the better man was.

William's gaze focused on the large patch against the side of the man's face. He hadn't killed him after all.

"Chuck." The goon elbowed his glaring partner.

Finally, "Chuck," with his gaze still locked onto William's, held out a photograph. "We're looking for this woman. Have you seen her?"

William kept his face tight, his grip on the ax's handle firm, while he allowed his gaze to fall to Josephine's smiling image. He frowned and hoped that he wasn't overplaying his part. "Never seen her before," he said, glancing back at the two men.

Chuck's gaze narrowed. "Are you sure?"

Despite his heart hammering in his chest, William cocked his head and refused to be intimidated. "I'm positive."

After a few more seconds of warring glares, the unwanted visitors finally thanked him for his time and ambled off his porch.

However, William waited until the strangers climbed into their black Escalade and drove off before he closed the door. His entire body slumped in relief as he rested his head against the door; but, once again, his attention was drawn to the footsteps on the stairs.

"Pack your things," William instructed curtly. "We're getting out of here."

"False alarm," Detective Hernandez said, entering Ming's office.

"Honey, let me call you back," Ming told Conan on the phone, then added, "I love you, too. All right. Bye." Once she disconnected the call, she gave Jorge her full attention. "Now run that by me again."

He handed her a report. "We just received the ballistics back on the Para CCW we confiscated from the Turner residence."

"That was fast." She flipped open the report.

Jorge straightened his tie. "Let's just say that I have connections down at the lab."

"A girlfriend?"

"Something like that." He flashed her a brief smile.

Ming's gaze lowered back to the ballistics report. Her temples pulsed with disappointment. The lab had run a test with the bullet recovered from Bancroft's body. The markings on the spent bullet versus the ones fired in the lab showed two different markings.

"Okay. That was a waste of time." She tossed the report onto the desk.

"Not really. Usually these setbacks can contribute to the process of elimination. If you look at the back, there's another report."

Ming picked it up again.

"Bullets from Bancroft, Turner, and *Thornton* are a match. Of course, I don't know why someone would shoot Thornton after he was already dead."

"So we're looking for one killer." Ming rolled her eyes. "Don't take this the wrong way, but I have a problem with being wrong."

"Yeah, Simmons may have mentioned that to me once or twice."

"Has he now? Did he also mention that it rarely happens?"

"He said you would say that, yes."

Ming rolled her eyes and made a mental note to get Tyrese back for that comment. "Well," she said drawing a deep breath, "I guess that means we move on to plan B."

Jorge's brows rose with surprise. "There's a backup plan?"

"Tyrese didn't tell you?" She reached for the phone. "There's *always* a backup plan."

In record time, William and Josie crammed what few belongings they had into the Lincoln Navigator and hightailed it out of Pine Mountain. To be safe, William instructed Josie to lie low in the back of the large SUV just in case the two goons were still in the area.

Neither spoke while he whipped around the curvy back roads. There was no need to. Each already knew what the other was thinking.

Josie battled guilt while William mused on what was the right thing to do. In this situation, there was no black-and-white answer.

Lost in his thoughts, he didn't hear Josephine climb from the backseat and into the passenger seat; but when her hand settled on his shoulder, his gaze shifted to meet hers.

"Thank you," she said softly.

"For what?" His attention returned to the highway.

"Everything," she added in the same gentle tone. "I can't help but feel that if you didn't save me when you did, I might not be here."

Once again, William's gaze returned to hers.

"Maybe the night your Dr. Bancroft died, they were actually coming for me."

He shook his head. "Don't say that."

"C'mon. You mean to tell me that you haven't thought about it?" She strapped the seat belt across her shoulder. "Don't tell me that you're the kind that believes in coincidences."

He didn't answer.

She turned to gaze out her passenger window. "Well, I'm glad you showed up when you did. I never had a knight in shining armor before."

William laughed. "That's pouring it on a little thick, don't you think?"

She shrugged and slid on an easy smile. "If everything happens for a reason, then maybe Paris wasn't a mistake after all."

Another awkward silence filled the space between them before William pulled over to the side of the road.

"What are you doing?" she asked. "What's wrong?"

Though they had stopped, William didn't pull his gaze from the road in front of him. "Paris was many things . . . but it was not a mistake."

Josie drew a deep breath as she stared at his profile. One thing she couldn't miss were the shadows of emotions that danced across his features. They pulled at her and destroyed the wall she kept trying to build between them. The wall was supposed to protect her.

"No," she said, finally. "It wasn't a mistake."

"Just lousy timing," he added. "You were, after all, an engaged woman—already spoken for."

"And you wouldn't take 'no' for an answer."

His cheeks darkened with his smile. "I was young."

"We both were."

Gazes locked, both sensed that the other wanted to say more. However, the words never came.

An hour later, William arrived at his two-story, redbrick home in the center of Peachtree City. It was a nice subdivision where most of the houses were exact replicas of one another. The moment William pulled into the driveway, the garage door opened.

He parked next to a black Mercedes, and the garage door closed behind them.

"Do you think it's safe for us to come here?" she asked, climbing out of the vehicle. "I mean with the neighbors and all."

"I don't see where we have much of a choice. It's either here or a hotel. Frankly, I think we would draw more attention to ourselves at a hotel. The great thing about my neighbors is they tend to keep to themselves." He headed toward the garage's side door and entered the house through the kitchen.

Josie followed close behind him. Her gaze quickly darted around. She was given a quick tour of the place before William noticed the time.

"I'm going to be late," he said. "I'm supposed to be at the hospital at noon."

"You're working today?"

"I have to." He opened a closet door and grabbed a clean shirt. "There should be plenty of food in the refrigerator." Next, he scrambled for a pen and paper. "I'm going to write down my pager number. If you need anything, just punch in code 9-1-1. Oh, I'll write down the address so you can have your medical records mailed here now. Wait, maybe that's not wise. Maybe we should get a PO box to have them mailed?"

"Isn't that going to take more time—or do you already have one?"

"No." He ran a nervous hand through his hair. The fact that he was losing control of the whole situation was sinking in fast. "Okay. We'll have them mailed here. I'll write down the address; but once they get here, we're going to the police. Agreed?"

She blinked.

"Josie?"

Belatedly, she flashed him a reassuring smile. "Agreed."

"All right." He nodded; his dilemma of whether to believe her was evident on his face. In the end, he made a quick change, jotted down the address, and brushed a rather awkward kiss against her cheek. "All of this will be over soon," he assured her.

His sudden closeness was all it took to short-circuit her senses, while she tried not to bask in the protectiveness his arms offered.

"You believe me, don't you?" he asked.

Josie's tearful gaze met his calm blue eyes, and in that instant, she would've believed they could live the rest of their lives on the moon. "Of course I do."

When William's gaze lowered to her lips, she couldn't help being drawn to his. Slowly, they leaned toward one another, each uncertain of what was happening to them and both unwilling to stop it.

The moment their lips connected, time ceased to exist. This was the second time life had thrown them together, and just like before it would eventually pull them apart. It was a sad fact that caused tears to trickle down her face.

"Hey, what are these for?" William gently wiped the tracks of her tears.

"It's nothing," she lied, and backed out of his embrace. "I'm fine. You better get going, or you're really going to be late."

He nodded but continued to watch her.

"Go. I'll be here when you get back," she promised.

After another nod, William reluctantly turned and left the house. "I'll call and check on you, but don't hesitate to page me if you need anything."

Josie followed him back to the garage. As he climbed back into the Navigator, her eyes darted over to the parked Mercedes, and she instantly wondered where he kept the keys.

After closing the door, she immediately launched into a mad search. However, her disappointment mounted as she went through one drawer after another. They weren't in the kitchen, living room, or any other room for that matter.

Frustrated, she slumped into one of the leather chairs in the living room. Hell, she didn't even know where she was trying to go. Where *could* she go?

A loud ringing filled the house, and Josie nearly jumped out of her skin. Once she realized that it was the phone, she pressed a hand over her heart and willed herself to calm down. She leaned toward the end table to read the caller ID, but the caller hung up before the answer machine clicked on.

As she stared at the phone, she was hit with an idea. *Call her.* Josie's anxiety kicked up another notch. What would she say if Michelle answered?

Don't say anything, she told herself. *I just need to know if she's there.* Josie picked up the receiver and actually felt her heart skip a beat. For a long moment, she just stared at the black buttons before she hung up.

She had no idea what the hell she was doing. She didn't know how to fight back against the kind of evil her sister possessed.

Josie closed her eyes while the war of what was right and wrong warred within her. It was a strange position to be in. She was uncertain what to do. It was very tempting to grab what she could and run, but a new voice in her head urged her to stay and fight. With renewed determination, she picked up the receiver again, punched star six-seven to block William's number, and then dialed home. It took everything she had to calm the swarm of butterflies in her stomach and slow her racing heart; but while she waited for the line to connect, she began to formulate a plan.

Suddenly, her sister's heavy pant came on the line. "Hello."

This was it. Josie was supposed to hang up, but she couldn't stop her lips from curling into a smile as she said, "Hello, Michelle. Missed me?"

" Josie?" Michelle asked, her amusement echoing through the phone.

"Were you expecting someone else?"

Michelle chuckled, but a nervous lilt prevented it from sounding genuine. "My dear sister. Where are you?"

It was Josie's turn to laugh, and she was surprised by how sinister it sounded. "That's not important right now. All you need to know is that I'm feeling *much* better."

A long pause hung over the line before Michelle spoke, and her tone gave Josie a new definition of evil.

"Why haven't you gone to the police?"

Josie swallowed.

Undoubtedly sensing that she'd hit her mark, Michelle continued. "At the moment, *sweetie*, you're a free woman; but if you rat me out, I'm taking you down with me."

Josie closed her eyes and clenched her jaw shut. Maybe she was biting off more than she could chew dealing with this woman.

"Are you still there, Josie?"

"Your threats don't scare me," she lied.

Michelle's laughter sounded like a witch's cackle. "It's not a threat, it's a promise. So why don't you be a good girl and get out of town before I find you?"

Josie's resolve hardened. "Don't forget, I already know where you are, *Michelle*." With that, she disconnected the call.

A few seconds passed while Josie stared at the phone and tried to control the wild pounding of her heart. It was official: She had lost her mind. She had just threatened a crazy woman.

"You can beat her," she repeated to herself, until she believed it.

Drawing a deep breath and slowly exhaling it, Josie moved her guilt to the back of her mind and focused on what she needed to do first. She picked up the phone and made the first call to hit Michelle where it would hurt most.

* * *

Michelle jerked open the medicine cabinet and reached for her much-used lithium pills, but then screamed in frustration when she discovered the bottle empty.

I told you yesterday that you needed to get a refill.

"Shut up," she hissed, and slammed the bottle into the bathroom sink. Her head was pounding while she felt as if she was spiraling out of control.

It's over. It's over. The voice sang in a ring-around-the-roses undertone.

"I can beat her," Michelle swore in a voice dripping with venom. "Josie doesn't know who the hell she's dealing with."

Oh, please. This was over the moment she escaped from Keystone.

"NO!" With both hands, she grabbed a fistful of hair on each side of her temples and pulled mercilessly. She had come too far to lose everything now. "I have to find her."

What—you have a crystal ball or something?

Out of frustration, she emitted another low scream and tugged at her hair again. If she could just think for a minute, she could figure something out.

Give up. You've screwed this up just like you screwed up everything else in your life. What was it that your adoptive parents used to call you?

"A lost cause." She slid her hands from her hair to stare into the mirror.

Slowly, a small smirk sloped the corners of her reflection's lips. "That's right," the woman in the glass said. "A lost cause. How could I have forgotten?"

Michelle seethed. "I'll show you. I'll show everyone."

Her mirror image laughed—a high cackle sound that rang in Michelle's ears. "You've never done anything right in your entire life, what on earth makes you think you can pull something this big off, Michelle?"

"It's *Josephine*." Michelle could feel tears in the back of her eyes. "I'm not a lost cause," she said with a shaky tremor.

The taunting woman's laughter waned as she met Michelle's eyes boldly. "Sure you are."

"No," Michelle said in a feeble whisper, and shook her head.

Her reflection laughed.

Michelle plugged her fingers into her ears, and her eardrums felt as if they were going to explode. When the sound intensified, she lashed out and attacked her tormentor.

For a moment she blacked out, but then the pain in her hand was the first indicator that something was wrong. She opened her eyes and was surprised to see that the mirror was gone. Her gaze dropped to the sink, where large shards of glass glittered up at her. Finally, she looked at her hand. It hurt like hell but she had come away with just a minor cut against the side of her wrist.

Temper, temper, temper.

Michelle drew a breath and tried her best to control the voice in her head. When she turned from the door, she jumped in surprise at the two large men who filled the entrance to her bathroom.

"Are you all right?" one of the matching gorillas inquired.

Hiding her hand behind her back, she flashed her new bodyguards a quick smile. "Yes, I'm fine."

Neither looked as though they believed her.

"Look, if you don't mind, I need a few minutes of privacy." She started to close the door, but was unsuccessful when one of them placed his foot in the doorframe.

"Don't forget you need to bring D'Angelo his deposit this afternoon."

Michelle could feel her temper slipping again, but she was able to rein it in to give him a curt response. "Fine. We'll go to the bank. Just give me a damn minute to get ready."

Gorilla number one removed his foot.

She slammed it closed and rested her head against the wooden partition.

You really are pathetic.

"Just shut up." She turned from the door and quickly cleaned up the glass, her hand, and even made herself more presentable.

An hour later, she and her "security guards" arrived at Bank of America. Decked out in her favorite cream chinchilla, Michelle walked through the glass doors feeling every bit like a diva.

She was immediately led to a cute account representative who introduced himself as Clark Owens. He seemed more than eager to help her with her banking needs. "I need to make a sizable withdrawal," she said, with a gleaming smile.

"Well, I'll be more than happy to assist you."

Michelle withdrew the bank information and handed it over. "I need one hundred thousand dollars from this account."

"Okay." Clark said, and immediately turned his attention to the flat screen computer on his desk.

However, it didn't take long before Michelle realized that something was wrong. She forced herself to sit still while he typed and frowned at the screen. Finally, after a few minutes, she couldn't take it anymore.

"What's wrong?" she asked.

Clark glanced back down at the account book she'd handed him and typed some more.

"Hello?" Michelle screeched, irritation sharpening her tone.

Startled, Clark glanced up at her with his frown firmly in place. "I'm sorry, Ms. Ferrell." He handed her back her small book. "But I'm showing that this account has been closed."

"**W**hat do you mean the account is closed?"

Clark Owens blinked, then glanced back at his computer. "I mean just that. The account was closed earlier today."

"Well, can't you just reopen it?"

His frown deepened. "No. According to the computer, you had all monies in this account transferred to a European bank. You are Josephine Ferrell, aren't you?"

In response, Michelle jumped angrily to her feet. "You saw my ID, didn't you?"

"I'm sorry, Ms. Ferrell." He jumped to his feet. "Let me just get the branch manager over here.

If you're saying you didn't authorize the transfers—"

"That won't be necessary." Michelle's heart leapt; suddenly she was afraid of drawing attention to herself—especially since she didn't know what Josie might have told the branch manager.

The young account representative frowned.

"I think I do remember closing this account now." She touched her forehead to feign forgetfulness. "I'm getting my banks mixed up today. I meant to stop by First National."

Clark relaxed a bit and gave her a relieved smile. "Well, we're definitely going to miss your business." He extended his hand.

Stiffly, she slid her hand into his, then turned away. As she walked through the glass doors, she hugged her fur coat tighter around her shoulders, but it didn't stop her from feeling exposed.

You have to hand it to her. You didn't see that coming.

Michelle's jawline hardened. Surely, she didn't close all the bank accounts. She rushed back to her car, paying little heed to her bodyguards, who tried to keep up with her. Her next stop was First National, but minutes later she left in the same angry huff.

"I don't believe this," she muttered, slamming the door to the Jaguar. As she clenched the steering wheel, she took a few deep, cleansing breaths, but her temper escalated.

"If I could just get my hands on her."

What's the point of being Josephine Ferrell if you're broke?

"Not now," she hissed. "I'm trying to think." Her inner voice quieted. As Michelle leaned her head back against the headrest, she couldn't help but wonder if Josie had time to cancel the credit cards as well.

She would be crazy not to, don't you think?

Michelle didn't respond. Instead, she started the car and drove to the nearest gas station. She pulled up to the pump and withdrew six platinum cards from Josie's wallet. Since gas pumps don't require pin numbers or verified ID, it was the perfect way to see whether the cards were still usable without any embarrassing scenes. But one by one, the automated pump declined them.

"This can't be happening." She jumped back into the car. A full-blown panic attack ruptured within her as a long stream of profanity spewed forth. Inside her head, all she could hear was a familiar cackle of laughter.

She didn't know how long her fit lasted; but when it was over, she found strands of hair in her hands and could taste the blood oozing from her lips. Panting, she glanced around and caught a few frowns from attending patrons—and two from D'Angelo's men.

Oh, this is classic.

Michelle drew a deep, calming breath, then used the rearview mirror to straighten her appearance. Other than having a swollen bottom lip, she pulled herself together quite nicely.

All this work, and it never occurred to you to move the money?

Michelle didn't answer. It was all she could do to control her rage. "D'Angelo can help me find her."

And how do you expect to pay him?

She had no idea, but her thoughts were interrupted when her cell phone rang. Briefly, she entertained the thought that it was Josie. Who knows, maybe she was getting a good kick watching her make a fool of herself.

Annoyed, Michelle dug through her purse and grabbed the phone. However, her anger evaporated into curiosity when she read Keystone Institute across the ID screen.

After hours on the phone, Josephine found the keys to William's black Mercedes in his bedroom on the nightstand. She clutched the keys tightly in her hand before she made up her mind about what she should do next, then finally decided to look up the nearest office of the Department of Motor Vehicles.

As she climbed in behind the wheel, guilt settled heavily onto her shoulders. William trusted her to stay put, but her head was clouded with thoughts of revenge.

She started up the car and promised herself she would return before William came home. Minutes later, she pulled up to the DMV. After reporting her driver's license lost, she obtained a new one with little to no hassle. Next, she stopped at a local Western Union, where she picked up the cash she'd wired to herself.

She was back in business.

Admittedly, she didn't have a concrete plan, but she did know that there wasn't enough room in the world for *two* Josephine Ferrells.

Locating an army surplus store was more complicated than she expected, but she finally found one next to a low-key shooting range. The minute she entered the building though, she felt completely out of her element.

At first, she thought the place was just a warehouse of army uniforms. Everywhere she looked were camouflage shirts, pants, hats, and even long johns.

"Is there anything I can help you with, ma'am?"

Josie turned toward a smiling blond female who took the edict "the higher the hair, the closer to Jesus" seriously. "Uh, I'm not sure. I was looking to purchase a gun."

"Sure." The blond clapped. "You came to the right place. "My husband, Buddy, will be more than happy to help you." She turned around and waved Josie to follow.

"I always say that a woman needs something to protect herself. Society tries to tell us girls that all we need is a can of pepper spray. It's crazy, I tell you. Oh, I'm Tammy, by the way."

Josie only managed to open her mouth before Tammy rambled off her conspiracy theory of how the government was trying to take away honest Americans' constitutional right to bear arms.

"Buddy! Customer!"

Josie wiggled a finger in her ear to stop it from ringing.

From the back of the shop, a General Schwarzkopf lookalike emerged. His slow smile never quite reached his eyes, and his firm handshake threatened to rip her arm from its socket. "Well, aren't you a pretty little thing? What can I do for you?"

"She's looking for some protection." Tammy supplied an answer for Josie.

His smile widened as he tilted back his camouflage cap. "Is that right? Do you already have something in mind?"

"No clue." Josie pulled her hand from his, then rubbed at her sore shoulder. "This is my first time buying a weapon."

"Ah. A first-timer." He led her over to a glass countertop. "Now, I have to tell you that Georgia requires a ten-day waiting period before I can actually sell you a gun. You can fill out an application, and we can go ahead and pick you out something."

Josie blinked. "Ten days?"

Buddy chuckled and shrugged. "Government. They want to make sure that we don't sell any weapons to convicts or any terrorist groups. They hold a monopoly on those sales."

"But I can't wait ten days."

Tammy and Buddy gave her a curious look.

Josie cleared her throat, but it didn't stop her from stammering. "I sort of need the weapon today."

There was new interest in Buddy's eyes.

"I'm not a convict or anything." *Not yet.*

"Then what's the hurry?" he asked.

"You know, that's okay." Josie backed away from the counter. "I'll go somewhere else." She turned away and rushed toward the front door.

"Just a minute." Tammy caught up with her and laid a restraining hand upon Josie's shoulder.

Josie faced the woman.

"We might not be able to sell you something today," Tammy whispered. "But if you need help, sugar, I know someone who can. We women have to stick together, right?"

Josie smiled as she winked back. "Right."

* * *

A bored D'Angelo leaned back in a metal chair and kicked his feet up on the corner of a table in the interrogation room. It was another day, but the same old b.s. He didn't know why he was dragged down here this time, and he didn't care. Whatever it was, he was confident that these people didn't have anything on him.

He was just too smart to get caught.

When the door finally opened, he recognized the tall, baby-faced Hispanic who'd interrogated him before.

"Please tell me that you guys didn't drag me back in here about Danny again."

Detective Hernandez said nothing as he swiped D'Angelo's feet off the table.

"Hey. I was just making myself comfortable."

"Well, don't. You're not at home." Hernandez dragged a chair back from the table and planted himself in it. "Tell me about your relationship with Michelle Andrews."

"Who?"

Hernandez's lips sloped unevenly. "I've always thought of you as an intelligent man, D'Angelo."

"Why, thank you, *amigo*. I wish I could extend the same compliment."

Hernandez shrugged. "I don't know. I'm pretty smart—made it through Yale okay."

Resentment curled in D'Angelo's belly. "It's just

like you college boys to throw that up in someone's face. Book smarts don't mean a damn thing in the streets. A certificate won't stop a speeding bullet, know what I mean?"

"So you and Michelle are from the streets?"

"Damn right. Nothing was handed to us on a silver platter."

"Unlike Michelle's twin sister."

Understanding dawned on D'Angelo, and in turn he gave the cop a stiff smile. "I got to hand you your props. You knocked me off my game for a minute."

"Is that what this is to you? A game?"

He shook his head and rolled his eyes. "I just call it like I see it."

Hernandez nodded. "Well, let me tell you how I see it. I see a man who's bitten off more than he can chew. And all over a woman."

D'Angelo laughed. "Man, you don't know what you're talking about."

"I'm talking about you two murdering Daniel Thornton, Dr. Meredith Bancroft, Dr. Ambrose Turner, and probably Michelle's twin sister, Josephine Ferrell."

"That's quite a list."

"Finally something we can agree on."

D'Angelo shrugged and laughed. "Hey, *amigo*. You got the wrong guy."

"I'm supposed to believe you? A minute ago, you told me that you didn't know Michelle Andrews."

"Look, I ain't saying nothing else. I want my lawyer. I get a call, right?"

Hernandez laughed. "Lines are down. Who knows when they'll be back up."

D'Angelo's eyes narrowed to small daggers, but Hernandez's smile only blossomed.

"So what's it going to be?" Hernandez braided his hands on the table. "Do you want to rot in a cell and hope that one day we'll remember you're there . . . or do you want to tell us what you know about Michelle Andrews?"

Josie returned to William's house while feeling the onslaught of a headache. She was proud of what she'd accomplished that day, but it wasn't without its emotional baggage. In fact, her tattered emotions were getting the best of her.

What she wouldn't give for William to hold her—maybe even tell her that she was doing the right thing.

After clearing a spot on the bed, she sat down and felt the gun holster at the center of her back. It was one of the best places to pack a piece according to Tammy. The other was around the ankle. Josie removed the new Glock from her back holster and the small .22 from her ankle. At this rate she would be ready to take on the Terminator.

On reflection, it was scary how easy it was to purchase a weapon.

A chill raced down her spine as she took a moment to step outside of herself. Suddenly, she couldn't find a correct angle in anything she'd planned.

Her hands trembled, and, before she knew it, the tremor moved up her arms. Just when she thought she could bypass William's advice and not take her shots this had to happen.

Josie searched and found the leather duffel bag, but hesitated in giving herself a shot.

She removed a vial and unwrapped a new hypodermic needle. But before she could administer the methadone, it was all over. *That wasn't so bad*, she thought. She released her held breath and relaxed back onto the bed.

It angered her that Michelle was responsible for her condition. She was tired of being a victim. The loss of her career, father, and nearly her life was slowly driving her off the deep end.

An hour passed before she felt a hundred percent better, but during that time, she'd decided to take a peek at Michelle's medical chart. She was disturbed by a lot of what was written. Most of it struck too close to home.

When she found herself feeling sympathetic,

her wrist itched like crazy. She looked down and was reminded of just why she was going after Michelle. It was time to settle a score.

Michelle entered Marcus Hines's office with glowing contempt and her patience hanging on by a thin thread. "This better be good," she said, then stopped short when she saw a team of men in black suits.

She turned toward Hines as he closed the door. "What's this all about?"

"Ms. Ferrell, I'd like you to meet some of our attorneys." He gestured to the only vacant chair in front of his desk. "Would you like to take a seat?"

"Attorneys?" she asked. "Did I miss something?"

Hines's smile fluttered weakly. "I invited you here to discuss a possible settlement."

She didn't budge from her spot by the door. "Shouldn't I have brought my own lawyers as well?"

"We just want to make an offer. You're more than welcome to discuss any of this with your attorneys later."

Michelle frowned, but then she realized that if Josie had contacted all the financial institutions, she just as likely had contacted her family's law firm as well. That meant all of this was moot, anyway.

"I would love to talk about a settlement, but I really think this sort of thing needs to be discussed when all our lawyers are present." She turned toward the door.

Hines jumped and blocked her exit.

Michelle took a retreating step and frowned. "Is there a problem?"

"No, uh. I just wanted to at least go over some items with you. Who knows, if we can agree, we could get a check to you as soon as tomorrow?"

"A check tomorrow?"

Hines's smile returned. "That's *if* we can reach an agreement."

Michelle said nothing as she mulled over this latest development and her palms itched with greed. "I guess it wouldn't hurt to hear you out."

"Great." He sighed with obvious relief. "Won't you have a seat?"

She turned toward the group of men. "Don't mind if I do."

Sashaying her way into the center, Michelle was certain the men were all drawn to her curvaceous figure. She peeled the soft chinchilla from her shoulders and lowered herself into the chair.

"Can I get you something to drink?" Hines turned to the cart beside his desk and reached for the glass pitcher of water.

"Some water would be nice." She flashed everyone a cordial smile as she slid her fingers from her gloves and accepted the offered glass. "Thank you."

"You're more than welcome."

Josie retrieved the spare key to her father's estate from a potted plant near the garage. She was more than a little disappointed and relieved that Michelle wasn't there.

Entering through the front door, she stepped into the spacious foyer and stopped. *Home.*

It was disheartening to see the place empty of life. Growing up, there had always been servants scurrying about while something delicious baking in the kitchen wafted throughout the house.

Now, the place was just . . . cold.

Josie closed the door and moved deeper into the house. The place was still reasonably clean, but that all changed when she climbed the spiral staircase and visited each bedroom.

Michelle had ransacked the place. The worst room was Josephine's old room. In no time at all, Josie had deduced how Michelle had gotten her hands on everything from financial information to Josie's social security number.

She found stacks of paper where Michelle apparently practiced her handwriting and even books on intermediate French.

"She left no stone unturned." Josie stepped over

a pile of boxes to open her old closet. It was just all stuff—nothing that meant anything.

The saddest thing in all of this, she thought, was how she would have gladly shared it all with Michelle. They were all material things anyway. All Josie wanted was a family, to be a part of something—just to belong.

Josie moved away from the closet and walked over to her old vanity. Melancholy, she picked up a few crystal bottles and sprayed their fragrances into the air. However, her mood worsened, and she fell the steady pulse of a new migraine.

Heaving an exhausted breath, she headed to the adjoining bathroom to see if she still had a bottle of Excedrin in the medicine cabinet.

William whizzed through his patient schedule. If it was at all possible, he wanted to get out of there early, but Hines wasn't kidding when he said that he was dealing with a diminishing and nervous staff. Everywhere he turned he was interrupting someone with the latest gossip about what had happened with Dr. Bancroft and Dr. Turner. The most popular story he'd heard was that their missing patient, Michelle Andrews, was knocking off the doctors to exact revenge on how she was treated while she was in Keystone.

After two hours of tolerating the low whispers,

William's nerves had sharpened to a fine point. To get through his day, he kept reminding himself that this would be over soon and everyone would know the truth. Of course, he wasn't entirely sure what that meant for him. Would he lose his job, or, worse, his license?

"Oh, Dr. Hayes."

William turned and saw Dr. Coleman racing toward him. "Can't talk now, Rae. I'll catch up with you later." He stepped onto the elevator and was grateful when the doors closed before Rae reached them.

His shoulders slumped with relief. If Dr. Coleman had managed to corner him, heaven only knows when he would be able to escape. The elevator slowed to a stop, but when the doors slid open William froze as he stood face-to-face with Michelle Andrews.

M ing entered Marcus Hines's office and extended a hand. "I can't tell you how much we appreciate your assistance in this matter."

Hines cleared his throat and smiled sheepishly at her as he accepted her hand. "I'm happy to do whatever I can to help the authorities."

She smiled and turned toward the other four officers who'd posed as attorneys. "Do we have what we need?"

One officer was still bent over and dusting for prints from Michelle's empty water glass. "Just about through."

Hines shook his head. "I still can't believe it. Michelle Andrews masquerading as her twin sister?"

"Technically, it's still a theory," Ming said. "That's what the fingerprints are for."

"But if she's Michelle, where is the real Josephine?"

Ming held little doubt that Josephine Ferrell had met the same fate as the others who stood in the way. "We're still looking," she said. "We're still looking."

"Oh, it's you again." Michelle smiled as she stepped into the elevator. "Going down?"

A faint smile curved William's lips. "As a matter of fact, I am."

"Perfect." She glanced at the panel and punched for the lobby. When her eyes darted back over to William, she turned flirtatious and sauntered toward him. "What is your name again?"

"William," he answered. "Dr. William Hayes."

She winked. "You know, I've always had a thing for doctors."

"Really?" *How ironic.*

"Uh-huh." She backed him into a corner and was bold enough to run a finger down the center of his chest. "You know, I'll be leaving town soon, and I'd hate to miss the opportunity to play *doctor* with such a handsome one like you."

It was odd for him to watch a replica of the face he adored be possessed with such a crazed malevolence. "I'll have to pass."

Michelle's brows rose as the elevator slowed. "Don't worry. No strings attached. I promise."

He forced on a smile. "As tempting as your offer may be, I'm afraid you're not my type."

Michelle's hands fell to her sides as all traces of her smile vanished. "Your loss."

The doors slid open, and Dr. Coleman stopped in the doorway. Her gaze zeroed in on the cozy scene in the corner, and her mouth gaped in shock.

Michelle winked, turned, and glided past the stunned doctor.

William drew a shaky breath, but he wasn't foolish enough to stick around to hear a lecture from the queen of gab. He stepped forward to exit the elevator, but was completely thrown off guard when Rae pushed him back into his corner, pressed a floor button, and turned on him.

"Have you lost your mind? Do you know who that woman is?"

"Rae, I don't want to discuss this."

"That woman might be suing us soon, or have you forgotten about that?"

Annoyance crept along his spine, but he was careful not to let the emotion show. "Rae, thanks for the advice, but nothing happened."

Once again, the elevator slowed to a stop, and William was spared more of his nosey colleague's comments when a group of formidable men and an uncharacteristically tall Asian woman stepped inside.

Rae maneuvered her way out of the cramped quarters and waved at William to follow.

"I'm going down," he informed her.

She opened her mouth to protest, but the doors slid closed.

William sighed and slacked his shoulders in relief. He darted a gaze to the other five persons occupying the small box. The only one who met his eye was the attractive woman, but her expressionless features quickly turned toward the door when the elevator returned to the lobby.

The lady and the four suits filed out and gave William the impression they were the Secret Service running late to protect the president.

"Humph. I wonder what all that was about."

Josie searched high and low through her old medicine cabinet for a bottle of Excedrin, and finally found it in the back of cosmetic drawer.

She walked back into the bedroom and, once again, stepped over a stack of boxes in the center of the floor. From the corner of her eyes, she recognized a pink storage container beneath one of the boxes. Turning toward it, Josie felt a warmth spread throughout her body.

She knelt and removed everything on top of the container, then popped it open. Piles of letters and pictures assaulted her memory and tugged at her heart. "Summer of '88," read the storage label.

Josie had forgotten she'd stored these things at her father's home. She reached inside and withdrew a poem that William had left on her pillow one morning.

A smile fluttered across her lips while the poem evoked the same emotions as it had sixteen years earlier. She reached for another envelope, but this time a small stack of pictures spilled out onto the floor.

She picked up a photo and blushed at the memory of her slinking across a grand piano in a red sequined dress.

"William and I really had a lot of fun," she whispered. They were perfect together. Her vision blurred beneath a thin sheen of tears.

Josie laid the picture against her chest and thought back to the first time they'd made love . . .

"There's no need for you to be shy," William whispered against her ear. "You're beautiful."

After weeks of dating, it was the first time that Josie had mustered up the nerve to invite him into her bedroom. It was the first time she'd invited any man in there, and now that they were there, she couldn't stop trembling.

"We don't have to do this if you don't want to," he said.

"No." She placed his hand across her heart so he could feel how hard it was beating. "I want to do this—I *want* to make love to you." As always, she melted at the sight of his dimpled cheeks and the gleam of his bright smile.

"I want to make love to you, too," he said. He looked into her eyes and tilted her face so her mouth could receive him.

It was the sweetest kiss ever and melted all thoughts of a fiancé.

Though the knots in her stomach unraveled, her heart hammered with anticipation. This was a big step, and there was no doubt in her mind she wanted to do it.

William's warm lips slid lovingly from her mouth and settled along the crook of her neck. As if he'd activated a switch, Josie's eyes rolled while her head dipped back.

Her breath thinned as he peeled down the straps of her dress. Shortly after, her knees knocked at the sound of him unzipping her dress.

"It's not too late, you know. You can still back out."

Her dress fell and pooled at her feet.

"I have to tell you, I'm praying that you don't."

Josie still didn't answer, and William stopped.

Their eyes met for a long, searching moment.

"Josie?" He eased a finger down her jawline and cupped her chin. "No pressure."

There was something about the calm blue of his eyes and the silkiness of his voice that assuaged her nervousness. Before she knew it, she was melting all over again.

"Don't stop," she whispered, and glided her arms around his neck. "Don't ever stop."

His smile was a mischievous one, and when his strong hands cupped her full breasts, she was eternally branded as his. She gently pulled his head down, and within seconds she was intoxicated by the simple taste of his kiss.

When William unhooked her bra, Josie was breathless. He turned his head to pepper kisses along the curve of her shoulder. Desire surged in impatient waves while his hands skimmed down the curves of her body and looped inside the lace of her panties.

Something new was happening, and she couldn't extinguish the persistent throb between her legs. She leaned back and allowed his breath to caress her skin and her Victoria's Secret to join the rest of her clothing on the floor.

"It's your turn," he said in a ragged whisper.

It was the first hint of the power she possessed over him, and she was emboldened by it. Taking her time, she unbuttoned his shirt, then peeled the material from his broad shoulders.

Josie drew in a breath and lightly ran her fingers through the fine hairs on his chest. He was a beautiful specimen of a man. She couldn't believe he belonged to her.

In no time, the lovers stood naked before one another. Both assessed, memorized, and loved what they saw.

He moved toward her. His sex brushed against her leg, sending sparks of desire clear to her toes.

Their lips met again. Each gave as much as they took and as a result created a delicious haze of pleasure. Everything tingled within her—everything was so new.

Impatient, William swept her into his arms and carried her to the bed. Laying her against the silk sheets, he lowered himself onto her. Their lips melded while his hands danced over the rise of her breasts, the flat of her belly, and the triangular nest of curls between her legs.

Josie quivered at his fingers' gentle invasion; but when they massaged her flower's aching bud, she unraveled at the seams. She moaned in wild bursts and writhed shakily beneath him. The more she moved, the faster his tempo became, and something fantastic built inside of her.

All at once, everything exploded. An array of multicolored fireworks burst behind closed lids. While her body struggled to extinguish the brush fires he'd ignited, a second orgasm hit and acted as an accelerant. In no time at all, she was dealing with a full-range inferno.

However, the biggest surprise was what William could do with his mouth: soft kneading across her dark nipples, gentle kisses peppered down the center of her body, and a cool tongue that eased her body's flames to mere cinders.

Through it all, her body still ached for completion, and she found herself begging that he give her the one thing she needed. In answer, he deserted the bed, then returned with golden-wrapped condoms.

Her body was still quivering while he sheathed his erection. When he lowered himself to her, she lovingly slid her arms around his neck. She thought she was prepared for what came next, but when his thick shaft broke through the barrier of her maidenhood, she gasped at the initial pain.

William held her and waited patiently for her body to adjust to his invasion. He ground his teeth and fought for control at the way her body pulsed around his snug fit.

"I'm okay," Josie whispered raggedly against his ear.

He nodded, but he hadn't gained control over his body.

She took the lead by sliding her legs around his hips and drawing him in even deeper. The feeling was excruciatingly divine.

William finally took over and moved with tormenting slowness. "You feel so good," he rasped.

She wanted to respond, but couldn't. Nothing in her life could've ever prepared her for this and she was more certain than ever that she'd chosen the right man to give her most precious gift.

Steadily, their tempo increased. Possessed by dual demons of pleasure and passion, William hiked her legs from his waist and settled them above his shoulders. His deep plunging drove her closer and closer to her peak.

At long last, an orgasmic cry tore from her soul. Suddenly, she felt as if she'd been flung into the wild, sweet oblivion when William gave a final thrust and emitted a mighty roar of his own.

Dreamily, she floated from a misty euphoria, sated and happy. As she shifted onto her side, William slid behind her so he could spoon her body.

"Thank you," he whispered, and kissed the back of her head. "I'm grateful and touched you chose me."

"So am I." Josie smiled and snuggled closer . . .

Josie pulled her thoughts from the past and once again felt an incredible loss. But was it really?

It's not too late.

The renegade thought was like a splash of cold water. Josie blinked, then stared back down at the pink box. While she could never go back to that magical summer, there was a real chance for her and William to create something new. And despite her earlier protest, she did want that. She still wanted him.

Ming marched through the doors of the police department and was approached by Detective Hernandez, who could barely contain his excitement.

"Today the gods are smiling down on us." He clapped his hands, then rubbed them together. "D'Angelo is about to break. I can feel it."

"That's good news." She smiled. "Why don't I take over questioning, and you follow these guys to the crime lab. I want the prints off that glass compared to the ones in Michelle Andrews's police record." Ming patted him firmly on the back. "Sweet talk whoever you have to, but get this done *ASAP*."

"Already on it." Jorge winked. "D'Angelo is in the first interrogation room. Good luck."

"He's the one who's going to need it," she joked, then headed toward the interrogation room. She took a few minutes to consult the two witnessing cops standing by the two-way mirror.

"How's he doing in there?" she asked, and glanced at D'Angelo lounging back in his chair.

"He's quite a character," the police captain, Amy Tompkins said, shaking her head. "But Jorge did a pretty good job priming him for you."

"That's good to know."

Amy nodded. "When you're through with him, I want to hear everything you have on this Andrews kidnapping. From what I'm picking up, it sounds like something for the record books."

"You got it." As usual, Ming took a few deep breaths and slid on her best game face before she burst into the interrogation room.

D'Angelo's gaze jumped up to meet Ming's hard stare seconds before she swiped his feet off the table and made herself comfortable. "Tell me about your relationship with Michelle Andrews."

"Ah, Detective Delaney. What happened to my little Mexican friend?" A sly smile sloped the street thug's thick lips. "I didn't scare him off, did I?"

"No one here is your friend, D'Angelo. You got something for me or not? And before you speak, let me warn you: If I find out that you've lied to me about knowing, planning, or aiding in any of Michelle's illegal endeavors, I'll lock you up for so long that you'll forget how to spell freedom—let alone remember what it means."

D'Angelo laughed, but fell silent when Ming's expression remained hard and serious. He cleared his throat. "I ain't got nothin' to do with any murders."

Ming crossed her arms and waited patiently.

D'Angelo looked uncomfortable. "All right. She came and saw me today. Is that what you want to hear?"

"All I want is the truth." She kept her eyes trained on him. "We already know she came to see you."

"Well, that explains why you dragged my black ass down here." He started to kick his legs up again, but thought better of it when Ming's gaze smote him. "Now that I've confirmed this for you, am I free to leave?"

"No."

"Figures." D'Angelo rolled his eyes and hardened his jaw. "What else can I do for you, Delaney? I live to serve you."

"I need to know whether Michelle Andrews is masquerading as her twin sister Josephine Ferrell."

He tossed up his hands. "I don't know."

Ming allowed a deafening silence to choke the truth out of him.

"She might be. She didn't confess if that's what you're getting at. I'm not a priest."

Nodding, she swallowed her irritation and attacked from a different angle. "What's your specialty, D'Angelo?"

His sly smile returned. "A jack-of-all-trades and a master at a few."

"Uh-huh. But you're pretty good at forging documents, right?"

D'Angelo laughed. "Now I have 'stupid' stamped on my forehead?"

"I see it pretty clearly. After all, you're trying to con me." She finally smiled. "Just because we haven't been able to put you out of business doesn't mean we don't know everything about you."

His expression quickly turned somber. "Big Brother?"

"Always around to keep you in check." Ming winked. "The question now is: What would Andrews want with a man in your line of work?"

He said nothing.

She lifted her brows in mild amusement. "Was that little piece today worth acquiring a new boyfriend down in lockup?"

Shock colored his expression with vibrant red hues.

Ming enjoyed being in her element. "Big Brother is always watching."

"Fine." His eyes rolled again. "This ain't worth it. Michelle came to see me about getting a passport. Said she needed it in a hurry. But I'm guessing you knew that as well?"

Already suspecting something along these lines, Ming nodded and waited for him to continue.

"She also said that she needed some protection."

"She purchased a weapon?"

"Nah. Michelle already had that covered, but she wanted to borrow some muscle, so I loaned her a few of my best men."

"That was awfully nice of you."

D'Angelo's smile made a dramatic return. "Let's just say that she made it worth my while. The girl is a freak in the bedroom. Knows just how a man likes it, if you catch my drift."

"Unfortunately. Did you provide her with a passport?"

"No, Your Honor," he replied, bitingly. "I didn't exactly have time since your lynch men stormed my place thirty minutes after she left."

"What was the name she wanted on the passport?"

He hesitated, but finally gave up the ghost after another lethal dose of the silent treatment. "Josephine Ferrell. Are you happy now?"

Straight-faced, Ming stood from her chair. "Ec-static."

The day might have started off pretty badly, but Michelle loved how everything had turned around. During her ride back to the Ferrell Estate she reviewed everything that had transpired at Keystone and couldn't help the smile that exploded across her face. Josephine didn't hold all the cards after all.

You know what happens when you get overconfident, Michelle.

"It's Josephine. And I'm not listening to you."

The cackling voice inside her head only laughed. *You still have to kill her, you know. The world isn't big enough for two Josephine Ferrells.*

Michelle hated to admit it, but the voice was right. How long could she bank on Josephine's fear of going to the police?

"That woman is officially a pain in the ass."

True. But we still have to deal with her.

Michelle nodded and drummed her fingers against the steering wheel as she tried to devise a new plan. "How in the hell can I find her?"

The voice in her head fell silent.

"I always have to think of everything."

She turned her beloved red Jaguar onto the estate's curvy driveway with her mind wrapped around finding Josie and the large check she'd receive, possibly as early as tomorrow. At least now she didn't have to start selling things in the house.

Michelle parked the car in the east wing garage and entered the house through the kitchen. But she stopped cold when the house alarm began its slow beeping. She never set the alarm. Quickly, she dashed to the nearest keypad. "What the hell is the code?"

She couldn't remember.

Josie had told her once, but . . . damn.

The steady slow beeps began to pick up speed, narrowing her time to enter the correct code.

"It had something to do with someone she met in Paris," she fretted. "Initials—someone's initials." On a whim she punched in C.H.W. with no clue to why, but was certain she was right.

An error message strolled across the small green screen and the countdown continued.

Maybe it's in the wrong order.

"Shut up," she hissed, but then punched in W.H.C.

Another error message.

Michelle's heart hammered. Why couldn't she remember this? She punched in H.C.W.

Error.

H.W.C.

Error.

W.C.H.

The alarm chirped twice and the beeping stopped.

Relieved, she slumped against the wall.

That was close.

Michelle agreed. If the alarm had gone off and the security office called, she had no idea what the Ferrell password was to prevent the cops from being sent to the residence.

Who set the alarm?

An icy chill slithered down her back. She certainly hadn't set it. She glanced around the large, spacious kitchen, half-expecting a gremlin or ghoul to jump out. When, at last, she found nothing out of the ordinary hovering in any of the nooks or crannies, she proceeded to tiptoe out of the room.

The rest of the house was a huge fortress. Someone could be hiding anywhere.

"Josie," she whispered. "She set it."

She's screwing with you. Oh, this is good. Instead of us finding her, she's come to us.

Michelle had the same thoughts. Where in the hell were those damn bodyguards she got from D'Angelo?

Where did you put the gun?

"Upstairs in my bedroom." She glanced around as she inched through the house. "I should have seen this coming," she chastised.

The voice said nothing, undoubtedly because it agreed with her.

One thing she noticed was that the house seemed to creak each time she took a step, and no matter how much she tried to control her breathing, its sound magnified and bounced off every wall. When she reached the spiral staircase, Michelle had the ingenious idea of sliding off her pumps.

Afterward, she hesitated to ascend.

Don't tell me that the big bad wolf is afraid of a little mouse.

Michelle bristled and took her first step, but her brave front didn't last long. Halfway up, she found herself wondering again about her absent bodyguards. Was she walking into some kind of trap? Had Josie somehow bribed D'Angelo's men?

Wouldn't this be a delicious game if she had?

Michelle's heart rammed in her chest, her palms itched, and a line of sweat beaded across her hairline. No, it wouldn't be a good game. The only games she liked were the ones stacked in her favor.

There was nothing fun about this at all.

She reached the top stair and surveyed the area. Was she alone or was she supposed to guess behind what door danger awaited?

I choose door number three: Josie's old bedroom.

"It's *my* bedroom." Michelle stormed toward it, but then slowed when she'd actually made it to the door. She drew a deep breath, prepared herself for a fight, and pushed through the door.

Nothing.

It took a moment for Michelle's heart to stop pumping so much adrenaline and for the blood to stop rushing to her head. No one was there. However, there was the unmistakable scent of perfume in the air.

"*Beautiful*," she whispered. "Josie's favorite." She glanced across the room to the dainty gold-and-glass vanity. The bottles had been rearranged.

"She *was* here."

I'm starting to like your sister. Now she's *a class act.*

Michelle swallowed her anger and eased farther into the room. She reached the pile of boxes in the center of the floor; but before she could step over them, something crinkled under her foot.

She looked down and frowned at a picture. Kneeling, she picked it up. It was of Josie smiling broadly at the camera. God, how she hated the spoiled little rich girl standing in front of the Eiffel Tower, with her arms wrapped around a handsome man.

She stopped cold.

The man's face—she knew that face. Michelle turned the picture over and read. "Josephine Lynn Ferrell and William Charles Hayes in love forever." She flipped it over again and stared into Dr. Hayes's baby blue eyes.

"W.C.H. Well, I'll be damned."

Josie barreled down the streets of Atlanta with tears blurring her vision. Her headache had returned and had escalated into a full-blown migraine under the stress of her decision.

She would stick with William's plan and go to the police once her medical records arrived. She would tell them everything—including her role in killing Daniel Thornton.

Her body trembled, and she could barely manage to pull over into an abandoned shopping plaza. She needed to get ahold of herself before she did anything. There in the parking lot, Josie allowed herself the luxury of a good long cry.

It would be the last time she would do it, she promised herself—the last time she'd play the victim. When her tears dried, she felt better. Her roller-coaster emotions had to be a by-product of her detox, and they were the most exhausting things she'd ever endured.

Beside her in the passenger seat sat her pink box of memories, and seeing it returned her thoughts to William.

Doubt and fear rippled through her mind; but then she remembered what had transpired between them last night and this morning. None of it meant that he would remain by her side.

She massaged her hammering temples and remembered the bottle of Excedrin in her purse. William warned her about taking painkillers while she was in detox, but this migraine was beginning to feel like it was burning into her brain.

Across the lot, she spotted a McDonald's and shifted the car into drive. She'd just get some water to wash down her pills. Once she got rid of the migraine, she would decide her next move.

Parked a relatively safe distance from the Ferrell Estate, Detective Tyrese Simmons heaved a frustrated sigh and called his partner from his cell phone.

"Who's supposed to take the night shift?" Tyrese asked as he watched Andrews's goons finally arrive. "I have to tell you it's lonesome out here."

Ming laughed. "You poor baby. Anything interesting happening?"

"Well, there was this episode at a gas station. She couldn't get gasoline or something and went berserk. When we finally arrest her, we might need a straightjacket."

"How was she when she left Keystone?"

"A blur," Tyrese joked. "I think she was trying to qualify for the Indy 500."

"Sounds pretty bad."

"You're saying the right things, but I hear sarcasm." He smiled and shook his head.

"I can never get anything past you." She chuckled. "But it looks like surveillance duty might be a one-day deal. D'Angelo confessed Andrews paid him a visit today. She wanted a passport under Josephine Ferrell. But I think he's played a bigger part in this than he's letting on."

"You'll get the truth out of him. If anybody can, you can. How did your master plan for the fingerprints go?"

"Waiting for a comparison to Andrews's police file right now. With a little luck, we'll have her in custody tonight."

"Before we find out what she's done to her twin sister?"

"Given the long trail of dead bodies, do you really think she's still alive?"

Tyrese thought it over and had to admit that the chances were pretty slim, but, "There's always a chance."

"True." Ming drew a deep breath, and when she spoke again, her voice sounded weary. "What would you prefer we do—follow her around for a few more days?"

There was a long strained pause while he looked past the curvy driveway to the handsome mansion nestled in the center of an immaculately manicured lawn. "Nah. The sooner we end this, the better for all involved."

"You got it. I'll give you a call as soon as I receive word on the fingerprints."

"You know where you can find me."

The moment William opened the garage door his heart sank. The Mercedes was gone. He pulled inside and climbed out of his vehicle and stared at the empty spot as if his eyes were playing some sort of trick.

When he, at last, turned toward the kitchen entrance into the house, he still called out for Josie. However, silence was the only thing that greeted him.

It didn't make sense, he thought. Why would she leave? His footsteps quickened as he rushed from one room to the other. All the while, a wave of denial wiped out reality. After he reached the last bedroom, he plopped down on the edge of the bed as stunned disbelief coursed through him.

As that emotion left him, anger and betrayal began its own war within his veins. He had placed himself on a limb, sacrificed his career and life for her, and this was what he got in return? When in the hell was he ever going to learn his lesson?

"To hell with her," he swore, jumping up and storming back to the master bedroom. As he entered, he ripped opened his shirt and paid no heed to the buttons as they cannonballed across the room.

Once again, Josephine Ferrell had made a fool out of him, and he had no one to blame but himself. He turned on the shower and set the temperature to scalding hot. It was a justified punishment as far as he was concerned, but unfortunately his thoughts refused to focus on anything other than Josie.

What was that? William stilled as his ears perked at an undistinguishable sound. Frowning, he leaned forward and shut off the water and strained to hear the noise again.

"Josie?" he asked, with measured trepidation. It had to be her, he reasoned; but he had no explanation for his hackles standing at attention.

"Josie?"

The sound of footsteps stopped when he arrived at the bottom of the stairs. He reached for a light switch and was stunned when the lights didn't come on. He needed a weapon.

He turned, then rocked back when something hard slammed into his chin. He quickly shook it off and came up swinging at thin air. His efforts were rewarded with a steel punch to his abdomen. Air rushed from his lungs, and, before he could refill them, something crashed against the back of his skull and knocked him out cold.

Josie struggled to get back to William's house. However, she was having very little success. Instead, she had once again pulled into an empty lot, where she tried to combat another withdrawal spell. It was a bad one. Behind her closed lids, a dizzying kaleidoscope of colors spun around her, and an eerie cackle of laughter pierced her eardrums.

Suddenly, Josie was pulled from the memory. Her body seemed to float above itself. Then she was soaring—faster, and faster until she woke up with a gasp. Darkness surrounded her in the vehicle; her labored breathing was the only sound. She glanced around nervously, then her head slumped against the steering wheel.

"Why?" she sobbed. Why did she shoot him? Why didn't he try to defend himself?

She glanced at the clock on the dashboard. Seven-thirty. She was missing nearly two hours. *What in the hell happened?*

"I need to get out of here," she said, though she didn't quite know where "here" was. Her head pounded mercilessly, reminding her she still hadn't taken anything to relieve the pain.

Josie started the SUV, but took a few more minutes to get her bearings. One glance in the rearview mirror, and she concluded that she looked as bad as she felt.

She drove out of the parking lot and tried to find out exactly where she was. Though she had managed to calm herself, she was still scared. What if whatever her sister had done to her was irreversible?

Her mouth was dry, and she reached for the small cup of water, and her arm knocked over the green bottle of Excedrin.

The sound of it falling and hitting the seat seemed as if it had happened in slow motion. Her hackles rose as a platoon of goose bumps prickled her skin. And then it hit her.

She pulled over to the side of the road and dug for the bottle next to the box.

For as long as Josie could remember, she'd suffered with migraines at least once a week. Everyone knew that. Josie picked up the bottle and stared at it with new eyes.

Michelle would have noticed her frequent headaches and her dependency on her favorite pain reliever.

"That bitch."

An angry Josie pulled herself together and started up the car again. After getting lost a couple of times, she finally pulled into William's driveway forty-five minutes later. At the sight of the black Navigator, Josie cursed under her breath. She had a lot of explaining to do.

At the door, she took a deep breath and stepped inside. Immediately, she sensed that things were amiss.

Her hands roamed around the walls in search of a light switch. When she finally found one, nothing happened when she clicked it on.

"William?" she called out in a shaky whisper. Her voice echoed hauntingly through the place. She continued through the house on shaky legs. When she walked into the dining room, she gasped in surprised at the overturned furniture and the crunch of broken glass underfoot.

The thought of William lying hurt somewhere in the house was the only reason she didn't bolt out of there. However, every muscle was coiled, while the tiniest of hairs stood at attention.

"William?" she called again. At the silence, her eyes blurred with tears. Had Michelle's goons figured out where she was staying?

Next, she entered the living room. The moonlight illuminated its total destruction. Her heart sank, while her search for William became a desperate need.

At the base of the stairs, she slipped on something wet and hit the floor with a loud thud. Timidly, she touched the sticky substance.

A horrified scream rang in her ears as she tried to scramble away. Glass cut into her skin as she pushed herself off the floor and went back through the house. When she was back in the living room, her gaze caught sight of letters printed on a mirror above the fireplace.

Josie stopped in her tracks and read the eerie message, "Tag. You're it."

Michelle smiled when the phone rang. "I wonder who that could be," she mused to herself. She stood from the bar and walked over to the dainty gold-and-white phone. She waited for the third ring before she picked up. When she answered, she made sure honey oozed off her words.

"Hello. Ferrell residence, Josephine speaking."

"Where's William?" Josie hissed through the phone.

"Ah, sister dear. How did I know it would be you?"

"You're insane. I'm calling the police."

"Ah, ah, ah, ah," Michelle sang. "I wouldn't do that if I were you. If you do, you'd be signing your beloved doctor's death certificate."

When Josie failed to respond, Michelle's high cackle filled the line. "You're not going to call anyone, or have you forgotten about Daniel?"

"Very clever how you replaced the pills in the Excedrin."

"You like that, did you? Too bad you didn't catch on sooner. Of course, I have to admit that was pretty smooth what you pulled off at the bank. It's a shame that you'll have to give it all back."

"Not on your life."

Michelle frowned as she twisted the phone cord around her fingers. "Don't push me, Josie. You're running out of places to hide."

"You're sick."

"No. I'm just ambitious. I see what I want, and I go after it. You weren't doing anything with your life, just sitting in some big apartment in Paris bitching about how you couldn't sing anymore. Boo hoo. Me, on the hand, I know how to enjoy money. I should've been adopted by a rich family, not you."

"Should I play my violin for you, Michelle? I can even play it when they sentence you to death. How many people have you killed now?"

"Two fewer than I should have; but I plan to rectify that tonight, starting with your handsome doctor."

Another silence hung over the line before

Michelle's mad laugh returned. "What's the matter, sister dear? Cat got your tongue?

"I didn't put two and two together—until now. Dr. William Hayes, the one that got away. You told me about him once. It's quite a coincidence that you two would run into each other again at Keystone. I have to admit, I was baffled how you got out of that hospital the night I came to kill you, but now it all makes perfect sense."

"How did you—?"

"Find him?" Michelle laughed. "I have you and your breaking and entering to thank for that. You dropped a photograph on your way out."

Josie didn't respond.

The playfulness evaporated from Michelle's tone. "I want the money back, and you have less than an hour to make up your mind. Otherwise, the handsome doctor will meet the same fate as my dear Daniel—may he rest in peace. And make no mistake about it, Josie. I will kill him. Call me back in an hour with your decision. *¿Comprende?*" With another high cackle, Michelle disconnected the call.

Rain sprinkled across Josie's face and hands as she slowly placed the receiver back on the gas station's pay phone. Tears slid from her eyes while her heart squeezed painfully.

"Oh, William. What have I done?" Still in shock,

she returned to the Mercedes and just sat there. Josie had no trouble believing that Michelle would kill William if she went to the police.

She closed her eyes and tried to think, but William's loving blue gaze stared back at her. William was her heart. She had always believed that, despite all her protests and their long separation. He had risked everything to help her, and she had no choice but to meet with Michelle. There was a very real chance her sister would simply kill them both—if she hadn't killed him already.

But not as long as she had the money. That was the last ace up her sleeve. Michelle had no idea where she'd transferred the money. That alone should buy them some time.

Speaking of time, she glanced at the clock on the dashboard. Michelle had given her less than an hour and as much as she wanted to call her bluff, she knew better. At long last, Josie started the car and headed back out to her home.

Josie wasn't crazy enough to roll up the driveway and ring the front doorbell. For the life of her, she didn't know how Michelle would've found him within hours of her leaving the house.

Familiar with her father's estate like the back of her hand, Josie parked on her closest neighbor's land and entered the Ferrell Estate on foot through the south side of the property.

Unfortunately, the rain followed her, and she had nothing to shield her from the steady drops. She also didn't have anything to help calm her speeding heartbeat. As she crept along the side of the man-made lake and around the estate's sparse trees and bushes, Josie was well aware that she didn't have a clue as to what she was doing, but was propelled to continue simply because she didn't have a choice.

If William was killed, the blame was hers.

She regretted everything that she'd done that day. Everything could've been avoided if she'd just gone to the police with William. Hindsight was always twenty-twenty.

Josie rushed past the small lake and reached the pool and sauna in the backyard in no time flat. When she finally approached one of the back windows, she was unable to see anything through the Venetian blinds. She still had the spare key that would gain her entrance through the garage, but what would she do if Michelle were sitting in the kitchen waiting for her?

All the what-ifs were going to drive her mad. She wouldn't know until she actually did something. But Josie never reached the garage. The minute she eased around one corner, a pair of arms wrapped around her like a steel vise, and something hard hit her on the back of the head.

* * *

"We have a match," Ming announced to her small team as she pulled the crime lab report from the fax machine.

A small whoop of victory went up among her five-man team, but she didn't dabble with them long. She rushed over to her phone and immediately tried to get the captain on the phone. With D'Angelo's confession and the fingerprint match, she was sure to have enough to get permission to haul in the phony Ms. Josephine Ferrell.

Ten minutes later, she and her men received the go-ahead. "All right everyone, listen up. This should be a simple arrest, but we're dealing with a mentally ill suspect and one who's likely armed and dangerous."

Once Ming and Jorge piled into one of the cars, she quickly gave her partner a call.

"I thought that you forgot all about me," Tyrese said groggily into the phone.

"Don't tell me you're sleeping on duty," she joked, but a note of warning hung on her every word.

"I'm tired, but I haven't fallen asleep. Please tell me you have good news. I wasn't prepared to pull a twenty-four-hour shift."

"Well, hang in there. The cavalry is on its way."

"Fingerprints?"

"It's a match. Is Andrews still at Ferrell's?"

Tyrese cleared his voice. "Yeah. Her goons left

for a while, but then returned carrying something heavy. Sorry, I couldn't get a good look at what it was, but I'm curious though."

"Well, hold tight. We're on our way."

"Be warned. She could go quietly or she could go out like Scarface. After what I saw at the gas station, I think the woman might have a few screws loose or something."

"Tell me something I don't know. We should be there within a half hour. Call me if something changes."

"You got it, partner."

"Josie, wake up. Josie."

Pain ricocheted through Josie's head as she pried her eyes open. She tried to lift a hand to see whether she was bleeding, but her arms were bound behind her back, and more pain shot through her wrist.

"Oh, thank God." William sighed. "You're still alive."

Josie's heart leapt at the sound of the familiar voice, and she struggled even harder to see through the mesh of her eyelashes. "Will—?"

"Yes, sweetheart. It's me. Are you okay?"

Josie's vision finally focused, and she was horrified at the sight of his bloodied and bruised face. "Ohmigosh. What has she done to you?" She tried to move again, but realized that, like him, she was tied to a chair.

"I'm all right," he said. His eyes softened as they roamed over her face, and then slowly lowered. "Some hero I turned out to be, huh?"

Tears swelled and seeped from her eyes. How she wished she could reach out and hold him. "I think you're a wonderful hero. I'm the lousy heroine. I should have confided in you. I should have trusted you more."

William swung his weight and scooted his chair over to her. "Never mind about me. How are you? When they brought you in I thought—"

"Will—"

"Please, let me finish," he begged, then licked his swollen lips. "It scared me. All I could think about was all the time we've wasted. My head filled with a list of things I've never said . . . all the things my pride wouldn't let me say."

"William, don't—" she blurted out, but winced at the booming sound of her voice. "There's something I have to tell you."

The room's door burst open, and a smiling Michelle sauntered inside. "Well, well, well. Just what I've always wanted: an attentive audience. I hope you're comfy, sister dear."

Hatred curdled in Josie's belly while her rage had her struggling against the tight rope.

"Relax," Michelle said, rolling her eyes. "My boys made sure those knots were nice and tight." Her gaze swung between the couple. "You know, neither of you have thanked me for reuniting you two lovebirds. What has it been fifteen . . . sixteen years? I should at least get flowers."

Josie frowned as she listened to Michelle's insane ramblings. "You'll never get away with this."

"I already have. You know, at first when Danny and I cooked up this scheme, I had my doubts; but I'm just amazed by how little people missed you. What did you do after your failed musical career—live under a rock or something?"

The verbal attack struck a raw nerve in Josie, mainly because it held a note of truth. She hadn't done much after her career, and now that she might very well be at the end of her life, she couldn't help but wish she had the wasted time back.

Michelle snickered as she eased farther into the room. This time her attention was centered on William. "I have to hand it to you, Josie. You certainly have a good eye when it comes to men." She reached out and ran her fingers through his hair. "Too bad *we* never hooked up. You look like you know how to show a girl a real good time. Of course, it's not too late."

William jerked his head away from her touch, but watched her through wary eyes.

"I take that as a no." Michelle sighed and lowered her hand back to her side. "You know"—she hiked her skirt up to midthigh and straddled him in the chair—"I've never liked the word 'no.' That's why I always *take* what I want."

She struggled to turn his head back toward her, and when she failed, she instead gave him a long, wet lick against the side of his face. Michelle turned her head and winked at her sister. "He tastes pretty good."

"Get the hell off me," he hissed, and tried to buck her off his lap.

Michelle's head rocked back with a hearty laugh. "This is the most fun I've had in months." She delivered another lick and a high cackle.

"You're crazy." Josie strained against her ropes.

Michelle "tsked" under her breath. "What's the matter? You don't like sharing your toys?" She climbed off William's lap and moved toward her sister.

Before Josie thought about what she was going to do, she pitched her body forward, stood in a crunched position, and hit Michelle in the stomach, head-on, like a wrecking ball.

"Josie," William shouted.

Michelle screamed as she hit the floor with a thud.

Pain exploded in Josie's body.

Michelle's two bodyguards rushed inside the room.

William assumed the same tactical position and

bowled sideways into them. They toppled over as William's chair shattered with a crunch beneath him and his ropes slackened.

Michelle gathered her senses, regained her footing, and batted her arms against Josie's head and body.

Josie couldn't defend herself, and it wasn't long before she tasted blood. Yet she wouldn't give her sister the satisfaction of knowing how hurt she was by crying out or begging for mercy, so she took each blow silently.

Though William was free from his binding, he was quickly restrained by one of the muscled bullies and turned into a punching bag by the other. He only managed once to rear back and kick his feet upward and clock his assailant hard across the jaw.

However, it was his only good move. His assailant shook off the blow as though a mere mosquito had stung him. The next punch William received nearly broke a rib.

Less than a minute after their brave attempt to fight back, both William and Josie were reduced to battered heaps on the floor.

The two bodyguards helped their boss back onto her feet.

"Get her up," Michelle commanded, while her body shook with uncontrollable rage.

The men lifted and righted Josie's chair just as Michelle wedged her way in between them and grabbed a fistful of Josie's hair.

Josie winced, but she didn't make a sound.

You need the money before you kill her.

"I'm only going to ask you one time," Michelle hissed. "What did you do with the money?"

Josie wasn't foolish enough to answer. It was her last playing card and an ace at that.

"Either you tell me, or lover boy gets it," Michelle warned.

"You're going to kill us anyway, and I'd rather die than see you with my father's money."

Michelle laughed. "Don't kid yourself. Your so-called father didn't want you around any more than mine. Mine shoved me into one hospital after another while yours shipped you to some foreign boarding school. So you can just stop looking down on me, because you're no better than I am."

Josie's eyes and heart hardened.

Michelle's thugs finished redoing William's ropes, but left him planted on the floor since his chair had been demolished.

"Why did you kill Dr. Bancroft?" William asked, interrupting the women's conversation.

She glanced at him with disdain. "Other than the fact that I never liked her? I figured since my darling Ambrose wouldn't kill Josie through a drug overdose as he promised, I knew it would only be a matter of time before my old doctor realized that Josie wasn't me. I couldn't have that now, could I?"

"And Ambrose?"

"Because he didn't keep his promise. Plus, after Bancroft's untimely death, he was a little too jumpy, and he knew too much."

"What about your *boyfriend?*" he asked. "Why in the hell did you kill him?"

"Daniel?" Michelle smiled. "Why don't you ask my sister about Daniel?"

"Shut up," Josie barked.

Michelle shrugged. "She did me a favor. I didn't want to split her inheritance down the center, especially since I had to do all the work. And it all ends tonight."

Josie shook her head. "It's not quite the speech to give when you want me to hand over a fortune."

"Actually, I don't care if you tell me where it is. As of tomorrow, Keystone Institute is cutting me a nice multimillion-dollar check; well, cutting you a check." She smirked. "It'll be enough to last until I find out what you did with the money. I'll apply for new credit cards, sell the house, whatever."

Swallowing, Josie's last ace was slowly turning into a deuce.

A lopsided smile shaped Michelle's lips. "For

what it's worth, I'm going to sure miss you." She leaned down and kissed Josie solidly on the mouth. "Keep a warm seat for me in hell." She winked, then turned to her hired hands. "Get rid of them."

Detective Simmons ignored his stomach's grumbling, but remained bored watching the distant house. He prayed that his partner and their small team would arrive soon. Suddenly, movement at the front door of the estate caught his attention and he reached over to the passenger seat and grabbed his binoculars.

D'Angelo's goons were loading something big and heavy into the trunk of a car. It was hard to make out, but their load resembled a body. He adjusted the focus on his lens but by that time, the men had closed the trunk.

"What the hell are you guys up to?" he whispered, trying to figure things out.

Michelle and the men piled into the car.

"Okay, something *is* going on." He reached for his cell phone and dialed Ming. "Where are you?"

"About three minutes out. Why? What's going on?"

"It looks like the gang is clearing out." He watched the car head off down the driveway, but it cut across the manicured lawn to head toward the back of the house. "Something is definitely up." He opened his car door.

"Any way that you can sneak on the property to see what's going on?"

"I'll probably have to go on foot, but consider it done."

"Okay, but stay on the phone with me."

"You got it."

Scared, bound, and crunched in a spoon position in the trunk of a car, Josie and William were faced with the realization that this could be the end. However, Josie was grateful for small mercies. Michelle and her men didn't gag them. In this moment where there was so much to say, she didn't know where to begin, and as a result, she didn't say anything.

"I love you, Josie," William whispered. "I know it's probably not what you want to hear, but if this is the end, I want you to know that I've never stopped loving you." He inched closer until their bodies touched, then pressed a kiss against the back of her head.

Fresh tears seeped from Josie's eyes. "I love you, too, William. I always have."

"Shh." He kissed her again. "You don't have to say that."

"It's the truth." She sniffed. "I never married Etienne. I couldn't."

"What?"

"When Etienne returned that summer, I couldn't go through with it. I broke our engagement and came to Georgia to find you."

Silence greeted her confession, but she continued. "I hired someone to find you and when I learned about your apartment near the Emory campus, I came to surprise you."

"Oh, Josie," he groaned.

"Sammy answered the door. She was literally glowing with happiness."

"I-I had no idea."

"Of course you didn't. How could you? I heard you ask who was at the door, and I made some excuse of having the wrong apartment. I didn't stick around for her to ask any questions. I just had to get out of there."

Josie waited for his response, but when he didn't say anything, she continued. "The first time I woke up with you by my side, I thought God was playing a cruel joke. I would've never believed in a million years our paths would cross again, but there you were again the next morning. It all seemed too good to be true."

After a brief moment of silence, she felt another kiss, and a flood of tears streamed down her face.

"But now look at what I've done. I'm responsible for dragging you into this," she sobbed.

"Don't say that," he commanded. "I was involved the moment I took you from Keystone."

"I killed Daniel," she went on. "That's the real reason I didn't want to go to the police."

"Shh. It's okay. I'm sure Michelle had more to do with that than you think."

Josie shook her head. "And I dropped a picture of you in the house today. Michelle put two and two together."

"Josie, we can go back and forth, and it's not going to change anything. We need to figure a way out of this mess."

That was impossible until Josie remembered. "I have a .22 in an ankle strap."

"What?"

"Tammy said a girl should always carry backup."

"Who?" He shook his head. "Never mind. There's hope. If I could just try and reposition myself, I can undo your hands with my mouth, then we can work our way from there."

Hope flourished throughout her body. "Do you think you can do it?"

"I'm going to give it a try."

Michelle was on top of the world as she drove down the hilly landscape toward the lake at the bottom of the property. In a few minutes, she would be rid of Josie forever and her transformation would be complete.

"Who's a lost cause now?"

It's not over until the fat lady sings.

She chuckled. "You just can't give me credit for pulling this off, can you?" Her laughter deepened. "It doesn't matter. Once I get to Rio or something and find a new quack doctor to prescribe my lithium pills, I'll be rid of you, too."

"Are you talking to us?" gorilla number one asked.

Michelle's eyes narrowed. "Did I call your name?" Not that she knew it.

The high cackle reverberated throughout the walls of her brain. *Is that what you think? You can get rid of me? Please, I'll always be here, watching you screw up everything. And trust me. You'll screw this up as well. You wouldn't be you if you didn't.*

"A lot you know." Michelle gritted her teeth and swerved to miss a bush.

The men in the car stared at her again.

Look at you. You're going to kill us before we even get there.

Michelle slowed, not because she agreed with her inner voice, but because they had reached the lake. "This is it," she whispered, and an anxious smile ballooned on her face.

Stopping a few feet from the lake, she and her men climbed out of the car.

"Are you sure this is such a hot idea?" the gorilla challenged. "What if the lake isn't deep enough?"

"It's deep enough," she assured him.

"What if the car doesn't sink?"

She stared at the clueless man. "And why wouldn't it sink?"

He shrugged. "I don't know. Luther?"

Luther hunched his shoulders. "All I know is that D'Angelo didn't say anything about killing nobody."

"I'll pay him later for the favor."

Luther shook his head. "Those type of things need to be negotiated up front."

"Fine," she hissed. "I'll do it myself." She stormed back to the driver's side door and pulled out the Glock they'd confiscated from Josie. She shifted the car into drive, then moved out of the way when it started to roll into the lake. When it passed her, she aimed the gun at the trunk.

"Watch and learn," she said slowly like freshly sapped maple, and fired two shots.

"Gunshots fired! Gunshots fired!" Tyrese shouted as he huffed toward the mansion. He dropped the phone and reached for the gun at his waist. He was still too far away from the house, let alone from whatever was going on in the back.

Behind him, two pairs of headlights appeared. He turned and instantly recognized the vehicles rushing toward him. The first one slowed long enough for him to open the back door and jump inside.

"Something is going on in the back," he shouted.

The car sped off and within seconds crested the hill and accelerated even more toward the three figures by the lake. Each stared up at them like deer caught in headlights.

"What the hell!" Michelle lifted the gun at the first car and fired straight at the driver.

The car swerved off course and her next shot missed the person sitting in the passenger seat.

Suddenly, the night was alive with gunfire.

D'Angelo's men found themselves caught in the cross fire. Luther was the first to go down.

Michelle didn't see what happened, nor did she care. She was too busy scrambling behind the bushes. She heard a splash and peeked around to see the car she'd shot at hit the water, but she also caught sight of a tall Asian woman rolling away from the lake.

I don't think it's wise to be shooting at the cops, Michelle.

"Shut up!" She glanced around, spotted another bush, and made a mad dash for it. After another glance, she saw the man she'd referred to as "gorilla" holding his own in the midst of the chaos.

Here's to another screwup.

Michelle rubbed the gun against her head. "Shut up!" Her gaze found the house off in the distance. "I just need to make it up the hill."

An unfathomable terror swarmed through Josie as she kept her head above the water that poured in around her. "William, where are you?"

She struggled against her ropes and tried to flip over. Was he hit? Was he dead?

"Dear God, help us," she said through short, asthmatic pants. She wiggled some more, hoping at least to feel William's body somewhere near her, but she was caught off guard when her hands unraveled from the rope.

William's head splashed above the surface. "Hurry up and undo me."

"Are you okay?"

"Hurry." His head slipped back under.

Seconds later, both were submerged in the dirty, silty water as the car plunged to the bottom of the lake.

The moment Ming had hit the ground and rolled away, she realized only she and Tyrese had escaped the car. "Jorge didn't make it out," she shouted to her partner.

"I'll get him. You go after Andrews!"

She climbed to her feet and sprinted for cover.

Tyrese dived into the muddy lake water like an Olympic diver.

A bullet zinged past Ming's left ear. Stunned, she cupped her lobe with one hand and shot at her attacker with the other. Her first bullet took one of the muscle-bound men down; the second one missed his partner.

The other two officers sprayed the perimeter

with bullets, though just like in a bad movie, somehow they all missed.

The initial numbness in Ming's ear morphed into an excruciating pain. Determined it wouldn't slow her down, she sprinted into the long line of short-cropped bushes and struggled to make out Andrews. It was hard to see anything while trying not to lose a chunk of her backside.

Michelle had to be headed toward the house, Ming deduced, and ran in that direction.

Josie was never good at holding her breath for a long time, but tonight all that changed. It seemed like forever undoing the tight knots around William's wrists. Afterward, she immediately reached for the .22 at her ankle. She had less than a second to worry about ricocheting bullets before she placed the nozzle against the trunk's keyhole and pulled the trigger.

The water pressure prevented the trunk from springing open. Josie rolled onto her back and pushed her legs up with all of her might. Her head started to spin from lack of oxygen, and her body begged for her to breathe. She couldn't tell if the trunk had opened; she was too worried whether her lungs would explode or not.

An arm wrapped around her waist and suddenly she was rising. However, they weren't reaching the surface fast enough, she needed oxygen *now*.

Josie gasped just as her head broke the surface.

She coughed, sputtered, and coughed again as her chest rose and fell with great heaving breaths. Beside her, with his arms still tight around her waist, William went through the same process to clear out his lungs.

Josie wanted to ask whether he was okay, but talking was an arduous chore. Belatedly, she became aware of short pops that sounded like firecrackers.

Someone was shooting.

She lifted her right hand and was grateful she still held the .22. She glanced at William, but neither risked speaking or drawing attention to themselves. Silently, they waded to the edge of the lake with the hope that the large blue car parked there would aid as cover.

William pressed a finger to his lips and boosted her out first. Yet, when it came time to pull himself out, pain blasted through the left side of his body.

Suddenly, the shooting stopped.

"William, what is it?" In an instant she forgot about the surrounding danger and focused on him.

He groaned and struggled again to get out of the lake. The task appeared too difficult.

"Here, let me help." Josie set the gun down and grabbed one of his arms and pulled.

It was a slow process, but through pain-filled groans they managed to get him out. William immediately rolled onto his back and clutched at his left arm.

She dropped to her knees beside him. "Baby, what is it? Were you hit?"

He nodded and sucked in air through gritted teeth.

"Where?" Panicking, she pushed open his shirt to see. His pale skin glowed in the night—so did the bright trail of blood that streamed from his left shoulder. "Oh my God. We have to get you to a hospital."

Remarkably, he gave a short chuckle and pushed her hand away. "That's going to have to wait."

"You're losing a lot of blood." His wounded growl tore out her heart. "There has to be something I can do."

He nodded. "We need to find something to slow down the bleeding."

Josie glanced around, then tugged at the sleeve of her shirt. Within seconds, she'd ripped the material cleanly from her arm and proceeded to tie it tightly around his shoulder.

Splash!

Josie and William jumped.

Josie also reached for her .22 and aimed it at the figure . . . the two figures in the water.

"Don't shoot. Police," a man choked out through heavy pants.

She froze at the preposterous declaration, but she didn't have time to ask any questions. Two short pops came from her left and she turned to see one of Michelle's bodyguards shooting at the cop.

Josie shifted her aim and fired. Time slowed as the shot missed its target, and the thug turned his attention to her.

Another shot came from the lake, and she watched with stunned fascination when the man spun like a marionette and hit the ground.

Her gaze traveled to the shooter, the man who'd identified himself as police. On guard, Josie took a protective stance before William and kept her gun trained on the man approaching them.

Josie frowned at the man's stunned expression. "Andrews?"

Her hand tightened on the gun. "Ferrell."

"The real one," William added weakly.

A smile ballooned across the wet cop's face. "You're alive." He heaved the man next to him out of the water. "Can you help me with him?"

Josie hesitated.

"Here, hand me the gun," William said. "I'll make sure he doesn't make any sudden moves."

After thinking it over for a second, she did as William suggested. Together, she and the cop managed to get the second body out of the water.

When the officer climbed out, he was a flurry of movement, removing the still man's tie and performing CPR.

"Do you need any help?" William asked, cautiously.

"One one thousand, two one thousand. I got it covered, four one thousand." The cop pinched the man's nose and blew into his mouth.

Josie itched to help as well, but had never learned this medical procedure. It didn't look like it would matter though, the cop's buddy or partner wasn't responding.

"Come on, Jorge. Breathe for me."

More gunfire sounded off in the distance, and Josie jerked in the direction of the house. "What in the hell is going on?"

"At this point, I have no idea," the cop said. He pinched the man's nose and blew into his mouth again.

To her surprise the man coughed and spewed out water. She watched as he then curled onto his side, and his body rattled with gurgling water.

"Are you all right, man?" the cop asked.

Jorge coughed and shook his head. "Hit."

"Where?"

"Arm."

In no time the cop also tore off some of the man's clothing to stem the blood loss.

Another round of gunfire came from the house.

"Jorge, I'm going to have to leave you here while I go and check on the others. I also need to get backup out here. I'm going to leave you with . . ."

"William and Josie," William answered.

"Yeah, with these guys, okay? Nod if you understand me."

Slowly, Jorge nodded.

"Wait." Josie caught the cop by the arm. "If you're going after my sister, I want to come."

The cop shook his head. "I can't allow that. I need for you to watch over these men. I'll get help," he promised.

She wanted to argue, but knew by the level of intensity in the cop's eyes that it would be a moot point. Forcing a smile, she nodded and encouraged him to leave. When he was gone, she returned her attention to William.

"You're going, aren't you?" he asked.

"I can't let her get away."

"Let the police handle it. If you go up there, they could confuse you with Michelle."

He was right. It made sense.

"I have to do this," she insisted. "I'll be fine."

"Josie, no. I can't lose you like this. Stay here, and let the authorities handle it."

She wanted to stay. Lord knows she did, but this was something she had to do.

"Josie, don't go," he asked with a wry smile.

"Please, try and understand," she pleaded. "I promise I'll be back."

Their gaze locked, and she was besieged with a list of things she wanted to say, but there wasn't time. "I love you," she said at last.

"Wait." He laid a restraining hand on her shoulder. "Take this." He handed her the gun.

He smiled, and his eyes lit with tenderness. "Make sure you come back to me."

"You got yourself a promise." She kissed him again, taking a little longer to savor the taste of his lips. She pulled away, but Jorge now placed a restraining hand on her arm.

"No," he croaked.

Josie pulled his hand away. "I'm sorry, but this is personal."

Once again, you screwed up.

Michelle had no sooner opened one of the side French doors when she heard two shots behind her. Close shots. Warning shots. She turned blindly and fired.

A lost cause. Your parents were right. You're a lost cause.

Michelle kicked the door closed and raced across the sunroom. In her mad dash, she abandoned her high-heel pumps. "I just need to grab a few things."

You need to get the hell out of here.

"My purse, car keys." She gasped. "The chinchilla."

A fur coat? Have you completely lost it?

"Stop talking. I can't think." She cupped her head with her hands.

Pathetic. The voice cackled. *You just declared war on the police and you still think you're going to get away with this?*

"Shut up. Shut up." Michelle stopped at the foot of the banister and hit her right temple with the butt of her gun.

The voice quieted while she drew several breaths and calmed down.

"Andrews?" A familiar voice called out.

Michelle jumped and glanced around. Someone had made it into the house.

Get out of the damn house.

"Give it up, Andrews. D'Angelo has already sold you out, and we lifted your fingerprints today at Keystone. There's no settlement money— just a nice eight-by-ten jail cell with your name on it."

"You're lying," she shouted.

The high cackle returned. *I knew it. You're an idiot.*

"It's the truth, Michelle. The four lawyers you met today were cops. Give yourself up."

"She's lying. She has to be." Michelle turned in time to see a curtain of black silk hair appear from around the corner, and she fired in its direction. She missed, then dodged out the way when Delaney returned fire.

"You're not going to win this one, Andrews," Delaney yelled. "Give it up."

Michelle crawled along the marble floor toward the foyer. She could win this. She had to win.

Didn't you hear her? There's no money, and you just drowned your last meal ticket.

"Michelle!"

She turned with her gun outstretched, but Delaney wasn't behind her.

"Talk to me, Michelle."

"My name is Josephine," she whispered, and rubbed the gun at her temples.

Maybe she's the last cop alive. Who knows, maybe D'Angelo's men were good for something after all?

"Where is she?"

Let me take over. If we kill her, then maybe we still have a chance of getting out of this mess.

Michelle warmed to the idea.

Ming had no idea where she was headed in the house. The place was like a fortress, and Michelle could be anywhere. However, if she could just keep the woman talking, she had a chance of zeroing in on her.

"Where's Josephine, Michelle? What did you do with her?"

A high, eerie cackle reverberated off the walls surrounding Ming. The laughter didn't help locate Michelle since it seemed to be coming from all directions. There was no doubt in her mind the tables had just turned, and she was now the hunted.

Ming drew a deep breath and reengaged in her tactical objective. "What's so funny, Michelle? Did you harm Josephine?"

In answer, a shot was fired, and a vase exploded near Ming's head. She turned to her immediate left and tumbled over a glass table. As she fell sideways, she fired her weapon blindly, but she was stunned when her head banged off the corner of another table.

Focus, focus. Stay in focus, she warned herself, but pain raced through her head like a locomotive and darkened the edges of her vision.

Michelle's voice floated threateningly in the air above Ming, and she fired at a moving blur.

"Say hi to Josie for me," Michelle cackled from the upstairs landing.

A gun fired.

Michelle slammed into the wall behind her with a shriek and dropped her weapon. Slowly, her eyes lowered to her blue chemise and stared in horror at the blossoming red rose.

"Anything you want to say, you say it to me," Josie growled, as she kept her gun trained above her. When Michelle fell back, she also disappeared from view, but Josie waited and strained her ears for the slightest sound.

Then suddenly she saw a gun and dived for

cover. Two quick shots were fired and punctured two holes in the wall, where Josie had last stood.

"You think you can take me?" Michelle's high cackle echoed through the house.

Josie crawled along the floor, hoping to find a spot not visible from the landing above her. *What in the hell is she doing?* she wondered belatedly.

She urged herself to remain calm, but the house had gone too quiet. *Where the hell is she now?*

Josie glanced across the room to the fallen woman. Was she another agent? Were there more?

"Peekaboo," Michelle sang.

Another shot rang out, and Josie felt the sting of a bullet graze her face, but she wasted no time in firing back in the same direction bullet came. At the sound of Michelle's startled gasp and a hard thud, Josie guessed she had hit her mark.

She inched out of her hiding place for a better view of the landing over her. She didn't see anything. *Is Michelle dead?*

Her attention flew back to the Asian woman on the floor, and she decided to first check on her. She knelt and felt for a pulse. The woman was still breathing, but one of her ears was bleeding.

A couple of minutes had passed, and Josie still didn't hear anything from upstairs. She needed to check on Michelle. She needed to see if it was finally over.

The Asian woman stirred.

Josie lowered her weapon to ask whether she was all right and was completely taken by surprise when the woman placed a gun at her temple. "Don't shoot."

"Come to finish me off, Michelle?" The Asian managed awkwardly to rise from the floor. "Drop your weapon."

"You don't understand. I'm—"

"Drop it!"

Josie slowly lowered her gun. "You're making a mistake. I'm Josephine Ferrell."

"Sure you are, and I'm . . ." The woman's eyes narrowed, then roamed over Josie's attire.

"She's telling the truth," a man's voice floated toward them.

Josie turned to see the same cop from the lake.

The female cop lowered her weapon, but she continued to look at Josie with a surprise. "Please, place your weapon on the floor," she instructed.

She glanced at Simmons again and at his encouraging nod, and Josie did as she was told.

"Where is Andrews?"

"Upstairs," Josie answered. "I shot her before she could finish you off."

The woman looked to her partner. "Check it out."

He nodded and rushed across the living room.

"Detective Delaney." The woman stretched out her hand.

Josie glanced at it, then accepted the handshake. "Nice to meet you."

"Got to tell you, I thought you were dead."

"I nearly was."

"We got a problem," Simmons yelled from the upstairs landing.

Josie and Delaney looked up.

Simmons met each of their gazes. "There's a trail of blood up here, but Andrews is gone."

Michelle crawled inside the red Jaguar and placed the gun in her lap as a river of sweat tickled down the sides of her face. The pain spreading across her body was nearly unbearable, but she was determined to get out of there.

You still could have finished them off.

She ignored the voice and struggled to put her key into the ignition.

She was right there in front of us. Right there.

"I need to get out of here," Michelle panted, still fumbling with the keys.

What are you talking about? We can't leave until we kill them. Go back in there.

"Please shut up." She finally slid in the right key and punched for the door of the garage to open. "I just need to get somewhere so I can think."

There's nothing to think about. You have to kill them all. It's the only way.

"N-no. I can't," she moaned. "I have to th-think. My chest hurts."

Stop whining. This is what you always do when the going gets rough. You wanted this, remember? You wanted to be Josephine. Suck it up and get back in there and take care of business.

"Shut up." Michelle groaned and shifted the car into drive. However, the moment she pulled out of the garage she stopped.

In front of her, and to her astonishment, a long trail of flashing blue-and-white lights charged up the driveway.

"The police."

The voice's high-pitched cackle rattled her eardrums. She pressed her fingers to the inside of her ears and tried to block out the sound.

What did I tell you? I knew you'd screw this up. What are you going to do now?

"Andrews, get out of the car."

Michelle glanced to her left to see Detective Delaney pointing a gun in her direction.

See? What did I tell you? You should have killed that bitch when you had the chance.

Michelle's hand lowered and drifted to the gun in her lap.

Shoot her now. We never liked her anyway.

"Shut up." She hit her head against the butt of the gun. "I have to think. I need to think."

"Andrews, lower the weapon."

Shoot her, dammit.

Michelle rocked in her seat and banged her head even harder while one side of her body seemed to grow numb. "Think. I just need to think."

There's no time to think.

"Shut up," she cried, desperately wanting some peace.

"Andrews!"

Michelle glanced at the agent again, and this time she noticed Josephine standing just inches behind her.

You need to take at least one of them out. It's only fair.

"I swear if you don't shut up." She placed the gun's nozzle against her temple.

I knew you'd wimp out. You're pathetic. A lost cause.

"Please, just shut up."

"Andrews, put the gun down. It doesn't have to end like this."

No. It's going to end with you in an eight-by-ten cell with a straightjacket on.

"I'm warning you," Michelle hissed, as tears rolled from her eyes.

That's where you belong, anyway. You know it. Your parents knew it as well.

"Andrews!"

"I said *shut up*," Michelle screamed, pulled the trigger, and finally quieted the voice forever.

"It's over," Josie whispered, and was surprised to feel the trickle of tears as she stared unblinkingly at the mess inside the Jaguar. When an arm weakly encircled her waist, she slumped into its familiar warmth and comfort.

"Are you all right?" William asked.

She nodded, not sure if it was the truth. She turned toward him and was shocked by his weakened condition. "Help! Somebody help!"

He collapsed, but help arrived.

Before long, ambulances and more police officers pulled Josie and William in two separate directions.

As Detectives Delaney, Simmons, and Hernandez conversed, the lake, the house, and even the garage area were taped off as crime scenes.

"I'll need to bring you in for questioning," Delaney said, drawing her to the side. "We have a lot of questions to ask you."

"Where are you taking William?" Josie asked instead.

"They're taking him to the hospital to look at his shoulder. We—"

"I want to go with him," she declared, pulling away from the agent.

"Ms. Ferrell, I understand your concern, but—"

"I'm not answering any questions until I know William is all right. Period."

Delaney held Josie's gaze for a lengthy spell before her demeanor softened, and she nodded in understanding. "Then let's get you to him."

They reached the ambulance just as they were closing the door, but she wasn't allowed inside until Delaney flashed her badge and gave the okay.

"I'll meet you at the hospital," Delaney said.

Josie nodded, and the doors were closed. However, during the race to the hospital, she found herself worried over William's blue pallor.

"Is he going to be all right?"

"We're doing all we can," the paramedic said. "He's lost a lot of blood."

She clutched William's hand, afraid more than ever that she was going to lose him. It would make sense, considering the hand life kept dealing them. She leaned over him and stared lovingly into his eyes.

"You're doing great." Her smile trembled. "They're going to patch you up, and you're going to be as good as new."

Amazingly, he returned her smile and squeezed her hand.

"You know, once you're all better, we have a lot of lost time to make up." She placed his hand across her heart. "I made you a promise, and now I want you to make one to me. Promise me that you'll pull through this."

He smiled again; his eyes were nearly closed shut. Could he understand her?

"Promise me, William," she urged, and batted back her tears.

His lips trembled but soon formed the words "I promise" before he at last passed out.

True to her word, Ming and Tyrese met Josie in the ER's waiting room. It turned out that one of the bullets Michelle had fired into the trunk was still lodged in William's shoulder.

The possibility of losing William forever unleashed a dam of tears and twisted the knife of regret deeper into Josie's heart.

His death would be all her fault and her undoing.

William had only wanted to help her and have a

chance at rekindling their love. And she . . . what—couldn't get over the fact that he had been married once?

She mopped her tears with an already-drenched Kleenex and gave her story to an attentive Delaney while they waited for news.

She told them everything. How she and William knew each other from Paris and how he saved her. She couldn't control her body's slight tremor as she talked, but the episode was mild compared to previous ones.

"I also have a confession to make," Josie said. "I killed Michelle's boyfriend." She started to cry. "I don't why, but I shot him in the chest."

"You shot him?" Ming asked.

"Y-yes."

"What else did you do?" she asked, gently.

"That's it. I just shot him. I don't even know where I got the gun."

"I do," Ming said. "It was Michelle's gun. Knowing her, she probably gave it to you. In your drugged state, she probably wanted you to think you had killed him so that your guilt could be used to get you to kill yourself." She reached for Josie's scarred hands."

Josie pulled her hands away, then lowered her face into them.

"The only problem is . . . is that you didn't kill Daniel Thornton."

Josie lifted her wet face and stared at her in confusion.

"According to Daniel's autopsy report, he was already dead when you shot him."

"Already dead?" Josie repeated. "But then that means . . ."

"That you're not a murderer."

Josie stared at her. "I didn't kill him."

"No."

Josie grabbed the cop in a fierce embrace and sobbed in relief. It seemed as if she held on forever, and when she pulled away, Josie smiled in embarrassment.

"Ms. Ferrell, after everything that you've been through, have you thought about enrolling in a rehab center to complete your detox efforts?"

Josie laughed through her film of tears. "No more institutions. I can handle a few shakes on my own."

Delaney nodded, and her voice softened as she spoke again. "By the way, Ms. Ferrell. I didn't get the opportunity to thank you for saving my life. Thank you."

"I did what I had to," Josie said simply.

Delaney winked and squeezed her hand. "That's all for now, but we'll contact you if we have any more questions. I'm glad you were able to survive this whole ordeal."

"Yeah. I just pray William will, too."

"I'm sure he will."

Josie gave her and Tyrese a gracious smile. "Thank you." Her eyes landed on Ming. "For everything."

"Don't mention it."

Ming and Tyrese stood and left Josie alone.

Tyrese shook his head as they walked out of the hospital's exit. "Now that I met both women, Michelle couldn't hold a candle to the real Josephine."

Ming nodded. "Yeah, it's a pity how differently they turned out. Well, partner, I'm heading home."

"Catching some Zs?"

"That and I have a houseplant that needs to be watered." She smiled.

"Come again?"

"I'm going to go home, take the phone off the hook, and make *love* to my husband."

Tyrese laughed. "Conan is going to be a happy man."

"Damn right he is."

William dreamed of Paris. He dreamed of dancing in the moonlight, kissing in the rain, and making love by candlelight. For the first time, the images weren't of the past, but what he hoped for the future.

At long last, he exited the dream and returned

to the present. However, he had a devil of a time opening his heavy eyelids. Light stabbed his eyes. Tensing, he slammed them shut.

"William?"

He struggled to open them again. "Josie?" His heart warmed as her image came into focus. "Is that you?"

"Of course, it's me, silly. I won't dare leave your side. We made promises to each other, remember?"

His laugh was stiff and painful. "How could I forget?"

"What about you?"

"I'm happy you kept your promise." Josie smiled and kissed him gently. She surrendered to all the emotions his lips drew from her. When the kiss ended, Josie slowly drifted down from the clouds.

"You finally have your life back."

She nodded, but her eyes lowered.

"W-what is it?" He licked his dry lips.

Josie immediately turned and poured him a cup of iced water. "It's nothing."

William greedily gulped down the water, then waited until she set the cup back onto the table before he continued. "You're not thinking about all that stuff your sister said to you, are you?"

"What? The part where she said I wasted my life away and that no one missed me while I was gone?"

William frowned. "Yeah, that stuff."

Josie shrugged. "You have to admit it had a ring of truth to it. It's like I just gave up, and I didn't even know it. There are lots of other things I could do. I can teach or write music, I don't necessarily have to sing."

"Then why don't you?"

The question threw her off, and after a second a smile ballooned across her face. "We shouldn't be discussing my career. We need to concentrate on getting you better."

"I'm already feeling a lot better," he said, and squeezed her hand. "Did you mean what you said about making up for lost time?"

"Ah, you *did* hear me."

"You were saying all the things I wanted to hear." He chuckled, but then grew serious. "So did you mean it?"

Josie stole another kiss before she answered, "I meant every word."

Epilogue

Four years later . . .

In a grand chateau outside the city of Paris, Josephine Hayes placed her first Grammy inside her custom-made trophy case and stepped back into her husband's arms to admire it. It wasn't the only award she'd received for songwriting, but it was the first *Grammy.*

"I'm so proud of you," William said, snuggling close and kissing the shell of her ear. "You know if we're quiet, we can continue this little celebration in the bedroom."

"Ah, are you afraid you'll wake the kids?" She turned in his embrace and slid her arms around his neck.

"Me?" He feigned incredulity. "I had to practically peel *you* off the ceiling last night."

Josie giggled as she accepted his puckered lips in a delicious kiss. In the next second, he swept her into his arms and carried her up three flights of stairs. Long before they reached the boudoir, Josie was making more than enough noise to wake Catherine and little Charlie.

With one kick, the door swung open, and William carried his beautiful wife across the threshold. Rose petals and soft candlelight set the scene.

Josie gasped. "What's this?"

"Let's just say that I called some friends to help our little celebration along."

"When did you call them?"

"Before we boarded the plane in Los Angeles. Do you like the surprise?"

"I love it." She giggled. "My hopeless romantic." She peppered his face with kisses. "And what about the children?"

"Out of our hair until tomorrow afternoon when we pick up Larry, Sheila, and Christopher from the airport."

"Once again, you've thought of everything, Dr. Hayes."

"I certainly try, Nurse Hayes."

Gently, he placed her on the bed and nibbled on all Josie's favorite spots. They took their time, playing and peeling each other out of their clothes. When their bodies finally joined, the magic that had always existed between them returned.

William knew that he would never tire of making love to this exquisite woman. He loved everything about her: the way she felt, smelled, tasted, and above all, he loved the way she loved him.

In the years after their reunion, she had rediscovered her talent and drive. She also committed herself to *live* her life and never take any of her blessings for granted. She had Michelle to thank for that lesson.

Night had dissolved into early morning before the husband and wife took a break just to cuddle. "If we don't get some sleep soon, we're going to be a wreck by the time Larry and Sheila arrive with their own little bundle of joy."

William chuckled. "I can't believe that knucklehead has finally made me an uncle. I was beginning to think he didn't have it in him."

Josie smiled and shook her head. "I can't wait to see the baby. Sheila said he looks a lot like you."

"Lucky kid."

"That's what you said about our babies."

"I meant it then, too. Of course, Catherine is starting to look more like you every day." He hugged her close. "Which means the next one—"

"The next one? How many do you think we're having?"

"At least six."

She bolted out of his arms and turned to him incredulously. "Six?"

"Fine, fine." He shrugged. "I'm a man of compromise. How about five?"

Her lips widened into a smile as she slid back into his arms. "That's much better." She kissed him. "You know our twentieth-year anniversary is just around the corner?"

William smiled. "Twenty years since we met. It took us a long time to make it to the altar, but I can honestly say I've been in love with you since that fateful night. I'm looking forward to loving you all the days of my life."

His words brought tears to Josie's eyes. She still couldn't believe God thought enough of her to reward her with such a man.

"I love you so much," she whispered.

The morbid truth was they had her sister to thank for reuniting them; then again, maybe everything happened just as fate had planned it. Josie tried not to think of Michelle, but she couldn't help it at times.

As usual, she was the first out of bed so she could have the bathroom to herself. She greeted her reflection in the mirror with a smile, then opened the medicine cabinet. She reached for her hidden lithium pills in the back.

When she popped the top, a voice startled her from behind.

"How long were you planning to keep this secret from me?"

Stunned, Josie's gaze found his in the mirror. "How long have you known?"

An easy smile curved William's lips as he stepped into the bathroom and slid his arms around her waist. "Baby, I make it a point to pay close attention to you."

Her heart hammered in her chest. "I was scared to tell you."

He turned her around to face him. "Just because you suffer from a bipolar disorder doesn't mean that you're going to turn into Michelle. Plenty of people with this disease get by just fine without turning into a mass murderers."

A smile fluttered to her lips. "You still love me even though—"

"Josie, Josie," he whispered, and brushed a light kiss over her mouth. "Don't you know by now that there's nothing in this world that could ever stop me from loving you?"

Tears splashed down Josie's face as she locked her arms around his neck and kissed him with every ounce of her soul. She nearly melted at the feel of his hands making those wonderful circles at the small of her back.

"Hey, come back to bed," William said huskily.

"Don't tell me you're ready for another round."

"Okay, I won't tell you, I'll just show you."

"Deal." She returned the bottle to the cabinet, winked at her reflection. "You're not a lost cause, after all." She smiled, then returned to bed with the love of her life.